By The Sea Shore

Sandra A. Morris

RISING
TIDE
PRESS

Rising Tide Press
3831 N. Oracle Road
Tucson, AZ 85705
520-888-1140

Printed in the United States on acid-free paper.

Publisher's note:
All characters, places, and situations in this book are
fictitious, or used fictitiously, and any resemblance
to persons (living or dead) is purely coincidental.

Cover art by Jude Ockenfels

First Printing: September 2000

Morris, Sandra A.
By The Sea Shore/Sandra A. Morris

ISBN 1-883061-32-6

Library of Congress Control Number: 00 133936

Dedicated to...

Gwendolyn J. Morris, who taught me the beauty and potency of language and supports my journey.
Diane Leah, who encouraged me to begin.
Ileana Grimm, who encouraged me to finish.
And the women of *Rising Tide*...Debra Tobin, Brenda Kazen and my editor, Laurie Field (who is the best speller I know).

In memory of...

My dad, my brother and my dog. Loved and missed...always.

About the Author

Sandra A. Morris (Sam, to those near and dear) grew up believing "Green Eggs 'N Ham" was written for her, (and yes...she would eat them with a goat, on a boat, should the opportunity present itself.) She lives in the resort area of Toronto known as The Beaches, in a seemingly constant cloud of drywall dust and paint chips. When not tearing down walls, Sandra is hard at work on her second Jess Shore mystery.

Sandra can be reached through Rising Tide Press, 3831 N. Oracle Rd. Tucson, AZ 85705 or www.risingtidepress.com.

Chapter One

"Provincetown Tower, Cessna 172 Golf Alpha Yankee, out of Boston, over Marconi National Seashore at two thousand feet with information Delta, landing."

Excitement bubbled up making me yawn. I focused myself for the landing. The shore beckoned like a gnarled finger from some nightmare, urging me into its depths. The crashing waves sent out a roaring invitation to enter into a watery embrace. It was a ruse, and I knew it. The sea, particularly at this end of the Cape, was dangerous and omnipotent; the ancient wrecks at its depths were fractured testaments to that truth. The sun warmed the cockpit and danced on my face.

I chanced a glance to my right and saw my passenger brace rigidly in her seat. It wasn't fear of flying I saw in her clenched jaw - but something...

A woman's voice crackled in my ear, "Golf Alpha Yankee, report Wellfleet, not below two thousand. Watch for Cape Air commuter departing Eastbound, clear to downwind...and welcome back Jess."

"Thanks Karen. Great to be back," I responded.

"You got that mangy hound with ya again."

I smiled back at the 'hound,' who looked miffed. He may not be a purebred but he is a noble looking beast just the same. Hound indeed. He was eclectic.

"Yeah he's here. Break out the biscuits," I laughed.

I began my pre-landing check. The Provincetown airstrip was shorter than I was accustomed to at the Island Airport, Toronto, so I adjusted accordingly.

I remembered, from previous summers, how the barren strip of pavement that was the runway leapt out from the coastline. It seemed like an impossible place to land a kite, let alone an airplane. The more hours I racked up in the air the more I acknowledged the sheer temerity of flying about with mechanical wings.

I smiled quickly back at my faithful hound, who was panting in delighted anticipation of landing at 'that sandy place with lots of water.' He could smell our destination. It was his fifth visit to Provincetown and he looked forward to it as much as I did. He favored me with a smile, which I returned. I wished, for the umpteenth time, that I too could wag my tail. It would mean so much to him, I knew.

I returned to my task. "Golf Alpha Yankee on the one niner decimal niner, established for right downwind."

"Golf Alpha Yankee, report right base, you're clear to land."

As I made my turn to the base approach I applied carb heat, lowered my flaps to 20 degrees and reduced my airspeed to 60 knots.

I heard a sudden intake of breath from the stranger next to me.

Her jet black hair fell loosely on her shoulders. It was the kind of hair that never required the assistance of gel, curling irons or Elmer's Glue. It was natural and shiny, framing a strong, roundish face with prominent, slightly protruding sapphire blue eyes. Her nose was long and straight, the nostrils flaring with the sharp inhalation of breath. Her skin was pale, not pasty, as if she spent most of her daylight hours in artificial light.

She had removed the headset I had given her and I was too preoccupied with landing to acknowledge her distress.

I had given her the requisite instructions during our flight... "in case of forced landing assume crash position, bend over, no oxygen mask will pop out, crack open your door, don't scream too loud"...blah, blah, blah. I attributed her distress to our descent. I shouted out, above the engine, what I meant to be a comforting statement, and turned back to my instruments. If she had heard me she gave no indication.

"Alpha Yankee, turning right base."

"Alpha Yankee, clear to land."

I applied a slight pressure on the right rudder to compensate for the cross-wind that always seemed to swirl around the runway, causing us to lose some altitude. The Cessna bounced once, slightly, and settled down to the runway. I love a good landing. Like a perfect tee shot, it's something you always expect, yet never take for granted. I taxied to the designated turn off point and tuned my radio to the Ground Station to receive my taxi and tie down instructions.

"Can I get out now?" croaked a voice from the right seat.

"No, not yet. Just a few more minutes. I'll let you know. In the meantime, you could fold up those maps and record our landing time, if you don't mind."

I sensed resistance, through the clucking of her tongue, and chose to ignore it. Tough noogies. After all she was the one who approached me at Logan International and begged a ride. She had seemed distraught, otherwise I would not have considered it. She had missed her connection to P-Town and no other flights were scheduled until the next day. Kelly, the charming Cape Air attendant on duty at Logan today had been relieved to shluff the angry 'suit' off on me, with an apologetic smile.

Chuckles the Frown had made a bee line for poor unsuspecting me as I was loading my gear and dog into the plane. She got right to the point, which impressed me. I always was a sucker for the direct approach.

Okay, I admit it. First impressions don't buy gas and she did offer me two hundred dollars for the short trip. I knew I didn't make her day when I told her that her smart luggage would have to join her later as Buster would be in the baggage area. I don't know what she had in those bags but it threw my weight and balance figures right off the chart.

She clung, in a proprietary way, to her one remaining satchel and snazzy briefcase, declining my suggestion that they be placed in the baggage compartment. When I had kidded her about its contents being stolen jewels she had shot me a glance that silenced me.

'Oh well Jess, not everyone can appreciate your sharp wit and winning charm.' The whole flight would only take about an hour, then I was on my own.

Flying was a solitary pleasure for me. For years, it has been me and my faithful pooch, soaring above the clouds whenever time permitted. My friends accused me, good-naturedly, of becoming a recluse. So be it, I muttered to myself. I liked being on my own. Sort of. Sometimes.

I taxied to tie-down and informed my sullen acquaintance that she was free to go. She thanked me, or burped, it was hard to tell, and scurried to the terminal building without a backward glance.

"The pleasure was all mine", I snorted out loud, only to be snapped back to brighter thoughts by a hot, wet lick on the back of my neck.

"Hey fella, whatta ya say you and me blow this pop stand and go for a swim?"

The thunk, thunk of his tail against the fuselage was all the answer I needed.

I gathered together our supplies and headed for the flight control office to complete my paperwork. Karen greeted me with the effusiveness of a friend and a fellow flyer.

We had known each other for years and although our visits were few and far between, there was an innate closeness that never dimmed with the light of passing months. Karen and I shared a love of flying and we greatly enjoyed each others tales of derring- do, or don't, as the case may be.

Karen was in her mid to late fifties, I wasn't sure, and didn't care. Her face bore the essence of her Pilgrim ancestors, apparent in the determined set of her jaw and the olive tone of her weathered skin. Her now white hair was worn in the same style as it always had been, with bits and pieces sprouting haphazardly from her head. Her eyes were bright and clever, their clear blue vision missing little and recording much.

Karen and her partner, Meg, had been my first friends in Provincetown when I arrived some ten years ago for a short vacation that grew to be a lifelong love affair with the town's character *and* its characters.

Regardless of her actual title, Karen ran the airport and I, and anyone else with an ounce of insight, knew this and respected her for her achievements. Karen had gone through her share of misery and heartache and that past kept her strong and true to her present.

The two of them, Meg and Karen, were a solid unit in whose presence one felt enveloped in the love and respect they had for each other. Their eighteen-year union had been virtually unmarred by scandal or recrimination. They were, and remained, an inspiration to those of us who felt jaded and cynical with respect to long-term wedded bliss. I count myself amongst that number.

It was wonderful to see her again and Buster, true to form, lay splayed at her feet, his big ham bone of a tongue lolling joyously as she vigorously rubbed his tummy.

We made plans to have dinner the following night, and, since Karen knew I was anxious to get settled - she ushered me out.

This done, the two of us, dog and dog-ma, made a beeline for the parking lot where we hoped to find our ancient Jeep, rusting placidly in the place where I had arranged to have it parked. True to her reliable self, Meg had indeed delivered the behemoth and there was a note tucked under the tattered wiper blade. Aahhh. I love getting notes. I unlocked the door, standing back to allow Buster to leap in ahead of me and letting the stale, humid air escape. I was distracted by the sound of angry voices.

"Don't do it Jess. Don't turn around. Just get in the jeep and get going. This is none of your business and you're supposed to be on vacation."

Fat chance.

I turned towards the fracas and was surprised to see my immaculately groomed passenger hurling abuses at a woman that I recognized to be the proprietor of one of the local fine dining places in town. Her name escaped me, for the moment, and I had to wonder at the connection of the two women. They seemed an unlikely pairing.

Sydney! That was it. Sydney Somethingorother. As most people with part-timers disease, I could recall various and trivial facts about her, however, her full name was lost for the time being in the quantum void. And what, pray tell, was she doing here, at the airport going toe to toe with my passenger? Did they know each other? Coincidence? I think not!

I remembered that Sydney had come to Provincetown some eight or so years ago, from Buffalo, and bought what, at the time, was a tiny shack on the East end of Commercial Street. I think it used to be a pizza place or something like that.

Grit, determination and a seemingly healthy bank account had transformed the ruins. It was now a popular bistro and after hours club that was popular with locals and tourists alike.

I myself, with various former side salads, had whiled away many an hour enjoying the seaside ambiance and delicious cuisine, prepared, if memory served, by Sydney herself. I had met Sydney on several occasions, and I wondered if she would remember me. It seemed that over the years I had either arrived with, or quickly met, someone with whom to share my days and nights. Single women, I have found, look different when they become part of a couple. Not so this year, I had determined. But then...I still had to see Catherine so, who knew.

Also, there was the fact that I had grown comfortably into my body over the past couple of years. I guess I was meant to be thirty-five, and my body and face had waited patiently for me to catch up to it. Maybe Sydney just didn't recognize me, period. Me?? Ego?? Nah.

I was getting used to people declaring that they wouldn't have known it was me... until I opened my mouth. Very nice. I had lost about ten pounds and had tried to get what remained in better shape. I was about five and a half feet, standing on my good leg. My hair grew blonder with the years, probably a precursor to going completely gray. I didn't like to spend more than ten dollars on a hair cut and it looked it. Lately I had found myself stopping for a moment when I looked in the mirror wondering who it was looking back at me. The dark brown eyes I saw revealed more than I would have liked and, as a consequence, I often felt like I was squinting. My smile lines remain etched on my face long after I have stopped smiling.

I was born with bags under my eyes as if the process of developing from a fetus had exhausted me for the rest of my life and my actual birth day simply lead to my first sleepless night. I have become accustomed to sleeping alone

Leaving the police force had been an impetus for me. I was my own boss now and loving every minute of it. I got up when I wanted and only took on clients who interested me and were willing to pay for my services. I was in good physical shape, finally, and had spent some difficult months with a shrink unpacking a lifetime of baggage. I was traveling light these days.

It was obvious that being on my own professionally and personally suited me for now. I felt good and it showed. Just like the shampoo commercials. I must remember 'to tell two friends so they can tell two friends and so on...'

I was trying real hard not to smoke. Having abstained for five years I had, one tipsy evening, indulged in the demon weed, only to be snatched back into its yellowed clutches.

After about six months of tar build up I had finally gone to my doctor and begged for help. 'Patches,' she said. Patches? I need patches? I felt like a tire that had just gasped out its final breath of foul air. I was weak but I knew it so I managed to view this as a strength. Perception is reality...say it with me!

The angry voices cut into my reverie and I turned just in time to see Sydney slamming the door of her very snazzy, black BMW Roadster, narrowly missing her opponent as she tore out of the parking lot in a great cloud of dust. I thought I saw her eyes meet mine as she spun by at Mach I, but no acknowledgment was forthcoming.

Buster barked at me to get going and I turned to get into the jeep, vowing not to pay any attention to my recent co-pilot, even as my head began to disobey.

I couldn't help myself. I wished that I could have but it would be like asking a dog not to chase a squirrel. Instincts are instincts and mine were spinning me towards a future that was as uncertain and dangerous as any I had ever encountered before.

CHAPTER 2

As if she could hear my thoughts, my new little buddy turned to face me and, to my utter shock and amazement, burst into tears.

"Ah geeez", I groaned. I fought to maintain my balance as a black and white streak of fur jostled me aside, loping across the parking lot to see if he could be of any assistance. That dog had great instincts and was always a sucker for a pretty face. I think he gets that from me.

I followed, reluctantly. Precious pooch that he was, my pal was on his haunches, trying to embrace his patient in the safety of his paws. I could see the dusty streaks on her jacket as I approached.

"Sorry about my friend. He hates to see people upset," I explained while attempting to drag him off before a seamstress and/or a lawyer would be required.

"Oh it doesn't matter," she lied, as a trail of drool formed on her cuff. She discreetly brushed it off with her hand. My opinion of the raven haired ice queen was beginning to thaw. Often I have relied on the good judgment of animals to lend me insights that may otherwise lay hidden to the human eye and Buster did seem to be bonding. She, in turn, was absently stroking his large Lab-like head in a gentle and familiar way.

"Hmmmm", I thought. A dog lover. Point one to the stranger with the long legs and gleaming too-blue eyes. Funny, I hadn't really noticed them before. She really was a striking woman...tall, ample and graceful, with a face that looked slightly worn down from years of grinding her teeth.

It wasn't just the tears that illuminated her sadness - it was deeper than that, beyond her eyes. I found myself slightly intrigued by this gypsy before me. My investigator gene kicked in and I made a mental note, shooing away the fly of warning that had begun to buzz around my mind.

"Jess Shore," I offered my hand.

Her answering grasp was strong and solid. She held my gaze. I held back. I love a challenge. We released simultaneously. A good sign. Hand shakes are an important form of greeting and she had the firm and solid grip of a pro. Just like my dad had taught me. Point two to the little lady from Crankytown.

"Jennifer Eastcott," she introduced quietly. "I guess I owe you an apology."

"For what?"

"I was pretty rude to you back there," she gestured vaguely towards the plane.

"No sweat," I assured her while trying not to sound smug or vindicated. "Could you use a lift into town?" I offered, the words springing surprisingly from my lips requiring no consultation, apparently, with my brain. I hate it when that happens.

She nodded in a sigh and, with Buster close at her heels, followed me to the jeep. Her step seemed heavy with exhaustion and resignation, her head lowered miserably, exposing an inviting and silky looking expanse of flesh below the sweep of her shoulder length hair. Yikes, I intoned inwardly. If it looks like trouble, and it feels like trouble....

I was woofed back to the present. Apparently I was dawdling and there was a panting, whimpering 80-pound reminder of my tardiness in the back seat, happily ensconced with Jennifer's arm slung comfortably around him. Ah, the life of a dog. They both stared at me.

I cleared my throat, if not my head, and hustled into the dusty interior, praying silently that the rust-bucket would spare me its usual belch of smoke and pyrotechnic protestations. As if reading my thoughts, the engine coughed daintily to life and I ground it into first gear.

I turned on the wipers in order to extricate the note that Meg had left for me. I may be lazy but at least I had finesse. As I flailed at the windshield, managing to secure a corner of the square under my index finger and drag it into my lap, I became aware of Jennifer's bemused expression at my machinations. I met her gaze in the rear view, and smiled

A real smile. It surprised both of us.

"Where can I drop you?" I queried.

"Oh God. I don't know. My plans kind of, um, fell through," she confessed.

"Mrmphhh."

"What?" she asked, leaning close enough for me to inhale her. She smelled like air conditioning and lavender soap.

"Any idea where you want to stay? It's early in the season; I imagine you could have your pick. How long ya here for?" I pried

"I don't know. I was planning on staying for, well, an extended period. That's why I had so much luggage with me in Boston. I don't know now. I don't know anything right now. Everything's screwed up," she said through clenched teeth. Buster licked her consolingly. I made a mental note to attempt, for the kazillionth time, to brush his teeth. He had, without a doubt, the worst breath in the world. I was kinda used to it, but an unsuspecting stranger could be forgiven for recoiling in horror at the first whiff. Instead - she laughed. It was an unexpected and wonderful sound.

I felt an uncomfortable nudge from my hormones and stifled them.

Again I put my mouth in gear before my mind was engaged. Oh boy...here we go. "Look. Buster seems to have taken quite a fancy to you and we have plenty of room at our place. (Who said that?) I have a little cottage thing on the beach, in the East end. There's a spare bedroom. If you like, you're welcome to bunk in with us until you get your plans sorted out," I offered.

She seemed genuinely puzzled. That made two of us, frankly. "Why would you do that? You don't even know me, and let's face it, I was a bit of a jerk before when you agreed to give me a ride from Boston. I'm grateful, really. I was just preoccupied with what I would find when I got here. It was bound to be, well, acrimonious, to say the least. As you may have noticed, it was. Sorry. You've been really generous, and yes, if you're sure it's okay, I don't really feel like checking into a hotel or B & B right now. If you're sure you don't mind," she repeated.

Buster gave me a look that I took to mean 'no we don't mind,' and I relayed his message to Jennifer.

Nothing else was said during the short drive to my little bit of heaven on the Cape. Just like our flight here, conversation was not indicated or missed.

I had bought the small, simple Saltbox cottage in 1985, when I was working undercover for the drug squad in Toronto. I had lead a simple if not uncomplicated life. Mostly I was at work or sleeping. I had my savings, and other benefits that befit an officer who sustains an injury in the line of duty. It had been a routine break and enter call that turned ugly. Kids with guns, all hopped-up on crack. My partner had shouted a warning that probably saved my life as the bullet lodged in my shoulder, not my heart. After the shooting I had spent my months of recuperation away from active duty, assigned to a desk job.

Surprisingly I had really enjoyed the 'inside' work. I had been part of a team that was responsible for building an on-ramp to the information highway for the Toronto force.

Our resources were woefully limited...my own computer would not have looked out of place in an episode of The Flintstones ...yet I persisted.

I had worked with computers while at University but only when absolutely necessary. I still remember the librarians drawing straws to see who would get the latest opportunity to show me how to use the microfiche. Heaven forbid I should have to photocopy something.

I loved having the chance to become functionally literate with my laptop and had lots of help easing into the cyber age. Going back to active duty with the force became an option in time, but I bailed instead. Time to strike out on my own. Becoming a P.I. seemed the most natural thing in the world, given my background. I loved the work and the toys were kinda cool too.

I had been cautious with my investments and still enjoyed a small degree of economic comfort that was great, considering the fact that legions of prospective clients had not been knocking down my door to enlist my investigative prowess. I was having, to say the least, a dry spell.

My little 'cottage' had been expanded and modernized, gradually and lovingly, through the years and was now a perfect fit for me. For the most part the interior was a reflection of myself, with small touches of past loves left behind in memory of our brief unions.

It was spacious enough, yet intimate and cozy. The French doors to the beach opened wide and fresh salty breezes would waft through gently caressing me to sleep each night. If it was cool, as it often was, a roaring fire in one of the two fireplaces was all that was needed.

There was a large stone hearth in the mistress bedroom, and a huge flagstone affair in the living room... a romantic or a pyromaniac. The jury is still out.

The cabin is my salvation. I was wary of the idea of having a stranger around, yet determined to be welcoming and gracious. The best of intentions and all that.

I was accustomed to having visitors off and on throughout the season - comes with the territory. Why stay at a guest house when we can crash at Jess's?

Why indeed, but those were friends. I assured myself that Jennifer would most likely be winging back to Boston before her luggage arrived so I needn't fret.

CHAPTER 3

The balding tires crunched on the gravel path that led into the cottage, the longer grass in the center of the ruts brushing against the undercarriage of the jeep. Before me was a sight that never failed to bring the curl of a Grinchy smile to my lips. The fishing fleet.

The 'fleet' precariously perched on dots of water, mere puddles left behind as the tide swept out. The boats had been abandoned for the latter part of the day, their duty being done in the pre-dawn hours, their owners long since gone to town to sell their catch to the local merchants. It was an odd sight. It looked as if the weathered vessels, leaning dangerously in all their shapes, colors and sizes, had been dropped out of the sky from the toy box of some celestial child, forgotten and left to bake in the afternoon sun.

I couldn't help but see a similar smile on the lips of Buster's new best friend, and again, I put my initial assessment of her up another notch.

Provincetown still had the look and feel of a small fishing village, although tourism was more a mainstay in the summer months. Many of the families that still had ties to the community could trace their lineage back to the Pilgrim's.

The scraggly path that was my driveway curved down to the left, and there, barely concealed by the unruly perennial garden sat my little Capey Coddy jewel. It appeared small and compact, from this vantage, as it winked at me in the bright sunshine.

Jennifer had a job of it trying to restrain her back seat-mate. He morphed himself into a butterfly and squeezed through an impossibly small gap in the back flap of the jeep, my luggage tumbling out with him. He was off like a flash, his geriatric shoulder and aching hips forgotten in his haste to dive deep into the cool waters of the Bay.

"See ya later pal," I laughed.

I saw Jennifer's gaze shift reluctantly from the dog, alerted by a rude blast from a car horn that sounded from Commercial Street. Her face drew in on itself in a painful grimace as if the blast was directed at her. I had to wonder what the honking may mean to her. Sydney, I wondered? Didn't seem to suit my impression of her, but who knew. Whatever story those two had, the final chapter was obviously not yet written.

As I made my way to the bright red front door I began a mental list of chores that would have to be undertaken over the next few months. Each year, it seemed, there was something else that needed to be done. I enjoyed the puttering. Last year I had, with help, completed the verandah that encircled my homestead. The yellow stain that we had used had faded considerably and appeared as weathered as the rest of the exterior. In true Cape Cod tradition, blasts of bright red highlighted the doors and window frames, giving the whole place the look of a Bazooka wrapper. Even the chimney conformed, painted wet-tar black and sticking up over the peaked roof like a piece of licorice.

I passed under Jennifer's black cloud and went to the front door. I never knew what to expect. After months of vacancy, my oasis could present me with a variety of surprises. These could range from the mundane raccoon invasion, with its inherent clutter, to the unexpected human guests who knew where to find a soft bed and warm hearth. I didn't really mind the turnaround that went on behind my back, rather, I was glad to provide shelter where and when it was needed.

Meg ran one of the more successful Real Estate companies in town and she had my consent to lend out the premises as she saw fit...an arrangement that worked well for all concerned.

As long as they cleaned up after themselves, I was not wont to make an issue of it. For the most part, they did. Mostly teenagers in the throes of adolescent angst or acquaintances needing a safe haven from an unpleasant domestic moment. Whatever.

Many a time I had found a small gift of appreciation on the premises. It could be as simple as a colorful stone or a perfect seashell, items made more precious when one considered the dearth of worldly goods available to my off-season tenants. I saved all, and had them scattered about the place, visible should my benefactors ever need to lay hold of them in the future.

It was obvious that some kind soul had come in recently and prepared the place for my arrival. "Meg," I grinned gratefully, "you are an angel."

The air was fresh, early spring flowers from my garden were scattered about in various containers and a bottle of chardonnay revealed itself chilling in the refrigerator, a note scrunched around the neck. There was also a healthy supply of staples and veggies filling the usually empty interior. I remembered the note that Meg had left on my windshield and rescued it from the deep recesses of my pocket. I laughed out loud when I read it.

deeR Buster
i **heRd that you weeR comiNg baK sooN!!** oh **boYs!! i just wonTd to let you no that i am alowD to go foR woKs. aLL bi miseLfl!!!! if Jes sayS it is OK!!!!! anD i hav a tReet foR you!!!**
yoR fRenD
HARLEY

I would have to pass the message on to Buster. He and Sydney's daughter Harley were great pals going way back. Ah-ha, perhaps that was why Sydney was there this morning and her run-in with Jennifer was just a coincidence. Young Harley must have somehow convinced her mother to play postmistress and she had been there to put the note on my windshield. Harley was a tough kid to say no to, and a good friend to many who lived in town.

"You weren't kidding about the view, were you?," Jennifer's voice whisked me back from my reverie.

"Ah, no," I cleared my throat. Witty Jess.

Her agitation had lessened and I could see in her the same appreciation and awe that I experienced every time I came back here. Provincetown was my second home. In Toronto I have a way cool apartment perched on the bluffs of the Eastern Beach with a coveted view of Lake Ontario.

I felt equally spoiled and at home in either location. Jennifer stood close to my ear and I felt myself unconsciously stepping forward, away from the whisper of her breath on my neck.

"Let me show you the spare room. I'm sure you'd like to change, or something," I fumbled. My knuckles seemed to scrape along the ground as I lumbered down the hall, my guest close on my heel.

As she followed along, a heavy sigh escaped from her.

"I'd love to change and freshen up, but my luggage, as you may remember, didn't make it on the same flight as I did. I have the basics but could use some clean clothes. "

I was prepared to take umbrage at her dig but when I turned I saw that she was smiling again and there was a twinkle in her bright eyes that disarmed me completely.

"I'm sure I have something you can throw on for now. Your stuff should be here sometime today. I'll have Karen give me a call when it arrives. Meantime you'll have to make do with hand-me-overs."

"Sounds fine to me. Thank you again. I still don't know why you're being so kind but please know that I appreciate it. A lot."

"Sure. No sweat." Fact is, I don't know why I'm being so nice either. Just my nature I guess, though I doubt many folks would guess that about me.

CHAPTER 4

Sydney lurched to a halt at the kitchen door of '*The Shooting Gallery*'. She turned off the car and cradled her head on the steering wheel, seemingly in no hurry to leave the sanctuary of the BMW's compact interior. She chastised herself for following Jennifer when she left the airport. She had not been surprised that Jess Shore had been there. Harley had spoken with Meg the other day and knew that Jess and Buster were expected sometime that week. Just Sydney's luck that she had arrived when she did, running smack dab into Jennifer. Did Jennifer and Jess know each other, Sydney wondered. She couldn't imagine how, but one never knew.

To make things even worse, Jennifer had probably heard the honk of warning Sydney had been forced to blast when the dark figure had darted from the bushes outside Jess's place, directly into the path of her car. Had she not veered suddenly, she felt sure, she would have hit the stranger in black. She would call Jess later in the day and alert her to the incident. Strangers, especially this time of year, and dressed like some movie of the week cat burglar, were likely up to no good. Sydney knew that break-ins in the off-season were a problem for Provincetown's summer residents, and hoped that all was well at Jess's place.

Moving laboriously, Sydney crossed the narrow path to the door and entered the hub of the bistro, her home away from home: the kitchen.

The usually comforting sight of the gleaming copper pots and pans, the redolent smells of hundreds of spices and flavorings and the barren quiet of the interior beyond failed to ease the tension between her eyes.

Sydney's anger had turned inward and threatened to manifest into a doozy of a tension headache. This pissed her off even more. Sydney had way too much on her plate right now, today especially, and could ill afford to be laid low for even a minute. Memorial Day Weekend was just around the corner and there was work to be done before the influx of tourists began lining up outside her door.

"Damn you Jennifer Eastcott," she seethed aloud. Your timing sucks, she thought.

She hadn't meant to get into a screaming match with Jennifer, it's just that she was so surprised to have seen her there that the tension of the last several months erupted and spewed out. She would have to track her down later and apologize. None of what had happened between them in the past was Jennifer's fault. After all, she had just been doing her job, but Sydney just lost it when she saw her at the airport.

She hoped she could make Jennifer understand and somehow make amends. They had seemed to be developing a friendship of sorts and Sydney regretted that she may have jeopardized that. She thought of the letter she had received just the day before and knew she would have to share the contents with Jennifer eventually.

Sydney turned her thoughts back to the restaurant in an effort to calm down. *The Shooting Gallery* was just hitting its stride, allowing Sydney, finally, the luxury of the odd day off during the week, maybe even two in a row. The collection she had booked in for the summer promised to be a real drawing card.

Two local artists, a brother and sister, had dug deep into their combined years of sculpting, casting, metal working and oil painting, unsurfacing an awe inspiring body of work. Once dusted off and artfully displayed, all involved stood to have a prosperous season indeed.

Sydney, with the help of Gilly, her magical chef, had designed and refined an entirely new bill of fare for their delighted diners. Also, added a few years ago, was a back room whose bank of leaded glass doors opened to a deck overlooking the beach. In it she had placed two antique pool tables; what was left from her grandfather's belongings.

Although each table had to be over seventy-five years old, their leather pockets and oak boarders were unmarked and gleaming. Over each table was a genuine Tiffany stained glass light fixture, which cast a pipe-scented glow over the room and invited lingering.

All the paraphernalia was from her grandfather's estate and evoked fond memories in Sydney whenever she hefted a cue in her hands or heard the familiar 'clack' of the balls, as they skittered around the green felt. Her grandfather was never far from her thoughts. He had raised her, single-handedly, and she had adored him as he did her. His death two years ago had not been a surprise; however, its suddenness was profound just the same.

The accompanying pain had become familiar to her and she actually feared its departure. What would it leave in its place? Harley, too, missed her great grandpa and Sydney had worried about how the loss would affect her at such a young age.

Sydney turned her thoughts to her chosen family. Sharron, who had started out as a waitress, had, in time shown her artistic flair and unique sense of design which had lead to her current role. She was responsible for running the front of the house for Sydney, as well as organizing the collections that were displayed throughout the season. Beth, a painter herself, had worked for Sydney since she opened, performing various tasks.

The Gallery family was rounded out by Gilly and Gilly's little helper in the kitchen, William, and sundry summer help as required. She liked most of her patrons and all of her staff. It was a family in the true sense of the word and one Sydney treasured.

She swore an oath and whipped herself into a flurry of activity. Sydney didn't like discord and was determined to pull herself out of her current funk. Whatever the special was tonight, it would surely be chopped, pureed, or diced to within an inch of its life.

Sydney showed no mercy, even as she cleaved into an innocent carrot, sending half of it across the floor only to stop dead against a sneakered foot. She squinted at the silhouette in the doorway, recognition dawning sickly on her.

"What are you doing here?" Sydney questioned.

"I have a message for you, Sydney," the voice whispered.

From behind her, too late, Sydney sensed the presence of another body. As she turned, a white hot pain exploded across the back of her head and all went dark.

CHAPTER 5

Gillian Belfontaine fumbled, as usual, with her keys to the restaurant. Balanced precariously on her ample left hip was the fresh produce she had picked up from a small shop in Truro. She was planning a gastronomic experiment tonight and looked forward to the ritual taste test she knew Sydney would insist on. "Try to figure this one out boss," Gillian laughed.

For six years now, Gillian and Sydney had maintained a friendly and heated rivalry in the kitchen. Gillian, with her Chef de Cuisine certification, had found Sydney to be a quick study. Gill appreciated the delicacy of Sydney's touch and had scrambled of late to reassert her dominance in the kitchen. If not for the moderating influence of Sharron, Gill was certain she would not have always felt so charitable towards her rival. Gill had always had a need to compete, especially if she knew she could win.

Sharron had introduced Gillian to Sydney. never one to judge and for that Gillian had always been grateful. Her youth had been wasted being wasted and that was that. She grew up and found an outlet for her talent in some of the finest kitchens along the East coast and Sydney knew she was lucky to have her.

Gillian nudged herself through the door. It always seemed a tight squeeze for her stout figure, although there was really plenty of room. She called out a cheery hi-dee-ho to Sydney, whose car she had seen at the back entrance.

The two women had for years now shared the companionable ritual of a quiet cup of coffee together in the dining room, before the front doors were unlocked and other staff began to filter in.

That precious fifteen minutes or so was something they both looked forward to. Whoever arrived first put on the fresh pot of the special Sumatra/Guatemalan blend and made ready for the other. As Gill called out to Sydney she felt a slight chill of apprehension as she realized that it was that smell, the rich dark beans being brewed into a steaming liquid, that was missing.

Strange, she thought, as she called out again, how some things are more noticeable by their absence. Gill quickened her pace to the kitchen. Halfway across the dining room she was startled by a sound that made her feel sick inside.

"Sydney... Sydney, it's Gill. Are you all right...I heard.."

The words froze on her lips as she swung open the door to the kitchen.

There in a heap, blood forming a puddle beyond the outline of her head, lay Sydney.

Gill's own blood turned to ice as she knelt close to her friend, searching desperately for confirmation that she wasn't too late.

"Oh God," Gill panicked, "don't let me be too late." No visible signs of life were forthcoming from Sydney as Gill cradled her close, the blood from her wound hot and sticky as it oozed onto her arm.

Gill gently lowered Sydney and, seconds feeling like days, rushed to the phone to call the Outer Cape Health Services. Her roommate Billy worked there and it was the only number she could think of.

To most mortals her words would have seemed incoherent, but Billy deciphered the code and reassured her that an ambulance was being dispatched and should arrive within twenty minutes.

Twenty minutes. Might as well be a week. Gill cursed out loud. She felt that life on the Cape was idyllic in almost all ways but at a time like this, when a part of her life was slowly draining itself away just a few dark feet from where she stood, she felt frustrated.

She swallowed these thoughts and hurried back into the kitchen. She felt shock and terror anew as she saw that Sydney was exactly as she had left her. She had somehow imagined that it had all been a horrible hallucination. Grabbing a cushion and afghan from the couch in Sydney's office, she covered Sydney and rested her head gently on the pillow. She hoped it would serve as a compress and staunch the continuing flow of blood.

Gill's mind raced wildly. What had happened? Gill looked around the kitchen. Nothing seemed out of place. The vegetables were still on the cutting board, a stark reminder of the normalcy that was no more. Nothing else seemed askew. No evidence was apparent to Gill that would indicate what could have lead to this tragedy. She did, however, notice something strange. The back door swung open on its hinges, swaying with the breeze from the bay.

Gillian cursed out loud, "Damn it all Sydney...you knew that lock wasn't worth squat."

Gill twisted herself around to give her a view out the open doorway. There was nothing amiss in the back lot. She heaved a sigh of relief. Who could have done such a thing? This type of violence was almost unheard of in Provincetown. Their community enjoyed a relatively placid existence and incidents of this sort were more a part of the evening news out of Boston than a part of their daily lives.

A voice called out from the front, startling Gillian as she huddled closer to Sydney. No matter what, Gill would not abandon her friend.

The door burst open as Sharron sauntered in, stopping dumbfounded at the sight before her.

"Holy frogs hairs, Batman, who knew?" she joked, not noticing the look of terror on Gill's face, or the unconscious form of Sydney. Thinking she had caught them in a compromising position, her laughter was raucous.

"Shut-up, for Christ's sake. Sydney's been attacked, you idiot. Get over here and hold her. I'm going to run for Catherine Hobbes. I can't risk getting her machine if she's with a patient."

"Go. Fast. I'll take over here," promised Sharron.

Gill's short legs surprised her and themselves with their great speed. She reached the ivy covered archway of Catherine's office and swung around it , dragging a goodly chunk of the greenery with her. She fairly tripped into the cool shade of the doorway. There was no reception area, no visible clues that this home was any different from its neighbors.

Gill almost knocked Catherine down as she barreled into the office and Catherine listened carefully to the few details that Gill could provide. She grabbed her medical supplies and pushed Gillian out the door in front of her.

Catherine Hobbes was once one of the most promising pediatric surgeons in the Boston area. Her career at Harvard medical school had been distinguished and she had been courted by leading medical institutions world-wide. Catherine had determined, even prior to her time at Harvard, that her talents would be best served in the inner city of her birthplace. Early on in life, Catherine had been involved with the problems and tragedies that often befall the oppressed. Through her parents, both professors in sociology at the University of Massachusetts, Catherine had spent her childhood and youth among the impoverished families that were championed by her mother and father. She knew the Combat Zone better than Beacon Hill and was more at home in the former.

Their research had done much to expose the inefficiencies in the American system that made assistance for those that were in need so complicated and bureaucratic. They illuminated their plight and forced reforms, tirelessly and tenaciously effecting change. Their efforts were applauded by their peers, if not their elected officials.

Catherine's parents had been instrumental in persuading their college, as well as others, to offer bursaries and employment to the children of the ghetto who might otherwise become members of one of the thousand-plus gangs in the Boston area. So many didn't make it, but those precious few that did provided the proudest moments of all the years of passion Catherine's parents invested.

Catherine Hobbes had spent five years at a free clinic in the Roxbury district, on Blue Hill Ave. She had done many of the complicated and sophisticated surgical procedures herself, as well as the more commonplace, and had worked out an arrangement with the Boston City Hospital.

They had provided her with the resources she needed first and asked for insurance information last. In return, Catherine accepted their invitation to join their board of directors and lent her well-respected name to their masthead. Her finesse and inventiveness had shone a prestigious light on BCH and they were happy to have her utilize their facilities.

Catherine had moved to Provincetown after the tragedy that had claimed the lives of her beloved parents. A drive-by shooting, all too common in the drug-infested Mission Hill area, had blasted away the foundation of Catherine's life and left her utterly devastated. It was a random act of violence, of being in the wrong place at the wrong time. Her father had been shot in the back as he threw himself against his wife, taking the bullet that had been meant for her, his body collapsing as another shot claimed the life of Catherine's mother.

She had spent a painful two months after the murders finding a suitable replacement for herself at the clinic, and, having accomplished that, she packed up the family home and moved to Provincetown.

Dr. Catherine Hobbes had entered life in Provincetown slowly, but when she opened her door to the world outside, it wooshed in. Unlike Boston, Catherine did not limit her practice to children. She took on any and all. Over half of her practice was women, the rest divided between men and children. In the beginning most of the men were beyond her resources or abilities to do anything but make what time they had left to them as comfortable as she possibly could. Advances in AIDS care and medical research have since brightened many futures, and Catherine kept herself well informed about new treatments for her patients.

Her attitude about death was necessarily philosophical and this was one of her finest qualities.

The children would, in contrast, mostly grow into men and women before her eyes, a process that gave Catherine a thrill. She loved to observe the process of maturation from her vantage, to aid and guide as she could, but mostly to marvel at their potential and take pride, vicariously, in their myriad accomplishments.

At first Catherine had spent her time cocooning in her new home on Pleasant Street, seeing few people. She had been there three months before she even got a phone. The 'Townies' had been curious about their new arrival. Her solitary walks along the beach did not go unnoticed by the locals.

She was a real looker, to say the least. Not just her physical appearance, which was striking, but also the way she carried herself. Stunning, would be the word that springs to mind. The townies knew who Catherine was. They knew who everybody was. It was part of their charm. They knew of her reputation, her work. They also knew from the sensationalist media coverage, of the tragic loss of her parents.

By tacit agreement, Catherine's need for privacy was respected by her new neighbors. Many let her know that she was welcome, day or night, to call on them if she should be in need of anything, and then left her to her demons. Her first real friendship had been with Sydney Ryan.

Catherine had spent that entire first winter in solitude. She sat alone for hours, remembering the sound of her parents' voices, their laughter, trying not to become lost in her grief. Come spring, finally, she felt in need of some human contact, and a good meal.

Catherine's skills in the kitchen were limited and, as a consequence, she was desperate for a well-prepared meal and a good bottle of an unreasonably expensive red wine. That was how she found herself one evening in early spring, being seated by Sydney at a table that, during high tide, seemed to float upon the water.

It was early and the restaurant was nearly empty. Catherine had a chance to drink in the warm hospitality of the room. The rich, yellow texture of the rough walls seemed to mirror the light of the fading sunlight.

The tables were draped with heavy linen, the settings laced with fine veins of gold. The long, elegant candles cast an even warmer shade of light on the polished silverware. The tables were spaced well apart from each other, allowing for intimate dining. The pine floors were pale and polished.

The billiard room in the back seemed to be built upon the water. The soft glow from the Tiffany lights danced across the sheen of the pine floors. The rough-hewn beams in the ceiling were thick and sturdy looking.

Gazing out from where she sat at her table, Dr. Hobbes really noticed Sydney for the first time. She was in the back room, enjoying a peaceful game of pool with herself. Sydney noticed Catherine watching her. She had tried not to stare back, but found herself captivated by Catherine's presence.

Sydney had heard the 'Catherine' stories and had felt a kinship with her sense of loss, having so recently lost her beloved grandfather. What Sydney had not anticipated was the great beauty that was looking back at her, the deep jade of her eyes holding her own fast.

"Would you like a game?" Sydney ventured.

"Ah, sure. I'm a little rusty but I think I still remember how to hold a cue."

As Catherine approached the table, Sydney took in the picture. Tall and graceful, Catherine walked with the fluidity of a wild cat. Hers eyes never left Sydney's and they flashed a green light that one intuitively knew didn't mean 'go'. The two women made their introductions and shook hands warmly.

Catherine placed her glass of wine on the mahogany bar and turned to the racks of cues.

She, too, had done an assessment of the woman before her who was lean and long, with wide set gray eyes that matched the gray in her shoulder length, curly hair.

Sydney dominated a room, not just with her height; which Catherine guessed at about six feet, but also with her crackling energy. Catherine smiled appreciatively at the fine craftsmanship, Sydney's as well as the billiards equipment, and selected a stick to her liking.

Sydney had racked the balls and gave Catherine the honors. A solid clack sent them scurrying for cover in the available pockets. Two solids went down. Sydney smiled with respect as Catherine followed up with two more deposits.

"And that would make me...stripes?" Sydney laughed.

"There does seem to be a surplus," Catherine allowed, with a smile that exposed neat rows of pearly white teeth sheltered seductively by full, generous lips.

Sydney lost that night. With grace. Catherine had asked Sydney to join her for dinner and the two had talked and laughed into the wee hours.

The staff, especially Gillian and Sharron, were beside themselves with curiosity but made no progress with Sydney, as their numerous attempts of butting in were waved off by their employer. So it was just the two women that night, and they became friends. Good friends.

These memories were now racing through Catherine's mind as she knelt over Sydney's inert form. For the first time since she had begun her medical career, Catherine felt panicky and inept. What she didn't feel was a pulse.

CHAPTER 6

Harley skipped down Winslow Street, cutting across at Bradford and down Ryder to Commercial Street. She slowed down only once or twice to confirm the amount of money she had clutched in her fist. Eighty-six cents. It was a fortune. Harley had been extra thrifty at lunchtime and was on her way to claim her reward. *Cabot's* was right on her way home. She knew exactly which flavor of salt water taffy she would choose today, but wisely allowed for the fact that maybe a new flavor had been born and she may need to try it. The door slammed behind her and Mrs. Nairn looked up, a fond smile on her lips.

Harley was a bright, intelligent, inquisitive and kind young lady. At the ripe old age of eight, Harley was a charmer. She had an active social life and made a habit of spreading her time and youthful energies around many of the local merchants and neighbors in her neighborhood. Many of the Townies had shared in Harley's upbringing since her arrival in their midst as a newborn.

They all shared in the pride and joy that was Harley's childhood. They welcomed the chance to feed her voracious appetite for knowledge; knowledge of their town, their heritage, their lives. She had no biases, nor did she judge.

Harley sought out the best in those she shared time and memories with, and it was these interactions which formed her feelings and opinions of the world that had come before her.

For Harley, it was a world of pilgrims and pirates and the birth of Provincetown's rich immigrant history. There was nothing in a history book that could approach the education Harley had already been privy to.

She chattered away to Mrs. Nairn as she scanned the overflowing bins of salt water taffy. The ancient machine twisted and stretched a bright red cinnamon concoction that would soon be cut and packaged for sale. It was a magical sight to Harley; every time she saw it was like the first time. The air in the store was thick with the smell of sugar and it made Harley's mouth water. It was only a casual glance at the large clock above the counter that drew her attention away.

She had promised her mother that she would not "lally gag," her mother's term, on her way home. She quickly made her choices. Two treats for herself and the others she chose for gifts. As always, her bag was jam-packed. Mrs. Nairn never bothered to weigh the packages that Harley purchased, and no matter how much money she had with her it was always enough.

She hurried out of the shop and planned her surprise deliveries. That was her favorite part. Harley could spend hours planning her hiding spots.

Oft explored pockets, frequently opened cupboards, and car seats to name a few, had all enjoyed the unexpected arrival of one of Harley's treats. For her it truly was better to give than to receive. It was part of who she was and one of the many reasons she was so treasured by the Townies.

The kitchen door of the restaurant flew open and Harley blew in. Her heart skipped a beat and a chill of terror coursed through her small body. She saw Catherine and Gill bent over her mother, their own fear visible on their faces and in their movements. She began to sob, calling out to her mother.

Sharron came through the door, scooped the child into her arms and carried her out to the dining room. Harley fought against her, the need to be near her mother overwhelming her.

"There now sweetheart. Your momma's gonna be fine. She just fell down and banged her head. That's why Dr. Catherine is here. You and me will just wait out here so's we don't get in their way, okay honey?"

"No," she screamed. "I want to see my mommy. She needs me."

Her tiny body trembled in Sharron's arms, her face was a chalky white under her freckles and her huge brown eyes were wide with terror, the long, blond lashes soaked with her tears.

"I know Harley. I know. You must be real scared, I bet, huh?"

An imperceptible nod confirmed this statement as a fresh flood of tears sprang from her eyes.

The approaching wail of a siren alerted Sharron to the approach of the ambulance and she clung tighter to the quivering child in her arms.

"Do you hear that honey? That siren is for the ambulance that's coming to help mommy."

"Why can't Dr. Catherine help her?"

"Oh, she can. It's just that she needed some special tools and supplies and stuff so she called the ambulance to come and get her and mommy and take them to the hospital where she would have everything she needs to make mommy better."

Sharron prayed to herself that this was true. That it wasn't too late. She felt Harley's fear combine with her own and struggled against the tears that were threatening to overflow from her own eyes. Sharron had felt helpless until now. Helpless to do or say anything that would help Sydney.

Here, with Harley on her lap, she felt her responsibility and swallowed down the lump in her throat. She may not be able to make Sydney better, but she sure as shit wasn't going to say or do anything that would make Harley feel worse.

Concern showed nakedly on Catherine's chiseled face as the paramedics pushed the stretcher through to the kitchen. Harley, who had begun to wail in the ensuing moments, became silent when the trio appeared with Sydney on that same stretcher.

"Mommy. Mommy," Harley choked as she broke away from Sharron and threw herself at her mother's still form.

Catherine knelt to the little girl, her heart wrenching at the shock and pain that was so apparent on Harley's face.

"Come on darling, you come along with me to the airport. A big helicopter is going to come and give you and me and your mommy a ride all the way to Boston. I'll answer all your questions in the car. I promise."

Catherine knew that this promise was the most challenging one she had ever made. She had no idea how she was going to tell this sweet, sensitive child how serious things were with her mother. How could she not?

One thing Catherine had never done, in all her years, was fail to keep a promise to a child. It was a lesson her parents had taught her, and a responsibility she treated as an oath.

CHAPTER 7

I called out to Jennifer and Buster who were sitting closely on the edge of the dock, both staring out at the horizon. Buster's nose hung over the edge, warily monitoring the undersea activities, his large puppy head resting on his left paw. In all of his twelve years with me he had never once managed to actually catch a fish, corner a squirrel or capture a cat - but still he tried. Bless him.

The two turned in unison at the sound of my voice and I signaled for them that lunch was served. Thanks to Meg, and her supply stocking, I had managed to make two of my favorite sandwiches for my guest and me.

Crusty calabrase rolls, the centers hollowed out, stuffed full with roast turkey, sliced beefsteak tomato, swiss cheese, mayonnaise, sprouts, salt, pepper, and finally, a dollop of hot horseradish, balanced precariously on top of the stack. Sandwiches are art, I thought; a chance to create, melding together flavors and textures that were a delight to the taste buds. A mound of Cape Cod potato chips, and a huge glass of cold milk rounded out the meal.

"Wow. Will that fit in my mouth?"

"Never fear. I haven't lost a rookie yet. I thought we'd eat on the deck. Can I get you a cold beer or a glass of wine?"

"That milk you have looks good to me."

"Comin' up."

I nearly tripped over Buster on my way to the deck. Jennifer had pulled the Adirondack chairs up to the table that my friend Leah had made from bits and pieces of fallen trees. It was a rickety piece and Jennifer looked quite comfortable sitting there gazing out at the water. Wherever she was, I decided, I'll let her be. This is my vacation and her business. Besides, I had more important matters to encourage the blood to my brain. Like getting to the gym, for one. And not smoking. There was a mental challenge if ever there was one. The gym intimidated me and I knew I would have to commit myself on a daily basis. The smoking thing distracted me. Damn.

In my day I had been threatened by some of the best. Psychotics, sociopaths, your run of the mill perverts, to name a few. You would think that facing my own weaknesses would be a breeze. Hah!

"What?"

"What, what?"

"You said something."

"Did I?".

"Thought so."

"Oh."

"Great sandwich."

"Mrmmh."

I munched happily, barely aware of Jennifer's presence. We managed a companionable silence that was broken by the whup, whup, whup of a siren. Strange, I wondered, straightening stiffly from my chair. Not a familiar sound around these parts. On auto-pilot I headed out the front door after the sound. It was in my blood, I allowed, following me like a lousy dog.

I turned at a sound behind me and saw Jennifer following close, a look of apprehension clouding her dark features.

"Where are *you* going?" I shot back over my shoulder.

"Same place you are."

"What are you, some kind of an ambulance chaser?"

"Something like that. I'm a lawyer."

"Ah-ha."

"Ah-ha what?"

"Just ah-ha."

"Uh-uh," Jennifer retorted derisively.

We reached Commercial Street on a run and didn't have to look hard for the source of the siren. An ambulance was parked out front of *The Shooting Gallery*.

Jennifer broke into a run, her gasp of horror lost on the wind. I wasn't far behind, with Buster fast on my heel.

As we made for the entrance we were pushed aside by the paramedics who were converging on their patient

Jennifer wailed. "Oh God, no, Sydney, not you. Please God, not you"

Odd, I pondered. What does that mean? Well, time enough for that later. I turned away from Jennifer and ran smack dab into Catherine Hobbes, a pleasant activity at even the worst of times, who protectively clutched Harley's hand.

"Catherine. What's going on here?" I asked.

"Not now Jess. I have to go with Sydney and Harley. We need to get her to Mass Gen as soon as possible. Gill can fill you in."

I yelled after her fleeing form, "Call me tonight. We need to talk."

A look passed between us. Our talk was long overdue and we both knew it.

"I'll find out what I can in the meantime."

Gill spooked me when she spoke into my left shoulder blade.

"I hope that means you're going to find out who the animal was who did this to Sydney."

I turned to Jennifer, who wore a look of guilt like a shroud over her eyes. I doubted that Sydney's condition had anything to do with an animal, at least not a four-legged one. "Yeah," I answered. "That's what it means. Jennifer, we have to have a little chat, too."

The three of us stood quietly for a moment as the ambulance pulled away. Catherine and Harley followed behind in Sydney's car.

Jennifer seemed torn between the departing ambulance and me. I won.

"Now...you and me, counselor," I whispered lethally.

I was pissed off. I don't like it when bad things happen to people I know and care about. Sydney and I may not have been best friends, but we were at least well acquainted. And Harley. Whew, what a gal that was. Even I had turned to mush at her ingenuous nature and spirited laughter. She had, more than once, inspired my biological clock into a cacophonous roar.

Harley and Buster were great friends, which accounted for his current moribund demeanor. He had, of course, followed me to the restaurant and stood pitifully looking after Harley, his tail hidden between his legs. She would come daily, when we were around, and play for hours with 'her pal,' digging deep into his canine heart and burrowing safely there.

She brought out the puppy in him and he the little girl in her. They *were* kindred friends and for this, if only this, I owed Sydney my best. I suspected that Jennifer knew something and I was determined to find out what that was.

They both followed me inside the restaurant. I motioned for Jennifer to sit while I went into the kitchen to reconnoiter. Work stations had been shoved aside, presumably by the paramedics. I called to Gill. I needed details and I needed them fast. Trails can grow cold quickly and I intended to hit this one while it was still warm.

Gill entered the kitchen. I looked in her eyes and knew that I had only a few precious minutes before the barely concealed hysteria I detected bubbled to the surface.

"Okay. Second by second, tell me everything." I encouraged her, my arm draping around her ample shoulder.

"I don't know anything," she wailed.

"You'd be surprised Gillian. Go ahead. Just go slow and tell me, from the moment you got here 'til now. Don't leave anything out," I encouraged.

Gillian sat heavily on a stool. "I got here around forty-five minutes ago. I knew Sydney was here because I saw her car around back. It's our routine. Every day, for years now, one of us gets here and puts on the coffee for the other. Every day! Anyway, I called out and when she didn't answer I came through to here and," her voice began to crack, "and there she was. Lying in a heap. She wasn't moving." The sobs began now in earnest.

"Okay Gill. Hang in there. There's gotta be something else. How would someone have gotten in. Did you see a weapon? Did you hear anything?" I fired at her, trying to shock her into attentiveness.

"Yes, yes there was something. The back door. It was open. Sydney never leaves it open. But that's all. Oh Jess, what are we going to do?"

"Well. You're going to go and keep an eye on my guest out there and I'm going to have a look around out back. Her name is Jennifer and she has to stay put 'til I get back."

"Oh, I know Jennifer. She's Sydney's lawyer. I met her a couple of months ago when Sydney and I went to Boston on a supply run. Sydney went to her office and kept me waiting for hours. She was in some mood all the way home in the car. Wouldn't talk to me or anything."

Hmmm. Curiouser and curiouser. Romance? Business? But that would have to wait. I treaded carefully through the back door. Unless I missed my guess, this was where Sydney's attacker had crouched in waiting for her arrival. I hoped he or she had been careless enough to leave some sort of a clue. I inched my way back to the bramble of weeds and sea grass that grew profusely at the edge of the driveway. Beyond this was the beach, which was never anxious to yield any imprints on a blustery day such as this. My eyes were on the ground below me, my concentration so intense that I failed to hear the distinctive crack of a dry twig. Until it was too late.

The first blow, just below my left ear, spun me around to face my attacker. The next blow brought me to my knees twisting my ankle painfully. I was gazing crookedly at black jeans, and really expensive looking leather boots. How original, I thought. Was there a black hat too?

One knee moved imperceptibly and I rolled away from it just in time to save my jaw from its impact. I grabbed at a foot as it turned to run and twisted it with all my strength. I heard a groan and felt the figure falling to the ground in front of me.

I held fast, although I was pretty sure those boots weren't going anywhere. Leverage, not size or strength, was on my side.

I observed that the knee and foot were facing in the opposite direction. Good for me, not so good for the owner of the leg.

"Ah shit," a rough male voice cursed. "You broke my fuckin' leg, you bitch."

I hated that. Now I was really pissed off.
"Wanna go for a pair?" I snarled at the sole of his boot.

"Just let go, will ya?"

"Not so fast."

I unfolded myself, spitting out a bucket full of beach, the finer particles crunching unpleasantly between my teeth.

I secured my attacker with what I think was my right foot, but unfortunately, due to a raging roar in my ears, a result of the blow to my head, I couldn't be sure of my footing. I suppose if he'd really tried he could have escaped, but he stayed put for the moment. I tentatively raised my hand to the back of my head and drew it away for a more in-depth examination. Blood. Just blood. No bony bits of skull or gooey bits of brain seemed to be present. This I took as a good sign. My vision blurred as I raised myself to an upright position. Otherwise, I seemed intact.

I turned my fuzzy attention to the prone body beneath me. "Get up."

"I can't. You broke my leg."

"Get up anyway." I nudged, not gently, with my good foot, feeling the play in his rib-cage.

He rose to his full height that I guessed to be somewhere from six to twenty feet.

Either way, the discrepancy in our physiques must have given him a pain in his ego that far and away ached more than the pain in his leg. Good. The man before me was big. Not big in a football sense, but big in a 'nice belt buckle you got there' kind of way.

His look reminded me of what, in the lexicon of the Brontes, would be called 'black Irish.' Brooding, dark and gorgeous.

"Who are you?" Always with the tough questions. Whatta pro, huh?

"What's it to you?"

"Nothing. Tell me anyway."

"Timothy Ryan." Amazing that anything intelligible could cram its' way through those tightly clenched, and, I surmised, capped, teeth.

"Ryan? As in Sydney Ryan?"

"Ooh, you are good"

I hate sarcasm...in others. This guy was not endearing himself to me. In fact, I don't even think he was trying. Shame, shame.

I heard footsteps behind me but kept my attention on my burly assailant. I heard a ragged intake of breath and Jennifer appeared at my side.

"What the hell are you doing here?" she accused Timothy, with no apprehension in her tone.

"Great. Two bitches for the price of one."

That tore it. I snatched at the front of his shirt and hauled Timothy Ryan toward me. He had the good sense to look surprised by my strength. That made two of us. My endorphins have always had a mind of their own, bless their hormonal hearts.

We stood, eye to sternum, where I firmly implanted myself in his space, thus blocking his proximity to Jennifer. "Before I call the cops, maybe you feel like having an enlightening chat with me." I was feeling generous. In truth, I would be happy to see Stretch hauled off in manacles by the local constabulary.

"Fine, whatever. For Christ's sake lady. What kinda nut bar are you?"

"Payday, since you asked." The thought of food brought a wave of nausea through my throat, stopping just short of my molars. My head throbbed and I chanced a quick swipe through my now matted hair. My hand came away damp and sticky with blood, smelling faintly metallic. I often had nightmares that involved bits of my brain, in the form of memories, seeping out of my ears and into oblivion.

I felt Jennifer close behind me, as she placed her perfectly manicured hand on my shoulder. I shook it off impatiently.

"You, start talking," I barked at either of them. Silence. Hmmm. That won't do. A more direct approach was obviously required. "All right boys and girls. Who wants to go first? Let's see, eeny meeny miny moe - I pick the one with the broken toe."

"Listen babe, I had nothing to do with what happened to Sydney."

"Babe? Babe?!? Lesson one, Magilla Gorilla, my name is Jess. Jess Shore. Not babe, or hon, or sweetie. Lesson two, nobody said anything about Sydney - so....for a guy with only one good foot, you sure have a knack for sticking it in your mouth. Lesson three, innocent bystanders do not thunk other innocent bystanders on the back of the head and try to run away - ergo...I find your presence here, shall we say, suspect."

"Maybe I can help."

"Okay Jennifer. I like that idea. Let's start with who the hell are you and what the hell are you doing here, if you don't mind." Boy. I really was pissed - and not very articulate as a result. Good.

"I'm a lawyer. Sydney's lawyer."

"Yeah. That's one name for it," snarled Ryan, contempt for Jennifer making his black eyes sparkle dangerously.

"Shut up Tim. I'm going to tell her everything. She has to know. Whoever did this to Sydney has to be caught. I have enough on my conscience - thanks to you, you bastard."

"That's enough." I snapped back. My head was swimming and felt like it was going under. I desperately wanted to lie down with my dog and have a little nap for a week or so. Later. Clearly these two would be best separated, which presented a little problem of logistics for me.

Gillian to the rescue, meat cleaver in hand..."Jess. Can I help?" The look in her eyes had gone from its earlier panic to something approaching rage. I liked it.

"Yeah Gill. Take the Unfriendly Giant here inside, will ya. Me and Jen Jen are going to have a little chat."

I noticed, with delight, that Timothy Ryan had the good sense to look intimidated by his guard, as he hobbled after her, wincing in pain. Gillian and her cleaver followed close behind.

I spun around to face Jennifer. She did not have the good sense to look intimidated. I must be losing my touch.

CHAPTER 8

"**I** met Sydney three years ago. She just walked into my office one day and started talking," Jennifer began.

The story goes something like this...Harley's father is Timothy Ryan. The Ryans still have the splinters under their nails from the Mayflower and like people to know it. They have money, scads of it, power and, most important of all, apparently, social standing. Timothy was their only male error. Oops - I mean heir. He was not an over achiever by anyone's stretch. He had a past that his family hoped to keep hidden from the masses, including the illegitimate birth of a daughter with a woman of questionable sexual habits, plus a quickie and ill thought out marriage. Blah, blah, blah.

Jennifer was never clear as to why Sydney and Tim got married. It may have been that he was doing the honorable thing but that seemed doubtful. It may have been that Sydney had forced his hand to give their daughter legitimacy. To give her a name and a history. Jennifer never knew the answer and didn't press Sydney for an explanation. It was never germane to her case in a personal sense but did muddy the waters legally.

As for his parents, Timothy Ryan, Sr. had taken the family-owned financial investment consulting firm and made it mega huge. Riding the wave of the bull markets over the years and tucking in during the bear times had assured Mr. Ryan Sr. of a place in financial history.

Ryan Financial Enterprises took the 'fun' out of mutual funds and dedicated their considerable resources to accumulating greater hoards of cash for themselves and their clients.

As for Mrs. Ryan, she was a bit of a mystery. Considering the family standing you would think she would have been an oft mentioned doyenne of the social scene. Not so. Her photo was snapped from time to time with her husband but mostly he was out and about on his own. There was no hint of marital scandal surrounding the couple but still it seemed odd that so little was known about Mrs. Ryan.

Okay, so...I get the picture. I'm quick that way. The past, especially his, only interested me insofar as it concerned the present. So. How did Jennifer fit in? I let her continue.

"Sydney has raised Harley herself, as I'm sure you know. Tim had only seen his daughter once, shortly after she was born. He had offered Sydney a financial package that, for all intents and purposes, concluded his legal and moral obligations. It always seemed strange to me that they got married in the first place. I suppose it would have been confusing if Sydney and Harley had different last names. Too many questions.

I came to wonder if Tim's plan had been to take Harley all along. It seemed unlikely though, he not being the fatherly type as far as I could tell, but you never know about people. Tim Ryan was raised in a world where power rules and having the most toys when you die *does* make you a winner. Maybe Harley was just another toy to the Ryans. An acquisition that was made more valuable by its inaccessibility.

Initially, Tim's parents had descended upon Sydney in an attempt to wrest control of Harley from her mother. Sydney had thrown them out that day and that was the last she had seen of any of the Ryans...until three years ago.

Harley was five and Sydney had been here, in Provincetown, for two years. She had no contact with Timothy and she hoped it would always stay that way. It didn't.

He showed up here, out of the blue, and told Sydney that he wanted to get to know his daughter - spend time with her. Sydney refused. Of course she didn't trust his motives. She suspected that there was more to it. The only 'bonding' Timothy Ryan was interested in was dental. Tim blew a fuse and threatened to get a court order. That's where I came onto the scene."

"Don't stop now, Jennifer. If I'm going to help Sydney I have to know everything. All of it." I could almost see the energy draining out of her. Whatever it was between her and Sydney, it had rented some big space in Jennifer's head for a while now. I wasn't sure about her as a person, but I was willing to concede that she was good at what she does. I would investigate her background further as time allowed but for now I would have to go with what she volunteered. And she volunteered a fair bit.

Jennifer is a good lawyer, as if that weren't an oxymoron. Like Catherine Hobbes, she attended Harvard but, unlike Catherine, used her prestigious education and vast smarts to land herself a big-time job with big time perks at a Manhattan firm. Robinson, Kline and Stone was and still is one of the largest and most profitable legal machines in the business.

She flew high for a couple of years and then: the incident. Jennifer had been having an affair with the wife of one of the senior partners.

No biggie in and of itself however, as bad luck would have it, things got a tad messy when Mrs. Senior Partner wanted to U-Haul herself over to Jen Jen's and sue Mr. Senior Partner for half of everything, including his share in the law partnership.

This did not go over well, so Jennifer took a big package of pay and perks and left to start her own business in Boston.

Although several of Jennifer's former clients followed her to Boston, she found herself moving away from the highly profitable and high profile cases of her past. What Jennifer moved towards was championing the rights of children caught in the middle of messy and complicated custody battles. I suspected that this choice had something to do with her own past, but that too would have to wait for confirmation.

Jennifer tended to work most closely with the children involved, regardless of who was paying the bills. She could afford to pick and choose her clients and she did, weighing the pros and cons from the child's viewpoint. If this didn't suit her client - so be it.

She didn't lose often and if she did she would go back and start from scratch, no charge, until she felt that the child had been placed in the most safe and loving home.

Jennifer's reputation had extended into Provincetown where she provided counsel for a handful of adoptions that friends of Sydney had gone through. For two women or two men to adopt a child together, a savvy lawyer was as important as a sound working knowledge of Dr. Spock. Jennifer was that and more, and Sydney knew this.

The same day that Timothy Ryan had darkened Sydney's door she had made a beeline for Jennifer's office, young Harley in tow.

Their initial meeting had lasted well into the wee hours. Harley had fallen asleep in her mother's arms and drooled endearingly on Jennifer's leather sofa. Sydney's case was not as cut and dried as some.

First of all, she was still legally married to Timothy Ryan. Timothy Ryan was the biological father of Harley. Timothy Ryan came from one of the most well respected and well-known families in Boston. Not so Sydney. She was an independent businesswoman. Her restaurant was just beginning to show some signs of success.

And Harley. The mother/daughter bond between those two was one of the most profound Jennifer had ever witnessed.

Jennifer had met and grown close to many children in her time but this one was special. There was no question in Jennifer's mind that Harley and Sydney belonged together but she did tell her new client that she would need to meet with Timothy Ryan before going any further.

Sydney had understood and agreed with this and provided Jennifer with Tim's phone number and address. The next morning Jennifer arrived at her office to find Mr. Ryan slumped threateningly behind her desk. The air in her office was thick with smoke and Jennifer had to count to ten before she trusted herself to speak.

"Mr. Ryan, I presume?"

"Wow, I'm impressed."

"You should be, Mr. Ryan. I am good, and you are trespassing on my private property. Please get out of my chair, open a window, go out to my receptionist and make an appointment to see me. Good day Mr. Ryan."

He was slow about it but he did, after all, comply. Jennifer had not achieved such a successful win rate in court without learning to assert her strong personality by way of body language and facial expression. She was not to be trifled with and this was apparent to even the densest observer. Her exotic appearance did not work against her in this regard. She was as darkly beautiful and absolutely self confident as Tim Ryan was. He was not sheepish mind you, but neither was he belligerent about it. Their eyes locked briefly as he passed by her. He seemed about to say something but thought better of it. After the door closed behind him, Jennifer exhaled and took up her place behind her desk. Her phone buzzed. It was Rochelle, her receptionist.

"Ah, Jennifer. There's a Mr. Ryan here to see you. He doesn't have an appointment but you are clear until one this afternoon. Shall I send him in?" She sounded peevish. Rochelle didn't care for being usurped in her fiefdom and if Ryan knew what was good for him he'd get that message and fast.

"Sure Rochelle, and could you please bring me a coffee. Strong. See what our visitor wants, will you?"

Tim came back in. He was a strikingly handsome man. He was well over six feet, with dark, chiseled features. His raven black hair was carefully groomed in a deliberately carefree style. His dark eyebrows partially framed deep-set eyes that sparked unpleasantly at Jennifer. He managed to look both threatening and harmless at the same time. His malevolence was practiced rather than profound. He appeared to have adopted a look that would speak for itself so he wouldn't have to. He used his physical size to provide shelter for his true personality.

He was dressed in a casual and, Jennifer suspected, expensive way. A man with no place to go but determined to turn heads when he got there. He walked with a grace that seemed rehearsed.

Jennifer felt like she had wandered into a lion's den and found the mighty beast to be declawed. Whatever lingering unease she may have felt upon finding Timothy Ryan invading her space was vanquished as she indicated a chair for Tim to sit in. She chose the one next to him and moved solidly into his personal space, nearly kicking him in the shin as she crossed her long and well-muscled legs.

Jennifer knew that tact and diplomacy would be crucial to the case. Her objective was clear. Harley belonged with her mother. Nothing would sway Jennifer from that opinion, however, she did subscribe to the theory that you catch more flies with honey than vinegar, or some such.

"All right Mr. Ryan. What was it you wanted to see me about?"

"And all this time I heard you were a bright gal. Guess you can't trust rumors, huh? " He had a distasteful, snorty kind of laugh. Jennifer concentrated on not letting her lips curl in distaste.

"Point taken. I assume you want to discuss my client, Sydney Ryan."

"Under the 'B' - 13...Bingo. Give the little lady a prize."

"Mr. Ryan. You and I can exchange barbs and see who draws first blood...or we can get down to the matter at hand. Here it is, in simple terms. Sydney wants an annulment and full custody of her child. She is entitled to the annulment given that the two of you have had sexual relations only once, and that was prior to the marriage contract being drawn up. This is, and I'll save you some time and energy here, a clean-cut and clear argument for the dissolution of your union.

Further, my client wishes to inform you that she does not intend, now or in the future, to seek any form of remuneration from you, although she is, by law, entitled to a portion of your assets. She is willing to authorize a contract to this effect. Sydney wants nothing from you Mr. Ryan. Nothing at all. Are you clear so far?"

"It's okay pretty lady, I have no problem with giving Sydney a divorce. Hell, I haven't even seen her for years. I only married her in the first place to piss off my family. She's a dyke, you know. Not much there for me, if you catch my meaning."

"I do Mr. Ryan, Rest assured, I will not allow her sexuality to become an issue in the divorce action."

"What about the kid? Dykes don't get the kids. I checked with my lawyer. Oh. Speaking of that, you may know my lawyer. In fact, I understand the two of you used to work together. He mentioned to me that you and his wife were quite close. Care to take three guesses?" Damn, damn, damn. Jennifer showed nothing in her countenance, but inside, a cold finger of fear traced its way down her spine. Lester Robinson. She'd always known that whole debacle would come back to haunt her. Well, if it's hardball he wants...

"If you're trying to blackmail me, you're using the wrong zip code. What happened in New York is history." She may or may not have been bluffing, she just didn't want him guessing which it was.

"Or 'her-story'." His laugh made Jennifer want to take a shower.

"Enough Mr. Ryan. My personal life has no bearing on this discussion."

" Okay. I'll buy that. How about this, counselor. No way, no how, and at no time will I give Sydney full custody of my child. She can have her divorce. That's it. In fact, my lawyer has prepared things from our end already. The demise is in the works as we speak."

Jennifer was instantly suspicious. This was too easy. She watched Tim Ryan get up from his chair and walk over to the window. Hmmm. No eye contact. Something's up. Jennifer wasn't surprised that Ryan was willing to agree to the divorce, what she didn't expect was the anger that had frothed its way to the surface when he had mentioned Harley.

Jennifer had already made the decision to remain detached from whatever emotions Timothy Ryan might evoke in her. To Jennifer, Ryan represented all that she hated about custody battles and dissolution of unions. The ugly. The petty. The art of separating out the hurt and anger from the real issues. This proved to be a challenge, as she was to discover.

"Mr. Ryan, I appreciate your cooperation with respect to your divorce. I am, however, interested in hearing your reasons for the statements you have made concerning Harley. I also think it would be judicious of you to request the presence of your lawyer for that discussion in order that all four of us may sit down and discuss the matter." He spun to face her, his anger turning him ugly. Jennifer met him iris for iris.

"There's no point in us sitting down together because there is nothing to discuss. I will not relinquish my paternal rights to my child. This is a non-negotiable point. What you can address with my attorney is the terms of the custody agreement that I will allow."

Jennifer made a grab for one of the many questions that were whizzing about in her mind. What she came up with was this. Why, after so many years was this man digging in his heels and fighting for his rights as the donor of sperm that lead to the miracle that is Harley Ryan? This proved to be the arrow that found its target."

I had listened to Jennifer's recollections in silence, no mean feat for me, I can tell you that. I had to interject...it's my nature. "Let me guess. If this was my case, I'd shove Tim aside and check what's hanging in his closet. Momsy. Poppy. Maybe a girlfriend or two. Maybe a boyfriend. Okay. I'll take a chance to bark up the wrong birch...he was in love, right? Is that it? Tim Ryan needed to get free and unencumbered?" I questioned her.

Jennifer barely hid her surprise, and I had the satisfaction of watching it turn to something closer to respect. 'Take that smarty pants.'

Women like Jennifer Eastcott were not usually accustomed to women like me. For myself, I preferred Levis to A-lines, Docs over pumps, and football to ballet.

I liked to conceal my intellect under an opaque drape of sarcasm and gruffness where it could keep my heart company.

"Well???" Is that it? Was Tiny Tim in love?"

"Yes. Well, I don't know exactly, but he was engaged to be married. I didn't find out until a few weeks ago who his fiancée was. Does the name Muffin DeWitt mean anything to you?"

"Bran or Oatmeal?"

"Huh?"

"Nothing. Listen Jennifer, I left my social register at home. Who, or what, is a Muffin DeWitt?"

I detected a smile knocking at the corners of her full red lips. I hoped she would let it in as I already knew a smile could well transform this beauty's face. Jennifer explained.

"The DeWitts are one of the richest families on the East Coast. Their fortune was built up late in the 1800's. Transportation. Muffin's father took over the family business about forty years ago and turned it into a mega conglomerate worth billions. His history is not unlike the senior Timothy Ryan. The DeWitts have their fingers in a lot of pies but mostly their mainstay is the mainframe. Computers and operating systems are their bread and butter.

Muffin is his only daughter from his first wife. She died when Muffin was just a child. If you can believe what you read, Mr. DeWitt was devastated by the loss of his wife. Anyone who knew the couple agreed that theirs was a true love story and her death at such a young age was a real tragedy.

In time Mr. DeWitt remarried and had twin sons with the new Mrs. DeWitt. Muffin grew up at boarding school, pretty much. Her choice, apparently. She was a bright student and seemed to prefer living away from home and her step-family. She's got a post graduate degree in business and does volunteer work, mostly for the A.S.P.C.A.," Jennifer explained.

There was something in Jennifer's voice while she laid out the story of Tim's fiancée. I felt a niggling in my head but couldn't nail it down. I decided to let the rest of the story unfold and listen carefully to what wasn't being said as much as what was.

"So, Daddy's little baked good has a good mind and a soft spot for animals. I'm starting to get a picture now. Tell me more," I encouraged.

It went something like this...Jennifer had put her firm's investigator on Ryan's trail. What she came back with was that Tim Ryan was not exactly the catch 'o the day as far as Mr. DeWitt was concerned. Even though Muffin had been shuffled off at an early age it seemed both parental units had a genuine concern for her future and well-being. Mr. DeWitt in particular sounded to be a little on the overprotective side and I thought that made sense given the events of Muffin's childhood. Chances are good that Muffin is a constant and fully formed version of her beloved mother. That's gotta be tough. Jennifer also had the impression that the second Mrs. DeWitt was an okay sort of gal and that the marriage was sound.

Tim's misspent adulthood and playboy lifestyle did not sit well with the elders of Muffy's clan and he was in desperate need of a bargaining chip. Pere DeWitt had not yet given his okey dokey for the marriage of his daughter to our Timmy and had confronted him with his own investigator's report.

Seems Mr. D.W. had found out about Harley and Sydney and was threatening to go to Muff Muff with the information. He figured Tim would have to act fast, assuming Muffin didn't already know. That part Mr. DeWitt just assumed: that Tim had not been honest with Muffin about his past. Add to this the fact that Tim's family was tired of his antics and the money train wasn't making as many stops as it used to. Lots of pressure for a fella that didn't seem to take responsibility well.

Mr. and Mrs. Ryan had informed Tim that it was time to settle down and get properly married or get out. A marriage to the little tea biscuit was the perfect pacifier for the elder Ryans. They not only approved of Tim's plans - they insisted that this was his last chance with them.

I would have felt some sympathy for him but the goose egg on the back of my head and still swelling ankle helped me keep my perspective. Young Tim was a bully. A ne'er-do-well. I figured it hadn't been easy being him, the progeny with its inherent pressure to succeed. Having to make a name for himself and, moreover, to live up to the name he had was probably no picnic. So he chose a girl that was not only obscenely wealthy, but rich in fiber as well. I didn't want to jump to any conclusions, and I was still unsure as to how Harley fit in. I asked Jennifer what she had come up with.

Mr. DeWitt had confronted Tim with his investigator's report that included the information about Tim's missing family. He knew about Sydney and he knew about Harley. The details of Sydney's lifestyle and Tim's involvement did not please Mr. DeWitt and he had presented Tim with an ultimatum. He insisted that Tim take responsibility for his actions and prove himself worthy of his daughter.

The child would be accepted into the family and Tim would be allowed to marry Muffin. To the DeWitts, a single father making good on his youthful lusty past and nobly raising his child was appealing. No thought seemed to be given for Sydney's role in all of this.

Mr. DeWitt sounded like a decent, if manipulative sort, but still...did he really think wrenching a little girl away from her mother...out of the blue...was the right thing to do?

Tim had agreed, at the time, to these conditions. At least that's what he told the old boy. Desperate times called for desperate measures. Harley had become a bargaining chip in Ryan's future. Without her playing the role of devoted and grateful daughter, Tim Ryan would be out on his ear. The scary part, as Jennifer found out, was that Timothy Ryan saw nothing morally wrong with his plans. He fully believed that Sydney would affix a price to the head of her treasured child, and that would be that.

Not!

Questions rattled around in my aching head. Something was not right about this little tale. Why would a prominent Boston family want to take on the child of a man who clearly fell well below their standards? Why would they welcome a grandchild of dubious background into their little coven? Nope. I smelled a rat. I decided to keep my suspicions to myself. I still wasn't convinced that Jennifer was as picture perfect as she seemed and I wanted to play my cards close to the chest.

When Jennifer had received the report from her investigator, she had contacted Sydney and arranged for a meeting. Things got ugly pretty fast, according to what Jennifer was telling me. Suffice it to say...Sydney had zero intention of giving Tim Ryan anything more than a divorce. The issue of custody was not on the table, nor would it ever be, as far as Sydney was concerned. To say she posed a flight risk would be an understatement. To keep her child with her, Sydney would gladly pick up and disappear in a breath. She told Jennifer as much. Jennifer continued.

"I tried to reassure her. She was so angry and frightened." Jennifer, as an attorney, could not openly encourage a 'flight'-type of a solution. Instead, she got Sydney to agree to let her try to settle the custody issue through the courts. Jennifer had sounded more confident than she felt. However, the mighty forces that would come to the party did not intimidate her. In fact, Jennifer looked forward to the eventual show down at O-Pay Corral.

Money shouldn't influence the courts decisions with respect to custody but Jennifer was savvy enough to know that it had in the past. She was determined not to let that happen to Harley.

I was about to probe deeper when I felt a cold and damp butt at my hand. "Hey there big fella, what's up?"

Buster's head bobbed up and down like a stallion about to charge. This must be important. He butted at my hand again and as I opened it up to his nudging, he dropped something into it. "Hmmm. What have we here?" I studied the discovery, while at the same time wiping the gooey strings of doggie goober off, yet kept it hidden from view. Interesting, I thought, as I slipped the object into the back pocket of my jeans.

I had never really trained Buster to be my assistant but he seemed to be a natural. He has good instincts and a great sniffer. In the past his help had been invaluable and it looks like he may have done it again. A clue, no matter how delivered is crucial, especially at the outset of a case.

"What a good detective. What say you and me go call Auntie Karen and ask her to order us up some fuel and we'll go for a plane ride? Wanna go see Harley?" His head cocked to the side, ears stiffened, in a vain yet worthy attempt to understand. The tail wagged wildly none the less.

Jennifer placed her manicured hand on my arm, her grip warm and familiar. It would have been obvious that I was discomforted by her touch if I had pulled back, so I made a conscious effort to stand fast. I will not flinch, I will not flinch. Sometimes with me I can't be sure if I really want or don't want someone to touch me. Either way - it could take lots of effort to let it be.

"What about me?"

Indeed, I thought.

"Can you keep Tim Ryan here for awhile? I have to go and see Sydney, talk to Harley and Catherine. I don't want to wait any longer. I will need to talk to him when I get back, though. Think you could manage that?"

I really didn't mean to sound sarcastic but I think the pain in my head and the hot burning spot on my arm, under her hand, were getting to me.

"I'd rather go with you to see Sydney." a look of sorrow curtains her eyes.

"I need you here Jennifer. You can't help Sydney by standing vigil over her, but you can help her by keeping her husband..."

"Ex husband."

"I stand corrected." I continued. "Her ex-husband, a detail by the by, that you neglected to apprise me of...I want Ryan here when I come back. What are the chances?"

"How does absolutely, with utter certainty, and unequivocally sound to you?"

"That works for me. You can either keep him here, or, if you feel safe with him, you can take him back to my place and wait for me there."

"Should I be afraid of him Jess? Did he do this?"

"I have no way of knowing that. His presence, to say the least, is suspicious, but I just don't know yet. Take Gilly with you, too. Between the two of you I'm sure our Mr. Ryan will be happy to sit quietly like a good little brute. What do you say counselor?"

"I say...see you later. Oh - and please, tell Sydney...tell her...oh skip it."

"I don't think she'll feel much like skipping, but I'll pass along the message."

A smile sped by her eyes and their color changed to moss. Maybe they were contact lenses. "Thank you Jess. I'll be waiting for you. We all will, don't worry about that."

I was already worried but kept it to myself. I checked in quickly with Sharron and Gillian and let them know what I was up to. I didn't have time for details and any questions I had for them would have to wait for the moment. I trusted them both implicitly and knew that they would be my eyes and ears in my absence.

CHAPTER 9

Karen had heard all about Sydney's predicament and my plane had been fueled, the pre-flight completed and Gold Alpha Yankee was lined up and ready to go when Buster and I arrived at the airport.

"Thanks Karen."

"Go Jess. You're cleared to take-off. Watch out for mid-level gusts, twenty-five to thirty-five knots, at about 5000 feet around Hyannis, otherwise, you've got nothing to worry about. I filed your flight plan with Logan. They're expecting you in about an hour. I arranged for a friend of mine to meet you at the airport. Her name's Kelly. Says you met her on your way out here. She'll give you a ride to the hospital."

"What, no catered meal on board. Geez pal, you're slipping," I laughed, as I threw my arms around her.

She moved me gently, yet firmly, away from her. "Better leave the flea bag with me Jess. They won't let him in the hospital."

Ooh boy. He's not gonna like that. It was just a brief infestation three years back, and his embarrassment was still acute. Poor fella. I must caution Karen against any further spurious comments vis a vis the flea thing.

"Good point. I guess I may be there for a while too. Thanks for everything Karen. I'll call you as soon as I have news. Oh, by the way. I've got some, ah, visitors at my place.

On your way home, if you could, just stick your head in and see that all the kids are playing nicely. Maybe drop Buster off too. Next to you, he's the one whose opinion I trust the most. Maybe he could enlighten me a little bit."

"Done. Bye."

"Love you too, Karen."

"Mrmpfh."

A woman of few words and many thoughts.

True to her word, as I was climbing the stairs from the basement arrivals lounge at Logan I recognized the face of Kelly, as Karen promised.

I must have been distracted before, what with Jennifer hitching a ride and all, otherwise I would have taken note of the lovely, younger than me woman who was now introducing herself.

Kelly belonged on a beach. Any beach. She had the look of the sand and the surf in her very short, naturally blond hair, eyes the color of the Caribbean from about six thousand feet, and a body that had not yet had the pleasure of meeting gravity head on. She was dressed in a form fitting white T-shirt and well loved cut-off Levi's. Right down to her gleaming Docs and grey work socks, Kelly was a dish to be served, and likely enjoyed, outdoors.

"Hi. You're Jess. Karen sure nailed your ETA. I only just got here."

"Hmmm? Oh, yeah. Great. Thanks." I wondered what had happened to my brain.

"Yeah, well, anyway, my car's right outside. I jacked my hood up and put my flashers on. I figure we have about twenty-seven seconds or so before they impound me. You all set?"

Bright girl for fourteen, I mused. "All set."

"Karen said to take you right to the hospital. Do you need to make any stops or anything?"

"No, thanks. The sooner we get there the better. Do you have a phone in your car? I'd really like to check in with the hospital."

"I called them just as you touched down. Dr. Hobbes is expecting you and she said she would fill you in then. Will that do or did you still want to stop and make that call. Unfortunately my car phone is a figment of my imagination, along with the car it's eventually going to be installed in," she laughed.

She had a great laugh. I'm a sucker for a great laugh. It was big and clear and free, like the beach she carries inside her. If not for the mention of Catherine's name I might have drooled. Her chariot awaited. I was not surprised to discover that Kelly drove a Triumph Spitfire that was probably made the same year I got my driver's license. An antique, I'm sure she thought. It was orange, of course, as I suspected all really old Triumph Spitfire's were.

I wondered if we would have to pull a Fred and Barney to get it started but it fired right up. The top was down and I was glad I had worn not only clean underwear, but a warm jacket as well. I managed to rally my social graces.

"So Kelly, how is it you know Karen?"

"Oh Karen and my mom have been friends for ages. I can't remember how old I was when I first met her but I was pretty little. She took me flying when I was about three years old and I still say it was the most thrilling day of my life."

Boy...do I feel old. I tried not to fidget in my seat for fear she would hear my ancient bones creaking. Mid-life is a bitch.

"I know what you mean. Do you fly yourself?"

"Grounded. Migraines," Kelly mumbled bitterly.

"That sucks." Oh good. Now I'm fourteen. "Can you appeal? It worked for me but the U.S. rules may be different from Canada's. When I first took the medical for my license the board turned me down. I guess there's some blanket medical exemption thing and migraines are on the list. Anyway, I'd give it a shot."

"I'm doing that now. It looks good. Dr. Hobbes is helping me out with the FAA. She says I have a good chance. In the meantime, I have all the hours and stuff I need to get my license. It's up to the board now. Karen keeps telling me to keep the faith."

"Yeah, that's Karen. Listen, I wouldn't worry. With people like Karen and Catherine on your side, the FAA doesn't stand a chance." I hoped I sounded reassuring.

We settled into a comfortable and wind blown silence for the duration of the drive into the hospital. I was grateful for the respite. I needed to get my thoughts in order. I laid out the facts, as I knew them.

One. Somebody nailed Sydney. Were they already inside? Did they gain access by force? Did she let them in? Did she recognize her attacker? Did someone that I didn't know about have a grudge against her? Okay, that's way more than one question, but the answers to them did represent the first step in my investigation.

Two. Timothy Ryan. A real pip. Smug, angry, rich and physically imposing. Is there more to him than meets the eye? Is anyone that black and white? Was his desire for custody of Harley enough to inspire him to violence? Did he have other motivation? What was he doing in Provincetown? I should have thought to ask him that earlier but I was too distracted. I chastised my lapse, briefly.

Three. I need to get the answers to one and two. And fast.

CHAPTER 10

There was no mistaking it. My heart did a little leaping kind of thing when Kelly and I entered the hospital and saw Catherine leaning there, barely holding up herself and the cup of coffee in her hand. She was an impressively beautiful woman. A head turner. Striking, in a classic way. Today she wore her golden chestnut hair back from her face and slicked down close to her head. I called it her Secret Service 'do.' Nothing, not even a bullet could break through that sheen of gel and whatnot. This look showed off her cheekbones and striking greenish eyes to their full advantage. In some lights, her eyes had a distinctly hazel tone to them, muted and flecked with brown and gold, but mostly they were Crayola green. Right now they looked sad and vulnerable. Her legs, which were tan and firm, seemed to drag your eye along forever, before coming to an end at what I still consider to be one the finest posteriors in the history of women.

As I came closer those magnificent eyes nailed me in a look that made me feel like I was going to seize up. All of a sudden every movement of my body seemed to take a lot of concentration and I felt like Pinocchio. The solid line of her brows framed her mesmerizing orbs and I would have stared right back, whatever the cost, if Kelly hadn't propelled herself past me and into Catherine's face. What ho?

Had I misread the look I had assumed was leveled at me? Was my myopia such that I didn't realize the Catherine was looking past me, at young beach baby?

Well. No time for that now anyway.

I worked my way between them, sort of, and waited until I was sure I had Catherine's attention. Her look said I shouldn't worry about trying to get her attention. She reached a hand past Kelly and took one of my sweaty, clammy ones in it.

"How is she?" My voice sounded like I should clear my throat.

"Fine thanks Jess, and how have you been? Let's see now, by my calculation, it's been about a year now, give or take."

I searched her face for some signs of amusement and didn't see too much. She was miffed at me and rightly so. That too would have to wait.

"Love-15 to you Cat. Could we pick this up later?"

"Count on it."

Kelly, looked...bemused. Funny, I hadn't noticed before but she did seem to have more teeth than a 12 pack of combs.

"Come with me Jess. I'll take you to see Sydney. Kelly, would you mind checking in on Harley? She's at the nurse's station just down that hallway. I told her you were coming and I think I actually saw her smile. She really needs to be with family right now."

"Family? Kelly is family? I *have* been away too long."

"You got it doc. I'll see if she wants to go for a burger or something."

"Thanks Kel. Don't count on much though, she's pretty upset."

Kel?

"Come on Jess. I'll fill you in on the way."

Indeed!

CHAPTER 11

We made our way down the corridor and my mind wandered back to when I had first met Catherine.

She was already a hero, of sorts, what with her reputation as a world-renowned surgeon. That alone would have assured her of a thriving practice so imagine that combined with a charming personality, empathetic listening skills and, pardon the objectification, but honestly, nobody would toss her out of bed for eating dim sum.

Catherine's personal life was of interest to many and known to very few. Her friendship with Sydney had, in time, extended naturally to Harley, Gillian and the rest of *The Shooting Gallery* gang. Almost every night Sydney and Catherine could be seen having their Courvosier in the back room, the only light coming from the Tiffany over the pool table. They would play a game or six and then Sydney would give Catherine a lift on her own way home. Rumors die hard in a town the size of Provincetown, but die off they did when even the most industrious Gladys Kravitzes had to admit that theirs was just a friendship, nothing more. Somehow this seemed to create a more solid wall around Catherine than if they had been having a romance. It seemed that Dr. Hobbes was quite content with the way her new life was unfolding.

Oh sure, there had been offers and invitations, flowers and cards. Someone had, for a time, even sent her baked goods. Catherine had been in Provincetown for about three years before any hint of a romance whispered its way along Commercial Street and beyond, starring yours truly.

I had arrived in April that year, recovering from a bullet wound to my shoulder. If I had thought that leaving the police department would make my life less dangerous I had come to know differently.

My arm was freshly bound and here and there angry bruises and cuts - soon to be scars -dotted the landscape of my body. I ached all over, the result of a particularly physical end to my last case. I had foggy memories of bungee jumping off a bridge without benefit of a chord around my ankles in a vain attempt to outrun the .32 slug that was screaming towards my heart. The perp was in jail and I was taking a vacation. I had called Karen's partner Meg ahead of time and asked her to arrange for someone to open up the beach house for us since I didn't feel up to it. Also, following Meg's recommendation, I had called Dr. Catherine Hobbes from Toronto before I left and made an appointment with her for the day after I arrived. My aversion to doctors was about to come to a mushy and starry-eyed conclusion.

There I sat, my records and x-rays on my lap, Buster asleep at my feet, in one of the three comfortable, cushy, chairs that made up Catherine's waiting room. It was actually her front porch that had been opened up to allow the warming spring breezes to circulate out the last of the dry winter air. I must have dozed off, (I blame the codeine) and I came to with Buster's tail beating a tattoo on my left foot. As I dragged my eyes open I was eyeball to eyeball with one of the loveliest faces I had ever seen. I think I may have gulped. I tried to remember if I had brushed my teeth.

That day Catherine had thoroughly reviewed my file with me and gently poked and prodded my injuries. She said little during the actual exam and I will always remember the smell of her hair as she bent close to my shoulder and the way her eyes drew me deep inside and left me feeling breathless. It was like time stopped in that moment of contact.

Her thick, wavy golden mane tickled my skin where it whispered past, giving me a wicked and embarrassing case of 'chicken skin.' I may have swooned, but again, it may have been the drugs.

She looked at me over the volume of pages that made up my medical history. Before I had gone out on my own I had been relatively fit and whole. Being a cop I had had the requisite broken bones and bubbly scar tissue. I had supplemented these injuries with ones I had earned as an entrepreneur. Shot twice, once seriously, twice lucky, a multitude of fractures and torn ligaments, deep cuts, concussions, etc, etc.,

It was all there and the real proof was visible to the eyes of few who had seen me in the 'all or nothing' in the right light. I often thought of marking the more visible scars, like when you're kids and your parents would tick off your height progress on a wall or inside the pantry closet door.

We chatted a bit as the examination was winding down. Catherine told me that Sydney had mentioned me to her on a couple of occasions and she had looked forward to meeting me. I blushed.

I admitted that I too had heard about her. I hadn't intended to meet *this* way but...such is life. Catherine was easy to talk to and seemed a good listener.

I made an appointment to see her the following week and made my exit. I was halfway down her wisteria vine covered walk when I realized I was alone. I turned to call poochy and saw him standing at Catherine's side, the two of them framed in her doorway. He looked at me, then at her and made no overt move to come hither and yawn.

"Come on fella...let's go."

Nothing.

Mutiny! As I mentioned earlier Buster has an innate sense of people and he had obviously decided that Catherine was worth spending time with. Now the question was what to do next. I had made an oath to myself, awhile back, to tread ever so carefully when it came to coupling-like behaviors. I wasn't just gun shy, I was downright paranoid and neurotically cautious. I still bore the scars, literally, where I had been burned before and I was not inclined toward traveling that dark road again. There was no doubt that my heart and my libido had chatted and decided that Dr. Hobbes was well worth getting to know better. As usual, they tried to leave my head out of the decision making process.

There were two pairs of eyes staring at me. They both had a sort of amused and laughing light to them, both their heads tilted questionably to the side.

"Okay fella, you seem to be trying to tell me something in your oh so subtle way...well Doc...how about it. We were headed for the beach, would you have the time?"

"Give me ten minutes." With that she disappeared inside, Buster holding strong his post at the step. I relented and climbed back up onto Catherine's porch and sat down in one of the comfortable chairs. I may have fallen asleep.

We drove out to the dunes and parked out by Race Point. Buster was whimpering in the back, desperate to get out. The back flap was open and he bolted, only the beacon of white on the tip of his tail visible through the growth. Catherine and I made a more dignified exit and followed silently behind where we thought Buster had gone. Her presence next to me was palpable and made my feet itch.

Catherine broke the silence.

"Your medical history is...interesting...to say the least."

I rushed in. Too often people could misinterpret my injuries and I wanted to set the record straight. The only victims in my life were the ones who hired me. I didn't want her to have the impression that I was, or ever had been, someone's boxercise dummy. I wasn't sure how much, if anything, Catherine had been told about me. I fully believe that what people say behind my back is none of my business but I wondered, just the same.

"I'm a private investigator. Sometimes it gets a little, ah, messy." I was always circumspect when talking about my work. Not that I didn't want someone to share it with, or maybe I didn't. Either way, Catherine didn't push.

"Aah. I see." We continued on silently, enjoying the thickening of the sand under our feet as we made our way closer to the roaring surf. I didn't feel compelled to fill the fresh spring air with words and neither did Dr. Hobbes.

As we came to a clearing in the sea grass we paused, in unison, and took in the majesty of the view before us. The water seemed angry that day, dark and roiling, shaking off the last vestiges of cold, cleansing itself from the winter's frigid influence. It was dark green and blue and steel grey, all at the same time, accented by the foaming white caps that undulated towards the shore.

The sky had become cloudy and the smell of rain was in the air, and in my bones. As though sensing my oncoming wave of exhaustion, Catherine suggested we sit for a moment before heading back. Normally I could walk the beach for hours but I was still pretty groggy from the pain medication and, admittedly, not physically up to snuff.

I tossed my jacket onto the cold sand and we sat. The next thing I remember was the sun going down and my head resting on Catherine's lap. I could feel, and smell, Buster's breath on my head and guessed that he was taking up space on the other side.

"Well, good morning." She smiled stunningly. I fought to shake off the codeine cobwebs that were making my head feel like a bowling ball and struggled to sit up. I was stiff and sore and my mouth felt like I had eaten a goodly portion of the sand that we were sitting on. Catherine's hand kept my head in her lap and my skin burned under her fingers

"Don't sit up too fast. I'm in no rush."

"Just so you know, I don't usually pass out on a first date." The words were out of my mouth before I could stop them. Stupid, stupid, stupid.

"I didn't realize this was a date?"

Before I could bolt up and explain, I noticed the smile playing at her eyes and relaxed again into her touch.

"That makes two of us." I too was smiling. I think I noticed a smug look in my canine companion's eyes.

Eventually the air cooled and I struggled again to sit up. Catherine helped me, my aching shoulder cupped gently in her hands. I sat facing her and our eyes locked, and in that nano-second I felt my whole soul rush through my body with the force of one of the mighty waves that had first lulled me to sleep. There was a profound absence of thought in my head. My lips invited hers over for a visit and she accepted. I almost passed out.

Her lips against mine were so soft I could barely feel them. My hand reached for the back of her neck, my fingers taking a great handful of her thick hair.

I pulled her closer to me, my lips parting in unison with hers. I could feel the tip of her tongue on mine and forgot to breathe. I felt as though I was watching us through the lens of a camera and rolling the film frame by frame.

I was falling into her eyes and leaned into her. We weren't kissing so much as allowing our lips to pause for a moment while pressed lightly together.

I guess I was staring...no, I definitely was staring but I couldn't tear my eyes from hers. I was getting lost and I saw her watching me go there...inside her. As I closed my eyes I felt my heart open. I couldn't speak, for that moment. I couldn't swallow. It was a feeling that was at once familiar and completely unknown. It made me feel vulnerable and strong and slightly dizzy. I waited longer than I should have to open my eyes, as if I could freeze the moment in time. I could feel her looking at me.

Slowly, I opened my own eyes and my heart stopped.

I found my hand on her face, tracing the outline of her strong jaw line, my focus intent on where my fingers met the fine blond hairs sheltering her perfect ear lobe. I felt her eyes on me still but could not look back. Not yet. I was frightened by what she would see there. The astonishment I knew even I could not hide.

I was shaking, or she was...or both. We held tightly to each other for an eternal moment as the world stood still and the shifting sand beneath my feet swallowed us whole in its sheltering depths.

"Maybe we should head back." I spoke quietly and there was a question in my eyes.

"I'm in no hurry." Her eyes answered my question and we stood like that - in each other's arms - while the sky turned black and rain began to fall, gently at first, then with authority.

We gathered ourselves and made our way back to the Jeep.

As I pulled up to Catherine's house I took her hand in mine. I was trying not to let myself feel confused. I am, as I mentioned, cautious, when it comes to affairs of the heart. This was, I sensed, different.

Not prone to bouts of insecurity or uncertainty, I was feeling adrift and awkward. Catherine saved me from drowning. Her hand squeezed mine and she said...

"Why don't you meet me at *The Shooting Gallery* at eight. If you're up to it we could have some dinner and try to figure out what all this means." Her own confusion and surprise peeked through and I felt relieved.

"I'll be there."

She leaned into my kiss and the warmth she left behind still hadn't cooled, even five years later.

I realized this as we made our way to Sydney's room.

CHAPTER 12

The sight of Sydney snapped me back like a slap in the face. She lay in the hospital bed, her skin as white as the sheets tucked in around her. She was wired for sound and there were machines beeping and gurgling, surrounding the head of her bed. Her eyes were closed and nobody was home. The stillness of her body was interrupted, in an alarmingly sporadic manner, by quick, shallow breaths. They didn't seem strong enough to sustain life.

I asked Catherine for the rundown, knowing that she would give me the straight goods, no holds barred.

"It's not good Jess. The contusion is at the base of her skull and she has developed a subdural hemotoma that is causing the surrounding tissue to swell. We're monitoring her closely to ensure that she doesn't develop cerebral edema. If that happens, we'll have to take her into surgery. We have her on anti-coagulants, to thin her blood. She's in a coma."

The words, although I had been expecting them, made my skin prickle with rage and frustration. I had known people with lesser injuries that had not survived. I knew the next question was unfair, but I had to ask it.

"Will she be all right?"

Catherine just looked at me. No words were necessary. Medically, Catherine was doing all she could for Sydney, the rest would be up to her.

I knew Sydney to be a strong woman and I had to believe that she could fight her way back to us...to Harley. If ever there was a reason to beat the odds, Harley had to be it. I felt somehow reassured. As if reading my mind, Catherine nodded with me.

"Yes Jess. The rest is up to her. The next forty-eight hours will be crucial. If she can maintain while the swelling goes down she may be out of the woods."

"Maybe?" I was being unfair but I couldn't help it. As a physician, I knew Catherine to be caring and concerned with all her patients. It's one of the major reasons, I believed, that she was such a great doctor. It didn't have to be Sydney lying there fighting for her life to invoke her compassion... but it was. Her best friend. I knew Catherine had suffered immeasurable pain at her parent's deaths and was emotionally scarred still from that. The thought of losing Sydney must be tearing her up inside.

"Yes! Maybe!" She sounded angry and I was instantly sorry to have inspired that anger. I put my arms tightly around her and she leaned into me; her breath on my neck was hot and, although I tried to banish the thought from my mind as it was totally inappropriate given the circumstances, way sexy. I held tightly, waiting for her to pull back, making a conscious effort not to release her before she was ready. There would be more time later, and I vowed to be there for her...if she wanted me to be. I loved the way she felt in my arms. They had missed her.

She straightened, gathering her wits, and made a methodical check of all the beeping and whirring machines. She made notations in Sydney's chart and tapped ineffectively at the I.V. that was dripping down a long tube, into Sydney's hand. Then she took that hand in hers and squeezed.

I held my breath, willing Sydney's hand to contract, her fingers to grip Catherine's, but they were still. Catherine closed her eyes for a moment, lost in her thoughts, or prayers, or both.

We both started when we heard the door open behind us. Kelly was there with Harley, and tears stained both their faces as they hesitated, for a moment, before coming in. Harley looked up at Catherine.

She knelt to the small child and drew her into her arms. Her tiny body, stiff at first, yielded to the embrace and two gigantic brown eyes looked up at Catherine. I wouldn't have switched places with her for all the Jif Extra Crunchy in the world.

"Can mommy come home now, doctor Cat?" she pleaded.

"Not yet sweetheart. Mommy is still sleeping. We still don't know when she will wake up."

Catherine knew it would be useless to try to sugar-coat anything for Harley so she explained her mother's condition as honestly as she could and Harley did understand. She stood next to the bed, stoically, her frame rigid and determined.

"Auntie Kelly got me a book from the gift shop. I'm going to read it to mama. Is that okay?"

Catherine gulped back the emotion she felt when she looked into Harley's eyes. She, better than most, knew what losing a parent felt like and her heart broke in empathy.

"I think reading mama a book would be the best medicine there is."

Harley smiled brightly at this and hopped up into the chair next to her mother's bed. Kelly slid in under her, allowing Harley to be up close to Sydney's face, her child's hand absently stroking the sheets, like a 'picky blankie.' Kelly turned gently, so as not to distract Harley and spoke to Catherine and me. "Why don't you two go grab a coffee and some fresh air. I'll stay here until you get back. Oh, and take your time, I haven't heard this story yet either," coaxing another smile from Harley.

My opinion of Kelly was going up and up every time she opened her mouth...or entered the room.

I put my arm around Catherine's waist, squeezing lightly, and lead her reluctantly from the room. The door had barely shut behind us when she collapsed against the wall, her head buried in her hands.

"Damn it Jess, damn it to hell. Who did this? I want you to tell me. Who did this to them? Why haven't you found him, or her, yet. What are you doing?" She was upset and angry. She needed to lash out, to find some control. I understood.

I took a deep breath. Catherine's words brought me back in a hurry. She was right, of course. Her work was here, with Sydney. My work was back in Provincetown. I had to get back fast, before the trail cooled even a little. Under normal circumstances I may have felt a little defensive. I don't take orders very well, never have, but I understood that Catherine was desperate for someone or something to blame...to make sense of what had happened. She was not attacking me, she was fighting for lives. I put aside my own feelings and said...

"I don't know who did this...yet. Let's have a cup of coffee and then I'll get back and I promise...I will find out who did this, Catherine. I promise."

"You never make promises." She smiled, sadly, remembering the last time we had been together.

"Maybe I'm changing." Yikes. Could that be true?

Catherine and I had a quick coffee in the hospital cafeteria. I couldn't persuade her to eat anything but I, bless my heart, did manage to wolf down a gigantic piece of carrot cake, with cream cheese icing, and the combination of caffeine and sugar had left my foot tapping and my brain humming. Catherine had spent enough time with me to recognize the signs.

"Why don't you come and say good-bye to everyone and get out of here Jess. You look like you could get back to P-Town without a plane."

I smiled at her familiarity and took her hand in mine. I looked deep into her anguished eyes and held her with my look. The hustle and bustle around us vanished and we were again alone together. I realized then that I had missed her. Way more than I had let myself believe up until now. I didn't mind the feeling, that was the strangest thing of all.

We returned to Sydney's room, quietly pushing open the door. I didn't have to ask Catherine to know that she too, in the non-scientific cell that lived in her brain, imagined seeing Sydney sitting up in bed, her eyes bright and clear. Hope springs eternal, or something like that.

Instead what we saw set off the snooze control on my biological clock.

Harley sat on Kelly's knee and was reading to her mother. The storybook had pictures and Harley, like every good grade school teacher, read on an angle so her audience could follow along with the illustrations, as if willing her mother to open her eyes and share in the joy of the colorful pictures. I nodded a good-bye to Catherine and promised to call her as soon as I learned anything - she promised the same to me.

I had almost made a clean getaway when Harley turned her too big and way too brown eyes on mine. Her tears from earlier had left her with a fevered and vulnerable look. She pinned me.

"Jess. Why would somebody want to hurt my mommy? Do they have a gun? Is Buster okay? Will you come back? Will you fix this?"

Oh jeez. I bent down so our noses were almost touching. "First off, I don't know who did this to your mommy but I am going to find out. Yes, they may have a gun but I don't think so. Buster is fine and misses you terribly. I will absolutely come back and, yes, I will fix this."

I hoped I sounded more convinced than I felt. It must have worked because Harley nodded at me once and returned to her reading. I felt too heavy to stand. Catherine's hand was on my shoulder and I rose up to face her. She of all people knew the weight of the promise I had just made, having made her own to Harley earlier in the day. We were in this together.

"I gotta go."

"I know. Be careful."

I wanted to hold her.

CHAPTER 13

Karen was waiting for me when I rounded the corner leading into the Provincetown terminal. She looked impossibly frazzled. I would have been less taken aback if she had appeared before me in a wedding gown with flowers in her hair. All my senses went on full alert.

"What is it?" No need for preamble with Karen, thank goddess.

"You better get back to your place. Pronto. I'm coming with you." This was not even close to being a question.

I looked past her and saw that my jeep was running and we both turned and dashed for it. I sped out of the lot, knowing that Karen would tell me all I needed to know, when I needed to know it. I waited, speeding too fast through the hairpin turns leading back into town. I was grateful for the new and improved asphalt on Race Point Road as it enabled me to grind away at top speed.

Karen began her tale as soon as we hit Commercial Street and I was forced to slow to mach I.

"About ten minutes after you took off for the hospital a private jet came in. One of those flying condo jobs. The call up was for Ryan Enterprises. Three people got off the jet. It had originated in Boston with a quick stop in Orleans. An unscheduled stop at that. It wasn't on the flight plan they filed."

"So how'd you find out about it?"

"I know everything Jess."

"Oh yeah. I forgot. Say Sherlock, does your good buddy Jamie still work the tower in Orleans?"

"Hrmpf."

"Back at ya. Anyway..."

"Anyway...an older couple and a young woman...a frosty looking bit of baggage, if ya catch my meaning, get off. They barely spoke to each other, or me, just asked for directions to the Sheriff's station and the phone number of The Provincetown Inn. They grabbed a taxi and took off."

As she spoke she pulled a flight manifest from the back pocket of her work-pants and read to me.

"The plane is registered to Mr. Timothy Ryan II. The passengers are listed as Muffin DeWitt and Jean Ryan. The flight originated out of Logan and no return flight plan has been filed. I didn't care for the look or the feel of them, Jess. They're trouble."

Karen had great instincts, not clouded by prejudice or presupposition. I trusted her implicitly. I urged Karen on, needing to have her articulate all that she had observed, leaving no detail out. She continued.

"It was the girl that I noticed the most. She was a snippy little thing, all icicle and tinsel. She was nattering away at the old man and kept trying to get in his face.

The wife, sorry, I know you hate that, just kind of followed along on her own steam. She seemed out of it, like she had just woken up or something. The girl though, she kept bringing up the name of some guy named Timothy, like a mantra. Whoever this Timothy is, I don't envy him. She looks like a nasty little bit of goods, if you ask me. Anyway, the old boy seemed okay, you know, he made nice with me, chatted for about a minute or so, asked me if I would be able to get the plane to a tie-down for a couple of days, have it fueled up, the usual. When they were making to leave he shook my hand and I swear to Goddess, Miss Snippety shuddered, like the old boy was going to catch something from me. He looked apologetic but hustled off with them and grabbed the cab that was out front. The wife, sorry, Mrs. Ryan, just kind of floated after them like an afterthought. That's about it Jess. Anything there?"

"Lots Karen. As usual your keen powers of observation have saved me hours of legwork."Her description of Tim Ryan's father stuck in my mind. Thoughts of my own father crept in like masked thieves, threatening, as they always did, to steal away my concentration. I shook them away, for the moment. The snippy one must be Cupcake, or whatever her name was.

I needed to organize myself - and fast. "Look Karen, I'm going to drop you off at the police station. See if you can't stall the Ryan entourage for me. Who's the new uniform in town? I heard he's a new recruit from Boston PD. What's his name again?"

"Alex Thorne. Nice guy. Young, bright. I like him. He's only been in town for a couple of months but I get a good feeling from him. We've had him up for supper once or twice. Meg thinks he's too skinny and spends too many nights alone. Her mothering instincts hit full stride when he came over that first time with wild flowers and a thirty-five year old bottle of single malt. It was love at first sight. I should be able to get him onside - buy you some time. Are you going to tell your house guest that his parents are here?"

"Not right off, no. Oh, and give me a call at the cottage when you get any info you can on the ice princess, will you. . Any trouble dropping off the fella?"

"None. Your passenger from before, the dark haired gal, met me at the end of your driveway and he seemed comfortable with her so I just left them. Pull over here, I'll jump out." We were at the corner of Shank Painter and Court. She was out of sight by the time the door thumped shut. Man she was spry, I couldn't help but smile after her. I punched down the clutch and sped for home. I wasn't worried about Gillian, but I wasn't sure how well Tim Ryan had survived his incarceration with her. Gillian could talk, literally nonstop, for hours on end.

She had a captive audience and I suspected that Ryan would, by now, be as pliable as if he had spent eight hours on the rack. Good. That's just how I like my aggressors.

I wondered, as an adjunct, how Jennifer Eastcott was holding out. I doubted very much that Gillian would have spared her a dip in her stream of consciousness. I looked forward, in a sick kind of way, to unwrapping the tableau that lay before me.

There was a strange car in my driveway. I mean it. It was a really strange car. It had been painted sky blue with a montage of clouds and sunflowers covering its surface. Protruding here and there were little birds. It could have been a Pinto or a Gremlin, it was hard to tell. I knew who the owner must be and jumped down from the Jeep to enter into what was sure to be, to say the least, the most eclectic gathering of individuals my little cottage had ever hosted.

CHAPTER 14

I could see inside my living room from the wrap-around deck as I crept quietly onto it and gazed in. Even with everything that was going on; Sydney's life in jeopardy, Harley, Catherine, Tim Ryan, etc., I couldn't help but smile at the sight before me and, more importantly, my stomach growled with a vengeance. What time was it anyway? Had to be about six, at least, though I felt as if I had been up for months.

Gillian was in the kitchen; every pot I owned, every dish I had, was out and in use, brimming over with what I knew would be an incredible feast. Timothy Ryan sat in my Adirondack rocker, his hands were not visible and I wondered if they were tied behind his back or he was wringing them furiously by way of blocking out Gillian's barrage. Sitting in front of him was my best friend, Leah Hughes, pianist, singer, composer, director and co-parent to Buster. I hadn't seen Leah for several months, since she had left Toronto to become the musical director for a new theater group in New York. I had missed her a lot and my phone bills from Toronto were a testament to that. We talked every day but still, it wasn't the same. I was overwhelmingly happy to see her. Leah had been my one truly significant other. We had met over two decades and too many lifetimes ago. Over the years we had suffered terrible losses together, celebrated great victories, and mostly, we had loved and cared for each other, deeply and honestly. Best friends, in for the long haul. Leah's career was finally starting to take off. Nobody deserved it more. Leah has more than played her dues over the years; the hotel lobbies, the dark, smoky bars, the scrambling for jobs. I looked at her now, undetected, and took in the picture.

Her short, choppy hair was sprouting out colors that were not on any color wheel I had ever seen. Her small frame was dressed entirely in black, and her hands, her instruments, stabbed the air around her, unconsciously conducting. Tim Ryan was her captive audience. Her freckles gave her a youthful look that was matched by the spark in her hazel eyes. Her ever-fluctuating weight seemed to be down, and I hoped this didn't mean that she was smoking again. I absently rubbed the spot where my patch had been. Between the two of us we have stopped and started smoking more times then Mt. St. Helen's.

Ryan said something to her and she laughed at him. Poor guy. Give it up pal. She will have her way, I mused. Leah had been a great support when I had decided to leave the police department and strike out on my own. She knew my restless spirit and encouraged its flight.

She had often come to visit me here, and stayed on until the next job offer came calling. I loved our time together and hoped that she would be staying for a while. I could use her help, personally and professionally. Leah knew all my secrets and made me feel safe and loved.

I took a deep breath and lumbered into the room. Actually it was more of a lurch. In all the cafuffle I had almost forgotten about my swollen ankle and the knot on the back of my head. Nothing serious, I was certain, but weariness was making me achy.

All eyes darted up. Gillian's were mischievous, Leah's expectant and Tim Ryan looked desperate. Jennifer and Buster were nowhere to be seen.

"See you've met Mr. Ryan. Did he give you any trouble?"

"Hello to you too, stranger." Leah struggled up from her crouched position and encircled me in her arms. It felt like home. I got a lump in my throat.

"For your information, I was ministering to this charming boy's face that you apparently shoved into the sand, as I understand it."

"Charming boy? Leah, are you drunk? This charming man may be the very person responsible for trying to murder Sydney Ryan."

A cry rang out behind me. Gillian was pale, or as pale as her dark beige features would permit, and she groped for a chair. It was as if she had managed to force the Sydney situation into one of her pots and had slammed the lid down firmly on it. The mention of her name, however, brought her fear back. I tried to assure her.

"It's okay Gillian. Sydney is holding her own. Well, sort of." It was tough to be reassuring when the facts didn't lend themselves to an optimistic outcome. I tried again.

"I'll tell you everything I learned at the hospital. Where is Jen Jen anyway? And, more importantly, where is my dog?" I couldn't believe he would have left Leah's side.

"*Your* dog?" Leah snipped.

"Sorry. *Our* dog."

Gillian explained. "Jennifer took Buster out for a walk. They left about an hour ago. He doesn't even know that Mommy II is here. Now don't give me the hairy eyeball Missy Shore. I trust that Jennifer girl even if you don't. She really cares about Sydney, and she needed some air. I sent Buster with her to keep an eye."

Surprisingly, this worked for me. I went to the front of the cottage, which, I guess, is actually the back, anyway the side that faces the road, and stuck two fingers over my tongue and blew. The ensuing whistle left my ears ringing for a full minute. Leah laughed. Gillian clucked her tongue and Tim Ryan sneered, careful not to let Leah see him. In the distance I heard a familiar jangle. Dog tags. I knew at least one of the happy wanderers would be home soon.

I closed the door and excused myself for a minute and went into my bedroom. I still didn't know what time it was. It was dark out. I hadn't noticed that before and suspected that the sun had dropped quickly, eking out a few extra minutes of light from the day before. I checked my watch. Actually it had been my father's watch and it was, chronically and chronologically, off the mark. By my calculation it was anywhere from seven thirty to eight fifteen, give or take. I also realized that the cornucopia of smells emanating from the kitchen were making me feel faint.

I went into my bathroom and splashed some cold water on my face. I dried my face and reached into my pocket to finger the object that Buster had discovered lying on the ground by Sydney. Where, if anywhere, did this little gem fit in? I returned it to my pocket for safe keeping and looked at my face in the mirror. What I saw made me smile, in spite of the lines of exhaustion around my bleary eyes. It was like looking at my mother. Her black eyes, her squarish jaw and - genes are such a bitch - her wrinkles. I also thought it odd that I had her thighs and, to the best of my knowledge, she was still using them.

I usually wear my hair loose and messy, still preferring my bangs hanging in my eyes as I had from about the age of four. When I couldn't be bothered, I would pull a Catherine and just slick the whole mess back and away. The first time I had done that the resemblance to my mother had frightened me. Oh well. The external similarity I could live with as long as it doesn't extend to the inside stuff. I am my own person, not because of, but in spite of, my upbringing. If I've learned anything over the years it's that I am who I am and tenaciously determined to remain so.

I closed and rubbed my tired eyes. What I really wanted to do was light a fire in my bedroom, draw a hot bath, dump in a cup of strawberry bubble bath, light about twenty bayberry scented candles, put on a stack of CDs and go to sleep. I was sitting on the edge of the tub indulging in this very fantasy when the door whapped against my aching leg and Buster bounded in. He was obviously trying to tell me that Leah was here. The grin on his face said it all.

He ran to me, then ran back to the living room...four times. Each time his cries of delight became louder and more insistent. I knew I would have to go and look for myself. I hoped I could act surprised so as not to disappoint him.

"What is it fella? Can you show me?" He had my hand in his mouth and I took that as a 'yes.'

He ran back and forth between Leah and me, his actions speaking for him... '...see, see, I told you...look who it is. Oh boy, oh boy. Both moms. Oh boy.' He was beside himself with glee. He made me laugh. I love that. I noticed Jennifer just coming in the front door, the haggard look on her face a testament to her distress. Maybe she really did care about Sydney.

I decided I might as well give her the benefit of the doubt, until proven otherwise. I paused lovingly and longingly over one of Gillian's pots and dragged myself into the fray. I laid it out for them...

"Okay. In a nutshell...you'll find a nut." Well, I laughed.

"Come on Jess. Save the stand-up," urged Leah.
One look at the naked concern on everybody's face, everybody including Timothy Ryan, interestingly enough, convinced me to play it straight, so to speak. We had all been through enough for one day.

I began. "I'll start with Sydney. The news is not good." I pushed on in spite of the gasps and sighs of concern that bounced around me. "I spoke with Catherine and she tells me that the next 24 to 48 hours are crucial. She is currently unconscious. Oh hell, she's in a coma. She has swelling on her brain and, for now, we all just have to wait it out. Catherine will keep us posted. Harley is...well, Harley. Catherine is keeping an eye on her and that Kelly girl is there too so that's covered. Catherine wants to keep things in Sydney's room as calm and quiet as possible so we should try to co-ordinate our schedules as far as visiting and what all goes. Now...as far as the attack on Sydney is concerned," I glanced purposely at Tim Ryan, who stared defiantly back at me...I'm guessing that she knew her attacker, or attackers..."

Gillian snapped out of her reverie, "What are you saying? Attackers? As in more than one?"

"Yes Gillian, that's right. I think Sydney was distracted by someone at the back door. That would explain the position she was lying in when you found her, but the blow clearly came from behind. I can't imagine anyone sneaking up on her if she weren't distracted to begin with, so, I'm thinking that there must have been at least a pair of them."

I took a breath and poured myself a glass of wine, swallowing dryly. The two person theory had just come to me as I said it and I needed time to mull it over in my head. I had learned, over the years, to go with my instincts. If my gut thought there was reason to suspect an accomplice, I was willing to play out the possibility.

Leah took up the conversational slack. "Okay Jess, what's next? What can we do to help?"

The words I dread. The thought of my investigation being 'aided' by the likes of Leah and Gillian was enough to make me crave the safety of the armed robbery call. I knew they would need to be involved in some concrete way; they just wanted to help, after all, however, I worked best on my own. How not to offend...I had a plan.

"I have thought a lot about this and here's what I've come up with. Gillian, first and foremost, you have to keep things running at *The Shooting Gallery*.

We all know that's what Sydney would want. That restaurant, next to Harley, is her life, and you are the one person who can pull up the slack while she recuperates."

Gillian's face took on a look of steely determination. She raised the spatula in her hand, like a Viking warrior and declared her commitment.

"Done. I'll just feed you lot and tomorrow, eleven AM, *The Shooting Gallery* will open for business as usual."

I was relieved, for myself and Sydney. "Great Gillian, but do me a favor. I need to get in there for a couple of hours later tonight or maybe first light tomorrow and look around again. Can I get a set of keys from you and drop them off later?"

"Better than that, I'll come with you. If something is out of place, I'll be able to tell right off."

I agreed with her suggestion. "Good point. How 'bout we head there in about an hour, after you feed me." I was hopeful and maybe a little pathetic.

CHAPTER 15

The food was laid out on my Parson's table in the dining area, next to the kitchen. There seemed to be enough food for a small army but experience had taught me that there would be scant leftovers for lunch. There was an awkward moment when we all finally sat down to eat. Tim sat down sullenly. Jennifer Eastcott was another stranger among us, but if she felt awkward she didn't show it. I suspected it was a well practiced facade that she crouched comfortably behind, both in her personal and professional life.

Leah's amused gaze slid back and forth from me to Jennifer and back again. She knew me well and I suspected she might be waiting for some sort of confrontation between me and the beautiful lady lawyer. Jennifer surprised me by starting first.

"I assume, Jess, that you have a lot of questions for me...about me. I've spent the day thinking about my part in all of this."

I was about to launch in when Tim shoved his chair back and headed for the door.

"I'm out of here...assuming that's alright with you, Miss Shore? I'm damn sure there's nothing Jennifer has to say that I want to hear."

"You're excused Mr. Ryan, but don't go too far for too long."

Jennifer didn't even seem to notice Tim's exit. She continued. "My first instinct was to get on a plane and get the hell out of here, but I knew that wouldn't help Sydney so I stayed. You can ask me anything you need to. I give you my word that I will answer your questions as honestly and forthrightly as I possibly can."

I figured I'd better strike while the iron was hot. I hadn't had a chance to organize my thoughts or formulate my questions but I leapt into the fray, nonetheless.

"Okay...thanks...first off, the coincidence of your arrival and this attack on Sydney is curious to me. Why now?"

She considered my question. I could see a flash in her piercing eyes as they locked onto mine. She was a beauty, no doubt about it, and I could just imagine the number of hearts, male and female, that had been set afire by her dusky, mysterious looks. I refused to blink and the effort made me want to sneeze. She took a huge breath, put down her knife and fork, pushed away slightly from the table, apparently needing some space between her memories and me. I countered by leaning over my plate, my right elbow coming to rest in my Chicken Vindaloo. There was nothing to be served by my pretending that I meant to do it but it did seem to ease the tension. Jennifer smiled, or Buster stepped on her foot - either way, she began.

"The Cliff's Note's version is...I'm in love with Sydney Ryan."

I tried to keep my expression neutral even though I heard Gillian drop her fork on the floor and Leah snorted in amusement. Jennifer continued, obviously not expecting anything interruptive to come forth from my gaping mouth.

"I think I fell in love with her the moment I opened my office door and saw her standing there. Over the last three years, I've kept my personal feelings to myself, it just wouldn't have been appropriate for me to have communicated them to her. Sydney had more urgent matters on her mind and she expected the same focus from me. I came here now because I couldn't stand it anymore. Her case with Timothy and Harley was beginning to wind down. We were, still are I hope, close to reaching a mutually satisfactory conclusion. I was going to surprise Sydney with some good news that I had just heard from the other side's legal team. I wanted to tell her in person and then I planned on telling her my feelings, in very non-professional terms."

Tears were now coursing down her face and her body trembled with the effort of not falling completely to pieces. Gillian was on her feet, estrogen in full flower, ready to offer 'mom' comfort to our bawling barrister.

Leah was picking the larger pieces of chicken off Jennifer's plate and passing them under the table to the four-legged compost. She assumed I was too distracted to notice. I wasn't.

Gillian was glaring at me over Jennifer's head, daring me to say anything snarly or churlish. I continued:

"I need to know what it was you were going to tell Sydney about her custody case, Jennifer. It may be one of the missing pieces I'm looking for."

She snuffled. "I can't tell you that. It's privileged information."

"Privilege smivlage," I retorted, showing off my facility with the English language. "This is important, lady. If we don't figure out who did this to Sydney her life could still be in danger from whoever whacked her in the first place. Now give.

She considered my words. I gave her all the time she needed, in a magnificent show of self-restraint.

"All right Jess, but just you." She looked apologetically at Gillian and Leah. I looked wistfully at my food. We both got up from the table and moved out to the porch. The Bay was still, the water barely lapping on the shore. The night was clear, or so it seemed at the moment, but this time of year one never knew. Storms could appear from nowhere and be swift and furious, turning the coast into a weapon that attacked itself.

We sat in the Adirondack rockers and faced out toward Long Point Lighthouse, our breath visible in the early spring chill. I had grabbed a couple of raggedy jackets on the way out and handed one to her.

"Look Jennifer, I understand what you're saying about protecting Sydney's legal rights and I appreciate how difficult this is for you. What I need is every detail of the last couple of months. Don't leave anything out, no matter how insignificant it may seem to you. If I have any questions I'll jump in, if you don't mind. Audience participation helps me remember better."

"No, that's okay. I'll tell you everything, as much as I can. It will probably help, actually, if you do ask questions. For months there was no give and take in the custody suit. Ryan had brought in the legal muscle from his family's law firm. It seemed to me that they wanted to keep all the balls in the air for as long as possible, until we finally gave in or Sydney ran out of money. Neither happened. Sydney and I made a deal. I would only charge her for administrative work if she agreed to let me publish a paper based on her case. I really believed, and still do, that her case could be instrumental in influencing some legislation in support of single and gay parenting. Anyway, things dragged on for the first two years. Motions were filed and filed and filed. The gargoyles that Ryan hired must have drawers jammed full of motions just needing a signature. I've never seen anything like it.

"The original deal we pitched to them was not only out of the ballpark of what they had in mind, apparently we were in a different league. Hardball and hardhead rules applied. In the beginning, Sydney was not prepared to allow Tim any access at all. No holidays, no birthdays, nothing. He had reappeared out of the blue and she didn't handle it well, as you might expect. She softened the blow by agreeing to waive any and all rights to the Ryan fortune, be it in her name or Harley's, in perpetuity.

"Tim came to my office, that time, and I laid out the deal for him. I'll never forget his reaction. It was confusing, to say the least. He seemed, I don't know, and believe me I've thought a lot about it, he seemed...defeated. Like he had lost control of the whole thing and he just wanted it to be over. If he was a witness on the stand it would have been the moment I knew I could go in for the kill."

"Unfortunately, he *had* lost control. His family, through their lawyers, had taken a stand that they wouldn't settle until they got what they wanted."

"The strangest thing was, in all those months of meetings and court appearances and what have you, not once did their side request any time with Harley. They never asked to have her visit and made it clear that they didn't want her showing up in court with Sydney. This whole thing was never about Harley, and that's what really stuck in my craw, kept me fighting as hard as I did."

"Was that the only thing that kept you there?" I asked gently.

"No, I've already admitted there was more. Sydney and I had spent a lot of time together, a couple of hours at least once a week. Also, Harley usually came along with her, and she and I became great friends.

I don't remember exactly when it happened, my falling in love with Sydney. I mean, I don't remember the exact day or anything. I guess I had become accustomed to feeling that way about her and not really being in touch with that. It doesn't matter anyway. It's not like I had the guts to tell her how I felt. I wanted to, though, hundreds of times. I didn't want to jeopardize our professional relationship by bringing my personal feelings into it. There just never seemed to be a good time. That's why I came here, oh God, was it only today? I can't believe it.

"Anyway, I came here today to tell Sydney how I feel and let the chips fall where they may. We had had a breakthrough with Ryan's legal team and I finally felt that the time was right." She sighed, as if exhausted.

"I need to know about that breakthrough, Jennifer. I need you to tell me." I had my 'tell mommy who broke the vase' voice. Works every time. She gave in.

"Tim Ryan is getting married this summer. His fiancée is Muffin DeWitt and, if you can believe it, her family has even more money than his. You see, all along I believed the Ryans were fighting so hard, not because of Harley or who she is, but that they felt she belonged to them...like chattel..."

"It was never about money or love or any of that...these people just don't like to lose. I guess when Muffin found out about Tim having a kid, she hit the roof. Her family got together with his family and they decided that the whole thing would be best swept under the rug...now and forever. They came to me with a proposal for Sydney. That's what I was bringing to her today."

I wondered if this was close to the truth of the situation or if Jennifer's biases were showing. It would be understandable, really. Here she had worked for months on a case that could greatly influence her own career; not to mention the personal attachment she had to Sydney and Harley. Fact or fiction...I had to ask.

"Can you tell me what it is? The deal, I mean."

She sighed deeply. I knew that she had been savoring this moment, to share it with Sydney. Her disappointment was likely personal, not professional.

"They've offered to drop the whole thing. No custody, no hassle, no nothing. We did up a contract for Sydney to approve.

"Without getting too technical, Tim Ryan is waiving all his paternal rights to Harley. There is no recourse for him in the future. Believe me, I've looked at this thing every which way and I'm confident that it's airtight. It's exactly what we were going for. What Sydney wanted."

My suspicious gene kicked in immediately but I managed to keep a lid on it. I pasted what I meant to be a winsome smile on my face and tried to share in her excitement.

"Wow." I think that about says it. The wheels had started to spin in my head. The package that Jennifer had just unwrapped was way too neat for my taste. I have often found mysteries can be solved less from seeking answers than by asking bigger questions. Right now I had plenty of questions.

If, as Jennifer said, the Ryans were out of it custody wise, then why was the clan gathered here on our fair shores? Cupcake and all. Did they follow Tim here? If so, why? My Spidey-sense was on full tingle. I was pretty sure he hadn't come to ask Sydney to be a flower girl at his upcoming wedding, so what was he doing here? Hmmm? I ask you? For the moment everyone, including Jennifer, is a suspect as far as I'm concerned. Oh sure, she spins a good yarn, but so do a lot of the bad guys.

I'd momentarily forgotten about Jennifer. I turned to her now. She didn't look like the happiest little piggie in the pen.

"Hey. You okay?"

She smiled sadly back at me.

"So...question..." I asked.

"Go ahead."

"Okay...if your news for Sydney was good why the toe to toe at the airport?"

"Oh God. That was so stupid. I was so excited to see Sydney there. To give her the good news. I knew it was impossible but I actually thought she had come out there to see me. That she had somehow found out that I was coming.

What a fool. It was just a freaky coincidence that we ran into each other. She didn't know anything about my coming here and started to give me a hard time about her case. I know her anger was borne of frustration but I was totally unprepared for her going at me like that. Truth is...I was disappointed and hurt. I don't handle that well, so I fought back. I can't tell you how much I regret that now."

I considered all that Jennifer had just told me. It was a lot of information and I wasn't sure how much of it I was buying. Whatever the truth I figured it would be up to me to sort it out. Alone, or at least without Jennifer Eastcott looking over my shoulder. I had a thought.

"Why don't you go to the hospital and be with Sydney? I could give Karen a call, I'm sure she could get you out soon. When Sydney comes to I'm sure you'll want to be there to fill her in."

If I expected her to leap at my insightful and sensitive suggestion, I had another thought coming.

"I don't think I can. Believe me, it's all I can think about, I just can't seem to bring myself to do it. I feel paralyzed, or something. I don't know what the hell's the matter with me...I came here to finally tell Sydney how I feel about her and now she's lying in a coma and I may never get to say what I had to say and I sit here like...I don't know what."

"Like someone who's terrified of losing someone they care so much about? Could that be it?" Might as well get her on my side for the time being.

She frowned and covered her face with her hands. I tried again.

"I really think Sydney would like it if you were there...to tell her the good news, if nothing else."

Jennifer's indecision was etched painfully on her face. I didn't feel compelled to add anything - this decision had to be hers and hers alone. I got up from my chair and felt her hand on my arm.

"Thank you Jess. If your offer still stands....I would like to go see Sydney."

I put my hand over hers and went inside to call Karen, giving Jennifer time with her thoughts and fears. Karen had a charter scheduled out of P-Town at 10:30. I could run Jennifer out there on my way to the restaurant. I stuck my head inside and said my good-byes.

As if on cue I heard the heavy thud of maleness on the porch. The prodigal had returned. I told Tim he was under no obligation to stay and the breeze he created as he limped past me blew my hair into my eyes, where it would likely remain.

CHAPTER 16

Gillian was there waiting for me when I arrived at *The Shooting Gallery*. It was lit up like a movie set and Gill was down on her hands and knees, feeling around the kitchen floor, as if she had lost a contact lens. I knew she knew that I was there...I had sounded a warning blast from my horn when I pulled in.

My teeth were still rattling from this afternoon and I ached all over. She barely gave me a glance.

"Ahh, Gillian. What are you doing, dare I ask?"

She sighed and sat back on her haunches, weebling back and forth like a jack-in-the-box, trying to maintain her balance. She gave it up and sat heavily on the floor.

"I'm looking for clues. I know exactly what has business being on this floor and what doesn't. "

"Any luck?"

She couldn't have looked more disappointed. "No. Nothing. All I can say is that whoever was here with Sydney either let themselves in or Sydney let them in herself. I locked up last night and both doors seem just fine to me."

Bad news for our side. Mind you, not everyone who does a break and enter leaves big clues behind. Locks are pretty easy to pick and the ones on *The Shooting Gallery* doors weren't exactly state of the art. As far as clues go I just have the one that Buster found earlier in the day. I fingered it like worry beads deep in my jacket pocket. The gold bracelet was more delicate than I had originally thought.

Not something a man would wear, or at least a man like Timothy Ryan. I felt safe in assuming that Alex Thorne, the young policeman that Karen had mentioned to me, had already been here and conducted what I assumed to be a thorough investigation. That and Gillian crawling around on all fours gave me a superfluous feeling and I realized that my presence would be best utilized elsewhere. I gave some suggestions to Gillian.

"Okay Gilly...you're on your own here. Check everywhere for anything that feels even a little hinky. You're doing a good job. Oh, and thanks for dinner. I'll be getting back to that as soon as I can. Remember what I said Gillian. You can be a great help to Sydney by keeping it business as usual around here. Now...I gotta run.   If anyone's looking for me, I'll be down at the Inn."

On my way to The Provincetown Inn, I spotted a Provincetown Police car in my rear-view. I pulled off on School Street and it pulled in behind me. A uniform started to step out. What a cutie pie. We hadn't actually met but I knew him at once from the way Karen had spoken about him. Also, he looked pretty darned pleased with himself. The words were rushing out of his mouth before he had unfolded his six foot and a little bit more frame from the car.

"Miss Shore, am I glad I ran into you...I'm just on my way to The Provincetown Inn...that's where the Ryans are staying. 'Course you probably already know that. Anyway, we got a domestic disturbance call at the station and it was from the room the Ryans are staying in. I don't know the whole story yet. Leave your car here and we can go together, if you like."

Phew. Anybody else exhausted? He didn't even take a breath.

I laughed out loud...

"You must be Alex Thorne. Pleased to make your acquaintance."

He blushed. He actually blushed. "I'm sorry Miss Shore, it's just that I know all about you from Karen and Meg and I figure we'll be working together on this case. Least I hope we can work together. I checked in with the Chief, he's a good friend of Karen's too, and he agreed to let me be your liaison with the Department. It's kind of a feather in my cap...my first official assignment and all so you and me are going to be working together.

I wasn't sure if he was asking me or telling me. Didn't much matter. I reassured him, if that was indeed what he was looking for.

"I look forward to it Alex."

"Great. I'm heading for the Inn now. We could go together, if you like."

"I like...I was heading there myself. We can fill each other in on the way."

I quickly laid out the facts as I knew them. I handed over the bracelet. Best to keep tangible clues in the hands of the authorities in case they can be used for evidence at a later date, and I knew this would. Alex didn't say a word, just nodded his head and tossed in the odd 'ahh,' and 'ah ha.' A man of few words and deep thoughts who smelled like Brut aftershave.

The ride to The Inn only took a couple of minutes and we pulled right up to the Ryan's room. Just as the car rocked to a halt the door flew open and Timothy Ryan bolted for the beach. Alex was after him like a shot. Better him than me. Twisted ankle or not, I had had enough of wrestling with the likes of Timothy Ryan. I didn't want to push my luck, after all. I hustled to the still open door and my eyes adjusted to the dim light within and widened in surprise as I took in the scene. It wasn't a real stretch of the imagination to pick out Cupcake and Ma Ryan even without Karen's earlier description. They were huddled together on one of the beds, both of them with streaky tears running down their faces a la Tammy Faye in a twister. The remnants of a lamp and a chair were scattered about. They weren't at their most fetching, I was sure.

Mr. Ryan, looking pale and shaken, was as far away from the girls in his life as he could possibly get. He had pushed himself into a corner of the room like a frightened animal. Wow. Family values. Am I missing something?

I went over to Mr. Ryan and gently put my hand on his arm. His eyes were vacant for a moment and then he seemed to snap to. I introduced myself to him, but if he heard me he didn't show it. I had to assume he was used to being in charge but this scene looked somehow beyond even his control.

Steel waters run deep and this was a man who had a ruthless reputation in the business community. I could see the wall going up before me. I knew I only had a second or two before he disappeared completely.

"What happened here, Mr. Ryan? Constable Thorne should be back any second with your son, so I suggest if you have something to tell me, do it now. I'll work with you to find a way for all of you *not* to end up being formally questioned by officer Thorne, but you have to give it up first. What the hell's going on here?"

I had him. I could feel it. Come on big boy...talk to Auntie Jess.

"Why can't you people just leave us alone?"

You people? What people? I surreptitiously glanced around the room, thinking perhaps someone else had arrived. Nope. Nobody there.

"What 'people' are you referring to Mr. Ryan?" He had a queer look in his eyes, like he had taken a cold pill and couldn't fight through the fog.

"All of you. Cops, lawyers...the whole lot. What happened here tonight was just a family quarrel, nothing more, nothing less. This whole place is crazy...I knew it was a mistake to come."

Okay, baby steps...maybe a wee push...

"Then why did you come here, Mr. Ryan?" I was pretty sure it wasn't the Early Bird Special at *The Martin House*.

"I came for the same reason I always end up in places like this. Places that I would never go if it weren't for him. I've been chasing that boy halfway around the world for the last twenty years, or so, but this really tears it. I'm fed up and I'm getting out of here today. Now."

At this he turned his now focused glare on the boo-hoo sisters and said...

"Alone, if I have to. In fact, that may be best all around."

If his bride heard his words, or understood their intent, it didn't show. I had the impression that not too much was getting through to Momsy. She was one spun bunny. She reminded me of those old golf balls that were layers upon layers of elastic. You picked and pulled for hours on little fragile strands of rubber, a laborious and addictive task.

Then, without warning, it would erupt in a frenetic and kinetic unraveling and careen madly about the room. Anyway...Mrs. Ryan was like that. Little bits and pieces of her had been picked at and snapped away, over the years, and she was about to blow. I got the distinct feeling that Pops was fed up...large.

Before I could get any more info, Tim was propelled through the doorway, his large frame blocking, not only the light, but the boot of Alex Thorne that was firmly, planted in Timmy's butt. Hence, the undignified entrance. I liked this boy. Alex, that is. Ryan I didn't really have a lot of warm fuzzies for.

Tim approached his father and got right in his face. Mr. Ryan seemed to recoil from his son but the wall he was against kept him pinned. Through gritted teeth, young Timmy dug into his father.

"What the hell did you tell this bit..." To his credit he opted not to purchase the other two consonants. I was gratified to think that he had managed, against his will no doubt, to attain some respect for me. I made a note. He continued. Or at least he tried to. He was cut off by his father who matched his boy, spittle for spittle.

"Enough Tim. Every time you open your mouth you dig a bigger hole, not just for yourself, but for the rest of us as well. This is the last time for me."

Tim stepped back as if slapped. My own head, quite of it's own volition, recoiled as well. No wonder Mr. Ryan had a reputation as a barracuda in the boardroom. There was something in his tone, his demeanor, that demanded one's full attention. He continued...

"I told you to work this out. This thing with Sydney, and, as usual, you've made a mess of the whole thing."

Tim's eyes darted between his father, me, and Alex Thorne, who was at this very moment scribbling furiously in his little black book. Tim glared at Alex...

"You can't use any of this, you know. Our lawyers will get those notes off you before the ink even dries."

"Good thing I'm using a pencil, Mr. Ryan." Gee, I really like this boy.

I took note that the old boy had not referred to Sydney as 'that woman,' a good sign. I couldn't help myself...now there's a surprise...I had to jump into the muddy waters and see what I could stir up just under the surface of what the elder Ryan was saying.

"What's the scoop Mr. Ryan? I assume this all has something to do with Sydney and Harley. Spill it." I talked like that because I read too many novels, and I can get away with it. I'm not sure this is a good thing.

Mr. Ryan turned to me. His thick white hair framed a ruddy face that seemed to darken to a dangerous crimson above a collar that I would have never gotten done up. He was a physically imposing man, although I pegged his height at a compact 5'11", or so. I suspected he may be a squash playing sailor, or some such. He had the feel of the wind about him, restless and hardy.

"There is no, as you put it, 'scoop,' Miss Shore."

I know I should be jumping in here and amending Papa Ryan's 'Miss' to the more PC, 'Ms.,' but saying it always makes me feel like sneezing, so I let it go. He continued.

"This is a family matter, and last I checked, you are neither a member of this family, nor for that matter, a welcome guest, ergo, I would like you to leave right now and take your muscle with you. That, Miss Shore, is your 'scoop.'"

Well shut my mouth. But not for long, I mean the man used the word 'ergo,' so I considered him fair game. I was just about to let fly when I felt a gentle squeeze on my burgeoning right biceps. I flexed involuntarily. It was Alex's voice I heard behind me.

"You're right Mr. Ryan. There doesn't seem to be a problem that would involve the police department. As you say, it's just a family matter. No sense wasting the taxpayers' money, now is there? Ms. Shore and I will just be getting along now. Thank you for your time."

My mouth was hanging open. I closed it with a snap and, instead, opted to grind my perfect pearly white molars to dust. I knew not to intercede on Alex's odd pronouncement so I said nothing, simply turning on my heel and stomping out of the room that had grown way too small. I was halfway to the road when Alex caught up to me.

"Hey Jess, hold up. You planning to walk back to town?" His eyes looked worried and I could see the outline of creases that would, in the years to come, deepen, adding a depth of character that was not present in his smooth as a baby's bottom skin. I was not pissed with him but I was pissed. He had done the right thing, after all, getting us out of there before the whole clan turned on us, as they had seemed poised to do. I was frustrated. I was also, I had just begun to realize, bone tired, in need of a really hot bath, a warm cognac and a soft bed. I let Alex off the hook.

"No, actually, I'd really appreciate a ride back to my car, or maybe right to my door. I think I may be too tired to drive. Would you mind?"

The relief on his face was disarming. I made a mental note to step carefully with young Alex as his emotional feelers protruded from his heart like magnets, pulling in any slight that may be within their reach. We walked to his car, neither of us breaking the silence of our own thoughts. When he couldn't stand it any longer, he asked,

"Do you think I did the right thing Jess? I mean, getting us out of there like I did?"

"You did exactly the right thing Officer Thorne. I wouldn't have been able to show that kind of restraint but that was definitely what was called for. Ryan's right. We don't have any legal right to question them about their comings and goings. I think that whatever information we need from these people we're going to have to get on our own. Together, if you don't mind sharing resources."

I hadn't worked with a partner since I had been a cop. The nature of the job caused you to form such strong emotional ties with your partner that I had avoided that sort of contact in my own work. Too many good-byes along the way. It was a commitment I hadn't been ready to make, until just now, apparently. I really did like Alex and I felt I could absolutely trust him. I imagined we would be good friends, no matter, so why not try working together. He brightened at the prospect of working as a team. He liked me too, I could tell, which may not speak well of his judgments about other people but then I tend to be pretty hard on myself.

We were both of us lost in our own ruminations on the ride back to my place. I was suddenly so tired I felt my eyes closing and my head lolling against the sweat scented vinyl of the police car. I was just about to start snoring when Alex cleared his throat in a gallant gesture to rouse me from my fog. I snapped my head forward which inspired a burst of cartoon stars before my eyes. Boy, I was pooped. I made a half hearted invitation for Alex to come in for a nightcap and he, kindly, declined, saying he wanted to get back to his office while the events of the evening were still fresh in his mind. I requested a copy of his report and he promised to drop it off to me in the morning.

CHAPTER 17

I entered my sanctuary, again, not sure of what I may find. Was it only a few hours ago that all my nearest and not so dearest were gathered around my table? All was quiet. I noticed an inert form on my couch. The light from the fire illuminated her enough for me to detect that it was Jennifer Eastcott...and she snores. One never knows when these facts will come into play so I stored it away for the moment. I was surprised to find her there.

Last thing, as I recalled, was that she was headed for Boston to see Sydney. Wonder what happened there. Buster was nowhere to be seen but I was certain I knew where he was. I peeked into Leah's room, as it was known, and sure enough, the two of them were in concert. His head rested next to hers, nose to nose. He barely lifted an eyebrow at my presence. Geez. I love you too fella.

All of a sudden I could barely walk. My ankle felt like the bones themselves were swollen, my head pounded, my eyes felt gritty and raw and every calcified bone in my body ached and moaned. I needed a bath and sleep...and a warm Courvosier. I went to the kitchen and found the bottle and snifter ready and waiting. Bless them. I lumbered down the hall to my bedroom. Bless them again...my bed was turned down and waited invitingly, a fire glowed in the dark and, miracle of miracles, the bathroom was lit by Bayberry scented candles, which illuminated the incandescence of the bubbles and steam which emanated from my tub.

The water was still a few degrees higher than luke warm and I could picture Leah and Buster winking and nudging each other at their successfully executed surprise. As if on cue, the big hound came into the bathroom and took up his place by the side of the tub.

"Okay, I know what you want."

I eased myself gingerly into the tub. A groan escaped my lips as my body sunk down into the Sandalwood scented water. I thought I would pass out. The last threads of energy unraveled and dispersed in the water and my eyes began to close.

Just then, I was snapped back to reality by a decidedly wet nose poking at my forehead. I made a cup out of my one hand and brought a puddle of soapy water to his smiling mouth. He lapped it up with glee. The best part is, while he is distracted by the warm and tasty water, my other hand is free to make soap-suds pirate hats on his flatish head. He hates it but will tolerate the indignity as long as he gets to drain the bathwater at the same time. A definite win-win. When his thirst is quenched he gives me a disgusted look and spends the next ten minutes rubbing all remnants of the offending suds from his coif. Small pleasures.

My mind began to wander as I slipped deeper into the weightless cushion. I was under water, out in the bay. It had been a wonderful day. It was the first summer that I had met Catherine. We had borrowed a friend's sailboat and Sydney had overseen the preparation of an overflowing picnic basket. We hadn't even made a dent in it yet as we intended to sail around to one of the many hidden sandy outcroppings that would be sure to give us the privacy we were seeking.

Catherine and I had spent some time together over the first weeks of my stay. A walk here, a dinner and nightcap there, but as yet, her schedule had been packed full.

Catherine was, and still is, tireless when it comes to tending to her patients.

To say she goes over and above would be an understatement. I had been tidying up three or four outstanding case files and the fresh air was a welcome relief for my strained eyes.

I was never very good at paperwork, always deferring it for a rainy day. Leah, as incongruent as it seemed, was a meticulous record and bookkeeper. She saw to it that my checks didn't bounce, too high at least, and that my filing system was at least thumbnail.

Catherine and I were taking each day as it came and simply enjoying each other's company; getting to know each other. I liked her a lot, that much I knew already. I was purposefully avoiding over analyzing whatever it was that we had between us and just going with the flow. We seemed to be in the same stress free zone and that was a real treat for me.

We sat close to each other, Catherine and I, while a gusty breeze gave us just enough umphf to pull the boat off an even keel. We tucked our ankles under the hiking wire and leaned out over the water in unison. We didn't speak, preferring the camaraderie of the sport over idle chit chat. It was a shock, therefore, when the small boat flung itself upside down in the water, pausing just long enough in mid flight to smack the boom across my forehead. I saw myself plunge into the darkness of the bay, the water clearing before my eyes.

I could see perfectly. I watched myself from the surface, breathing deep lungs full of water that sustained me like oxygen. This process did not surprise me. I had always believed that I could breath underwater, but had as yet not had an opportunity to test the theory... and there I was, both of me, watching the miracle occur. I will always remember how calm and safe I felt there, my limbs entwined with the rigging from the mainsail.

What I don't recall is Catherine hauling me unconscious from under the sail and, with superhuman strength, as it occurs to me, flinging me across the exposed hull of the small craft. I do not recall her administering mouth to mouth. I do not recall Joe Silva coming up in his small fishing skiff and rushing me to land as Catherine maintained a rhythmic CPR to my waterlogged chest.

I do remember opening my eyes and seeing the most beautiful face I have ever seen in my life, tear streaked and panic stricken, looking down at me. I do remember taking that magnificent face in my hands and pulling it to me, my lips seeking out hers. I do recall how the sobs of relief shook her perfect body as she held me to her.

I have, of course, conveniently forgotten throwing up my Cafe Heaven breakfast of granola, strawberries and yogurt all over her sodden Reebok's but, hey, it's my memory, after all. I also remember, that was the moment I fell in love with Catherine Hobbes.

My romantic meandering was washed away with the mouthful of now cool bath water that I had just inhaled. Buster looked indulgently at me, as I sputtered and spit my way back to wakefulness. I gripped the curved edges of the large claw foot tub and eased myself up. I hurt everywhere. My head was pounding so hard that even the slightest movement of my bloodshot eyes inspired yet another moan of pain to escape my lips.

I toweled off and padded to the bedroom. I pulled on my boxer shorts and the remnants of a T-shirt that bore the crest of the Ontario Police College. I eased myself back against my pillows and passed out. Fade to black. No gradual closing of the curtain of wakefulness. Nope. I stayed that way until my REM was cut short by the sound of raised voices coming from my kitchen. I recognized one as belonging to Leah; the other one, however, was not as familiar yet, somehow, I knew it too.

CHAPTER 18

"Well, color me caught off guard. What are you doing here Muffin?"

I must have been quite a sight as both Leah and Muffin stared open mouthed at me, neither seemed capable of responding to my question. Go figure. I caught my reflection in the hall mirror and had to smile at what I saw. My blondish hair, so expertly coifed just the week before, shot from my head in spiky explosions, making me look like a crazed Phyllis Diller gone to seed. My black and brown eyes, usually so expressive and bright, looked flat and opaque. I could have packed enough for a month-long cruise in the bags under my eyes.

My body, though in pretty good shape over-all did bear the traces of my years of over use. One leg shorter than the other gave a lop sided tilt to my hips, making me look like I was always walking in a Westerly direction along the beach. Both knees had what looked like an abandoned tic tac toe game on the surface, my arms and shoulders, though 'buff' by my standards, still stuck out from my body like chicken arms. Can't fight genetics. At five feet six inches, (or five three, depending which leg I stand on), my 122 and a half pounds was fairly well distributed. My daily or so 'ab' routine had kept my stomach fairly flat, and my legs were well muscled from pounding the dirt on my every other day runs.

Not bad for an old broad, if I do say so myself. Now, if it weren't for gravity....but more on that some other time. Leah recovered from her appalled fugue state first. There was something askew. Ah yes. She had coffee grounds in her hair.

Very nice. I bit my tongue. Hard. Obviously, I had slept through something good...or bad, depending on your perspective.

"Jess, this woman was prowling around outside our place this morning, skulking about like a thief."

'Our' place. I let it go. Leah continued, not seeing the balloon of words over my head.

"If it weren't for Buster, who knows what she might have done."

Who knows indeed, I mused. I couldn't stand the suspense any longer. I had to know.

"Leah, why do you have coffee grounds in your hair, if you don't mind my asking?"

At this Muffin took center stage.

"She was coming at me. I had to defend myself."

"Ah hah," I knew there had to be more so I waited. Cupcake continued.

"She was trying to force me to stay in this...this hovel until she had woken you up. I, quite frankly, have nothing to say to you, so I declined her invitation to stay. She attacked me, plain and simple. I did what I had to do."

I really wanted to laugh but sensed that may be an inappropriate response. Instead I looked past the DQ Blizzard and speared Leah with my 'if you don't tell me the truth, I'm gonna be mad at you' look. This was about as antagonistic as Leah and I got. She, however, was not to be intimidated by the likes of Muffin DeWitt. Her words, when they came, resided on the border of petulance and righteousness, a place she always had a passport for and was ready to cross at the drop of a hat.

"Jess Shore, if I have learned anything from you over the years it's that individuals who snoop could well be individuals who shoot. Frankly my friend, I am getting too old to spend sleepless nights in strange emergency rooms waiting to find out if you are going to live or die. And so, yes, I did insist that this intruder wait for me to get you up to see what you wanted to do about her. Is that so unreasonable?"

I smelled tears on the horizon and put my hand on Leah's arm, squeezing her lovingly.

"No Leah, you did exactly the right thing. Thank you. Now, you may want to go jump in the shower or your hair's never going to get to sleep. Don't worry about our guest. I don't think she wants to make trouble, do you Muffin?"

She glowered at me and sniffed derisively at Leah. Not a smart cookie, our Muffin. I decided that the whys and wherefores of the tossing of the grounds was better left between the two of them. I gently nudged Leah on her way, Buster plodding morosely behind her, taking up a post midway between the bathroom and the kitchen, ready to defend whichever mom needed him most. What a great guy.

I turned my attention to my uninvited guest. Geez. What a snippety looking thing she was. She had premature 'pursed lip' lines around her mouth and had the countenance of a much older, and bitter, woman. I figured her to be in her mid twenties but her dour personality was aging her in dog years.

"So, Muffin, what brings you to my, how did you so eloquently put it, humble hovel, if I remember correctly?"

"I don't have to tell you anything. It's a free country. I was simply out for a stroll when your rabid hound attacked me. There are laws you know."

What ho?? Bad move. Insult me. Make fun of my puny, yet fit, legs, criticize my Filene's Basement drapes, but don't, not ever, malign my dog. My jaw clenched painfully as I fought to maintain my composure, as I knew there would be nothing gained by reacting as I truly wanted, which would likely involve clumps of hair and heavily soiled clothing. Hers, for the record, not mine. I could tell by the look in her eyes that she sensed the rage that simmered hotly below the surface of my calm demeanor. Smart gal. My words, when they came out, were tight and I would like to think, threatening.

"Here's the scoop Muffin. You were trespassing on private property. My property. I don't like people trespassing on my property. I don't like people who trespass on my property tossing compost at my best friends. I don't like you. As to your comment about there being laws, I concur, and in this particular case the laws fall on my side of the fence. The side you were trespassing on. Believe me when I tell you that I wouldn't hesitate for a moment to pick up the phone and call Officer Alex Thorne of the Provincetown Police Department and have him come down here and charge you with trespassing. Don't try me on this one honey, 'cuz I would love an excuse to see you posing for a mug shot, so, here's your only other option. And here's a tip. Don't put your mouth in gear before your mind's engaged, got it?"

She reluctantly nodded her assent, or did one of those frightening 'innie' sneezes that can't possibly be good for you. Either way, I intuited it to mean I should proceed.

"I assume you didn't drop by for tea and scones, so let's see...if I had to guess, I would think you were looking for something. Now, further along those lines, I would assume that what you were looking for was somehow connected to the attack on Sydney Ryan. How am I doing so far, Ms. DeWitt?"

She glared at me through her pale eyes, the perfect arch of her eyebrows exclamation points to her pinched features. If I had owned an infra-red scope, I'm sure I would have been able to see the smoke coming from her brain as she worked out an acceptable cover story. This may seem unfair, but young Muff struck me as being about a twenty-five on a Tri-Light bulb. I remembered what Jennifer had told me about Muffs education. I knew she had to be a fairly bright gal but she sure did a good job of hiding it. I awaited her response.

My father had been the consummate salesman. He had dedicated his life to business and taught me many valuable lessons, many of which I didn't quite figure out until after he had died, but, better late than never. Anyhoo, he always said that once you ask for an order, picture a big sign over the head of your client that says "SHUT UP!" the theory being that the first one that speaks loses. So, I waited, the imaginary sign firmly nestled in Cupcake's brittle bouffant.

"I came to find something that Tim had lost the other day when you attacked him."

Again with the attack thing. Can you say 'persecution complex?'

"What might that have been, this thing that Tim lost?"

I thought about the bracelet that I had turned over to Alex just last night. In and of itself it didn't implicate anyone, but I hoped Muffin may be about to inadvertently shed some of her twenty-five watts on the situation. That must have been what she was after, anyway, either the bracelet or, failing that, whether or not I had found it. Silly Billy, did she actually think I hadn't 'sleuthed' out that clue yet.

Oh ye of little faith. I waited with bated breath...which always makes me think of eating worms but I'm sure that's not the original idea behind that expression. How gross.

"He lost a credit card. He told me how you had manhandled him over here and that your, ah, friends treated him like some mass murderer, or something, so we thought that maybe it had fallen out of his pocket around here somewhere. That's what I was doing outside. Nothing more."

"Ah hah. A credit card hmmm? What brand?"

"Huh."

"What kind of card Muf? Stripe, checker, polka dot?"

"What are you talking about? It was an American Express. Platinum!"

"Do Timmy's platinum club cards have a habit of jumping free from the confines of his Vuitton billfold and hurling themselves in a kamikaze dive, to the ground, and pulling a half inch of foliage over themselves? How cool. And I thought they were for buying stuff with. Who knew they were stringers for The Cirque du Soleil. Nope, sorry Muff, I'm not buying it, on credit or otherwise."

She got too close to my face. I wondered if there were any coffee grounds within the radius of my reach. Her breath smelled like bananas and red Dentyne.

"I don't give a flying fuck what you think, you lousy two bit dyke…….

"Ah……that's 'dick', as in the vernacular for private detective, right Pumpkin Pie? You do realize the difference, I assume."

I could see the drops of my spittle on her face. She had so much pancake on I was tempted to pour syrup on her. I liked the look, in my mind of course. It's not that I have any problems with the actual word 'dyke'. I know that it is one of those words that we Sisters of Sappho have reclaimed ownership of, however, somehow on Muff's lips the word seemed hard and ugly and not even a weensy bit empowering, which I knew was her intent.

My 'newly acquired as a result of becoming middle aged' political sensibilities were stirred up. She was crossing more lines than Thelma and Louise did. A baked good with a spine and a dirty, smelly mouth. Perfect.

I had more to say but internally I had already had the conversation so I didn't feel compelled to include Muff in my thoughts. Instead I made another stab at the truth.

"Are you sure that's the answer you want to stick with? The credit card in the foliage one? You must know that one of my friends is in a coma right now and you must know that *I* know that you and/or one of your coven, is somehow responsible for this unfortunate reality. You must also know that I will not rest until the truth is revealed and whoever is responsible is scrubbing filthy bathroom floors with a toothbrush for the rest of their lives. With that information in hand, would you care to change your answer?"

"No I wouldn't. What I will do is get the hell out of here and go straight to a phone and call my lawyer and have you charged with...something."

"No, no! Not the 'something' charge. Could you be so cruel? Now get out of my home, and oh, take a message back to your people. I'm coming and I'm coming hard and fast. I don't care how many pin stripes you throw at me, I'll dodge each and every one until I see justice done. Got it?"

She didn't bother to answer, how rude, rather she shoved past me, her pumps making infinitesimal horseshoe shaped dents in my beautiful pine floor, and stormed out. I went immediately to the phone. Just the mention of Sydney's name caused a fissure of panic to re-open inside of me.

I would let Muff go, for the moment. I had slept for about six hours and was frightened by how much could have changed in that time. I dialed Catherine's pager and punched in my number. I knew she would call me as soon as she could. In the meantime I should get a move on. I started for the bathroom, and almost made it, before Leah intercepted me in the hallway, her hair freshly de-caffeinated.

To her credit, and my abject appreciation, she didn't impede my progress.

"Go ahead Jess, get yourself ready. I'll bring you a coffee."

"Thank you. I'm so glad you're here. Why are you here anyway, or should I ask?"

"Later. For now, you have work to do and I have a lawyer to comfort. How does one do that, do you suppose? Well, no matter, I'll put her to work. This place could use a little freshening up."

"No tie-die. Promise Leah. Last time you 're-arranged' my place I felt like I had fallen into Laura Ashley's delicates drawer and couldn't get out. It's not my thing."

"Oh for Pete's sake Jess. Not everything in this place has to come from the land. It's okay to purchase material that you didn't peel off a birch tree. Now go. I'll listen for the phone."

"How did you know...oh skip it."

I peeled off my sleeping suit and turned on the shower. I imagined it may be the last free time I would have for many hours.

I composed a mental list of the things I needed to do. First and foremost, I had to get a status report on Sydney. Also, although I knew I didn't need to worry about Harley, what with Catherine and Kelly on the job, I did want to touch base with her as well. I may not be able to fulfill my promise to her today, but I would give her as much information on my progress as I could. Next, I was a little more than curious about Jennifer's reasons for not being at Sydney's side. If it was personal, fine, none of my beeswax, however, if there was more to it than that, I wanted to know about it. And, last but not least, the Ryan clan. How odd for Tea Biscuit to show up at the crack of dawn like that. Her behavior was suspect, at best.

My first stop would be to meet with Alex and go over whatever the information we had so far and discuss our next moves. The shower massage threatened to lull me back to sleep so I cut the hot and gave myself an invigorating blast of cold water, full pulse. Just as my teeth began to chatter the bathroom door opened and a hand appeared between the drapes of the shower stall, a steaming bowl of cafe au lait precariously balanced in it. If I didn't love her already, I would love her from this moment on and forever after.

"Thanks Leah. You are the best."

"Yes, I knew that. Now shake a leg Five-0, you've got work to do."

"Any word from Catherine?"

There was a moment of hesitation. It hung there in the steamy room. I cut the water and peeled back the curtain. Leah's eyes were still moist from a recent spell of tears. I urged her to come clean, so to speak.

"I spoke to Catherine, briefly Jess, so don't drill me, and she said there was no change. Nothing. She said to call her on her cellular when you were on your way out. You should really dedicate the rest of your life to worshipping that woman or I give up. Now, go!"

I wanted to pepper her with questions but, as she had already stated, she didn't know anything more and was obviously upset enough as it was. I smiled weakly and I'm sure not reassuringly at her and she left me alone. I stood and drip-dried for a moment, trying not to let my mind wander to any place it may not like the look of once it got there. With a deep sigh and painful gulp, I went about my business and tried not to think about how good a cigarette would taste right now.

I dressed quickly and sat on the edge of my bed, hitting the speed dial for Catherine's cell phone...hoping it was the same as before. She picked up on the first ring, her voice sounding as bone tired as my body had last night. My heart broke a little for her and my arms ached to hold her tight to me. Yikes. What does that mean?

"Jess, I'm so glad to hear your voice." Her own voice cracked with the effort of speech. I knew that Catherine's demons must be wreaking havoc on her. The personal and professional losses in her life would have to be overwhelming, especially at times like this. I wanted to comfort her but didn't know how.

"I'm glad to hear yours too Cat. You sound wiped. Leah passed on your message. Is there really no change at all?"

"Nothing. I sat with her all night. The only positive thing I can say is that she isn't getting any worse. The blood thinners seem to be working and the swelling on her brain is slowly subsiding. Other than that..."

Her voice trailed off. I closed my own eyes and saw her face so clearly I felt I could reach out and touch it. I wanted to touch it. I wanted her to feel me there with her, even if I couldn't be. I realized I hadn't responded and snapped back from la la land.

"Cat I know you are doing everything you can for Sydney. Please baby, try not to beat yourself up over this. You're the best and you will do the right thing. How's Harley holding up?"

"Like a soldier, the little angel. We brought in a cot for her to sleep on. Kelly just took her out for some air and hopefully she'll be able to get her to eat something. Oh God Jess, her faith in me is terrifying. I can't let her down."

"And you won't, no matter what happens with Sydney. Now listen to me Dr. Hobbes. I know you well enough to say that you better remember to look after yourself as well. Take a break. Why don't you go and find Harley and Kelly and take a little breather yourself?"

Yeah, I thought, that's about as likely to happen as me riding naked down Commercial Street on a Unicycle, but at least the words were out there.

"Sure Jess. I'll do that. What's happening on your end? Any progress?"

"Hard to say at this point. For now, I just have a lot of little pieces. I'm off now to check out a few more things. I have a hunch or two but that's about it. I should really get going. Ahh, Cath..."

"Yes Jess?"

"Ah, just, well, oh hell Catherine, I love you, okay? That's all, and I know what you're going through and, oh, whatever. I gotta go."

"Ever the romantic." But I was pleased as punch to hear the smile in her voice. I would think about what I had just confessed to us both later. Much later.

"See ya Jess. Oh, I wanted to ask you about Jennifer Eastcott. I thought you said she was coming in last night. What happened?"

"Good question Doc, and another answer that I need to get. I'll keep in touch."

I hung up the phone and headed out to the kitchen to track down my houseguest. I still couldn't get a handle on Jennifer. I think she's on the level but there's something else niggling at me and it looks a lot like her. Leah was out on the beach with Buster playing an enthusiastic game of fetch. Leah that is, not Buster. He had never quite mastered the bringing back part of the game, but still we tried. There was no sign of Jennifer, but her stuff was still in the living room, her briefcase tucked away next to the couch. Hmmm. Should I? Would I? Yes to both, but later. The phone rang. It was Karen.

"Hey sleepy head, why haven't I heard from you today?"

"Because it's only 7:16 in the morning and I just got up."

"Hmpfh. Well, while you were napping Cape Air brought in that Eastcott gal's luggage. Cripes Jess, this one doesn't believe in packing light. She has enough stuff here to set up a small camp. Want me to have it sent over to your place?"

"Ah, no Karen, if you don't mind, could you just keep the delivery under your hat for the time being. I'll loan her the essentials for now. I want to keep her a little off balance and this may help."

"No sweat. Anything else I can do? Have you heard from the Doc yet?"

"Yeah I just talked to her. No change I'm sorry to say. By the way, did Jennifer ever make it out to the airport last night, do you know? She was on her way to Boston last I saw her and next thing she's catching forty on my couch."

I could hear Karen shuffling paper, looking, no doubt, for the flight manifests from last night.

"Nope. She was booked and never showed. Is that it for now?"

"Yes thanks. I'll be in touch."

Karen assured me that she would call me if anything I should know about came up, and if it happened within a twenty-mile radius of the airport, she would indeed hear about it.

I went out to the deck and called to Leah. She gave a wave and headed up to the house, dripping wet black dog at her heels, listening intently with his eyebrows to whatever it was she was saying to him. Oh to be a flea on that collar. I swear, those two talk more than Leah and I do. This doesn't seem strange to me somehow.

"Where's Jennifer?"

"Fine thanks, and yourself? Yes, I slept well too. Geez Jess."

"Not now Leah. Please. Where is she, do you have any idea?"

"Of course I do silly. She went for a run about ten minutes before you came to. She should be back soon. Do you want to wait around for her? Maybe lace on your shoes and join her?"

"No, I don't have time. Did you two talk last night at all? Did she tell you why she didn't go to see Sydney?"

"Yes we talked. It was kinda odd actually. I mean she just showed up back here about an hour or so after she left. Needless to say I made polite inquiries...."

"Needless to say...and?"

"Well, not much I guess."

"Leah, could you just try to give me the blow by blow and we can put it under the Bat Analyzer later? Hmmm?"

"Cranky old broad...okay, okay, don't glare at me. Gracious, what if your face froze like that?"

"Leah Hughes...spit it out." I really didn't want to laugh but sometimes the more frustrated I got with Leah the more I wanted to guffaw. I restrained myself. Barely.

"Jennifer Eastcott, thirty something and stylish, arrived back from Provincetown Airport at approximately eleven thirty PM. Allegedly. Aforementioned then proceeded to the bathroom, where she remained for eight and a half minutes. Upon exiting the facilities she made her way to your Courvosier and asked my permission to pour herself a shot. I granted said approval and she sucked back enough of that plonk to bring tears to her eyes. It was then that I surmised that the tears were not alcohol induced. Shall I continue?"

"Yes, pray continue..."

"Well, here's the thing. I asked her why she didn't go to Boston and she told me that she just didn't have the intestinal fortitude to see Sydney in that condition. She did, really, seem quite distraught, yet...I don't know, I kept hearing a little bell going off in my head and it wasn't Avon calling, if you catch my drift."

Now I did laugh. Such a way with words. I tried for the most direct questioning I could, otherwise I sensed I would be here all day.

"Was there anything specific that she said? Anything, I don't know, askew?"

"Yeah, the whole thing seemed slightly left of center. It wasn't that she was lying, I just didn't get the feeling that she was telling me the whole truth, know what I mean Jelly Bean?"

"Yup. Do me a favor. I can't stick around here all morning waiting for her to show up. Can you see that she doesn't leave town until I get back? If you have any problems, call Alex Thorne. He'll know how to get hold of me."

"Done. Bye bye. Oh, will I expect you for dinner?"

"Hard to say, why, are you cooking?"

"Not in this lifetime. Call me and I'll get the toaster warmed up"

I went back to my room and dragged the small stepladder out from under my bed. I set it up in my closet and reached in the back, knocking seven thousand or so empty shoeboxes onto my head. I just couldn't bear to throw them out. The last box was the one I really wanted. I pulled it to me and hopped off the ladder. I could feel the lethal weight of the contents. Inside was a locked steel box, the combination known only to me.

I don't like the idea of leaving the gun unattended but transporting it over the boarder all the time got pretty tedious. It was registered and all that and the local cops knew where it was and how it was stored, but still...

I peeled back the layers of tissue paper and removed my 9mm from it's cocoon. It's still as ugly and deadly looking as I remember. Usually I favor a smaller caliber, something like a .22 but I kept that stashed under the driver's seat of the jeep in a special compartment that I had added years ago. It wasn't exactly easy access but it was there, none the less.

I didn't like carrying a gun, nor did I really mind it. I was used to firearms and my police training had taught me to respect their power. The thing about a bullet is when you first meet one, you may be saying good-bye at the same time. I have had occasion to fire my weapons and yes, I have killed people. It's part of the job. Not a great part but hey, there's always the snappy military issue footwear, so all's not lost. I checked the .9mm out carefully.

I was meticulous about cleaning and maintenance but it always paid to check. I kept my ammunition buried in my Pot Pourri basket in the bathroom, of course, and grabbed a handful of bullets. I tucked the gun into my waistband, the butt nestling into the small of my back.

I would forget it was there in a minute or two, but for now I felt its full heft. I threw on what remained of my favorite denim shirt to cover the bulge and headed out.

I waved good-bye to Leah and Buster who were back at the water's edge and climbed into the Jeep. It coughed and sputtered to life and I scooted up Cottage to Bradford so I could pull over by Pearl at Commercial and run into The Portuguese Bakery for something fresh and hot and really greasy.

Next stop, Spiritus for a couple of jumbo Lattes. Breakfast of champions here I come. After the supplies had been purchased I headed up to Shank Painter Road to find Alex.

CHAPTER 19

He looked like he had spent the night at his desk, which indeed he had as it turns out. Ah youth. He still looked pretty chipper to me. Even with six hours sleep under my belt I still looked like I fell over during my Boxercise class. I was pretty sore from my little run in with Tim Ryan. My ankle was a bluish color and my toes looked like little cocktail weenies. As for the knot on the back of my head, it was tender to the touch but otherwise, miraculously, I didn't have a headache. Lucky for Ryan. I get enough headaches all on my own, thank you very much.

There were a couple of officers that I had met and worked with over the years going about their various tasks and the new summer recruits were starting to filter in for training. It was a beehive of activity and I felt the energy in the room. I recalled the earnest faces of the young officers; many taking the first step to fulfilling a dream to wear 'the uniform.' A flood of memories swept me back to my days at the Academy in Aylmer Ontario. I would never forget the first time I put on my new uniform. It was one of the proudest moments of my life and I felt completely at one with myself for the first time. A false sense of omnipotence emanated from each crisp crease, and every squeak of the stiff leather of my utility belt gave me shivers. The hat, however, was another matter all together.

Honestly, you could balance a tray of draft on one of those things and never spill a drop. Slave to fashion that I am, I remember thinking that for the rest of my working life I would have really bad "hat head."

I envied their youth and empathized with what I knew were bats flapping about in the deep recesses of their bowels.

Provincetown may not be a mecca for crime but it was, for many, a starting point for their law enforcement careers. In my heart I wished them all well. For their sakes and the sakes of their friends and families, I said a small prayer for their safety. I unconsciously rubbed my shoulder where I had last had a bullet removed. Well, I survived and hopefully so would they. I plonked the coffee and pastries in front of Alex and he jumped about two inches into the air.

"Oh, geez, Jess. Hi. I didn't see you come in. Is this for me? I could sure use it. Thanks."

"You look like you've been here all night. Anything interesting?"

He looked so pleased with himself I thought he might bust.

"Wait 'til you see this."

My heart did a little flip flop. I would love to close this one down fast and get out to Boston with some good news for Harley and Catherine. Also, I felt torn not being able to be there for Sydney, not that I could do anything if I was there but none the less. The other thing to consider was that the longer these things take to figure out, the colder the trail gets. I knew we couldn't count on the Ryans sticking around forever and I didn't feel like playing the game on their home field.

Alex had pulled around a chair for me and as I sat down he passed me a sheaf of papers that he had piled in front of him.

They were print outs from VIPAC, the computer system cops use to gather information. It's amazing to think that 'Big Brother' is alive and well and living in the United States of America, even if you don't have a criminal record.

Alex had requested information on the whole Ryan clan, including Muffin. I leafed quickly through. Reading reports like this are like taking a multiple choice exam. Read through all the info from the get go, then go back and whip through the easy questions, saving the toughies for last. I was following this golden rule until a name leapt off the page and slapped me across the face. Jennifer Eastcott! What the h - e double toothpicks was her name doing on Muffin's bio? Uh oh.

Alex must have been waiting for me to make my discovery. When I looked up he was grinning back at me like Buster when he plants a slimy bone on my pillow. I figured he was already a step or two ahead of me so I asked for the skinny. (The skinny. Don't ya love it?)

"Interesting huh? I checked it out first thing this morning. I knew you'd want to know what the connection was. Seems Muffin and Jennifer knew each other years ago in New York. They were both in their early twenties when they met. Near as I can find out they had some friends in common and did the party circuit together. Jennifer was still at Harvard and rumor has it the two of them became quite "close.""

My Spidey sense started to tingle again.

"How close?"

Alex frowned. He must have anticipated this question and I could tell by his expression that he hadn't found the answer. Not yet at least.

"That I don't know Jess. I've put in a couple of calls but so far nobody has gotten back to me. I found the connection from an old list of names that the Boston PD put together years ago. Kids mostly that got involved in some animal rights protest or something. Nothing came of it but they were both there at the same time.

It all seems to be on the up and up but I thought it was pretty strange that Jennifer never said anything to you about it...or did she?"

I didn't blame him for his suspicious tone. Partnerships, be they of a romantic nature or not, are built on trust and the original foundations of that trust are laboriously built up one brick at a time. We had only known each other for a blink of an eye and were still mixing the mortar. I would have had the same reaction. I put his mind at ease as best I could.

"No she didn't say a word. In fact, I would go so far as to say she hid that little bit of information from me. Damn. I knew something was hinky with her but her heart on sleeve story about Sydney and all that threw me off. Must be losing my touch. Course there was the chance, slim I reckoned, that they never actually met each other. Just in the same place in the same time. Nah. I doubt that."

Alex sipped thoughtfully at his latte while I read the reports. Tim Ryan had lots and lots of entries over the years. Stupid stuff mostly to begin with. Shoplifting at an early age, theft etc. Most of the charges could have been attributed to many teenage boys growing up in an urban center like Boston with too much time on their hands and not enough attention at home. No biggie. Then, he hit his stride in his eighteenth year. Assault, assault with a weapon, and more assaults. Barroom brawls, street fighting, you name it. Seems he ran with a tough crowd.

A pattern had begun to emerge that spanned, according to his DOB, about eighteen years. My initial assessment of Tim had been officially confirmed. Tim Ryan is not what you would call a nice guy, not by any stretch.

All the legal representation he had received over the years was from the same firm. The name rang a bell and I made a mental note to check them out. Robert Stone was the attorney of record and I jotted it down in my notepad.

Up until about ten minutes ago I would have asked Jennifer if she knew them but now even her presence was, once again, suspect.

I was aware of Alex clearing his throat. It sounded like when you take a too big bite of something with lots of chocolate in it and it gets jammed in your throat. I didn't know if he wanted my attention or the Heimlich...

"Got a date for the phlegm ball?"

"Huh?"

"Skip it. You wanted to say something?"

He rifled through his papers and held a piece up, triumph shining on his adorable and smooth like a baby's bum face.

"I saw you were reading Timothy Ryan's sheet. What you won't see there, however, is that part of his record has been expunged."

"Translation?"

"When Ryan was sixteen he was involved in a car accident. His passenger was killed, and, you'll never guess who that passenger was..."

"Well, I assume it wasn't Curious George...I would have heard about that.....come on Alex. Don't toy with me."

"His sister."

Look up dumbfounded in the dictionary and you will see a picture of my face as it appears at this moment. I actually flapped my lips, and until this time, I never really knew what that meant. Now it was my turn to clear the chocolate gob out of my throat.

"His sister? What sister? Why expunged? How? When???"

"Yes. His only sister, Sarah Ryan. Parental request. High priced legal help, and, finally, June 12, 1976. Next salvo?"

"Wow. Was he charged with anything?"

"Nope. Actually it wasn't his fault. The other car came flying through a red light. The driver was drunk. He smashed right into the passenger side of Tim's car. That kid didn't have a chance."

I felt sick in the pit of my stomach and my heart lurched painfully in my chest. Man. Poor guy. Whatever opinion I had of Ryan notwithstanding, something like that's gotta mess you up pretty bad. A new vision of Timothy Ryan began to present itself to me.

Maybe that thing, that thing that I thought was anger or hatred in his eyes was pain. Man. I just sat there for a minute or two, Alex allowing me the space. I'm sure that he was feeling something akin to sympathy himself. He could do no less. I eased back into my thinking brain and considered whether or not this information did, or should, have any impact on my suspicions about Ryan or not. Damn. It did change things. Alex spoke what was in my mind.

"You know Jess, I was pretty much comfortable with my suspicions about Tim but I've got to say, right or wrong, this makes it different, don't you think?"

I noticed that he referred to 'Tim' as Tim...as opposed to 'Ryan.' I get paid big bucks to make these observations and I knew that the times they were a'changin.

"Okay officer. Let's not get too swept up in emotion here. Ryan was, and still is, a viable suspect. He has a motive, he can be placed at the scene, and his family is nuts. It still works for me," I said in a voice that didn't even convince me.

Alex stared steadily at me and I defiantly back at him. No way was this young whippersnapper gonna win a visual arm wrestle with me. Sure enough, he turned his eyes away first. Ha! God, I could be so petty. I let him off the hook.

"Let's take a look at what else we have. We'll operate, for the moment, as if Ryan had an airtight alibi and look elsewhere. Let's start with the rest of the family...What do we really know about them? Not what they do or how much money they have, I mean, them as people?"

"Not much really. There's tons of stuff in there about the business and the society stuff, but other than that..." His voice trailed off.

Getting information can be like doing a jigsaw puzzle without having the picture on the box. You have to start on the edges and work your way into the center of the design. Even when you know what the finished product looks like, you still have to build your way towards it piece by piece.

You try to rely more on your other senses, the deeper senses, like intuition and reason. Often the most important things about a person's life are only known to those nearest and dearest. The stuff that gives you insight. Information like, say, that Pa Ryan had a heroin habit, or Mrs. Ryan was a transsexual, stuff like that. I was having another thought.

"Who's the one person in all of that that actually has a connection to the Ryan family and may benefit from giving us a hand, say to sway suspicion away from himself and get on with his life?"

It was Alex's turn to look dumbfounded.

"You mean you're gonna ask Tim Ryan for help? Am I missing something here Jess?"

"No. I admit, it's a little left of center but look at it this way. If we keep going on the assumption that Tim is innocent, he wouldn't lose anything by helping us out. Besides, who better to fill in the blanks than a family member? That and the fact that without his help, we've got bubkus.

It's a long shot but I'm willing to throw it into the air and see if it flies if you are. What can go wrong? If he is guilty, our implied trust in him may cause him to lower his defenses and give something away."

"Teach me oh master."

I chose not to think of his tone as sarcastic, rather, respectful. Hey, it's my ego and I'll delude it if I want to.

I gathered together the research that Alex had done while he put in a call to The Provincetown Inn, checking on the whereabouts of the clan. Seems Alex was friends with a gal that worked on the desk during the day.

If I didn't know better I would say he blushed at one point. Her name is Beth and she told him that Ma and Pa Ryan were present and accounted for but she hadn't seen Muffin or Tim since she arrived that morning. Alex covered the receiver with his hand.

"What do you want to do Jess? Beth can put me through to their room."

"Yeah, go for it."

I listened in on Alex's end of the conversation. My guess, judging from his tone, was that he had Mr. Ryan on the line. He hung up abruptly, or somebody did, and grabbed for his keys.

"Tim and Muffin are having breakfast at Galerani's. They just left a few minutes ago so we should be able to catch up with them."

Hmmmm. Breakfast. Now there's a thought. I usually went to *Cafe Heaven* for their 'to die for' home-made granola and thick as Clam Chowder yogurt, but they didn't usually open their doors until the May two-four. No worries. I'm sure I'll be able to find something delectable on the menu at Galerani's.

An added bonus is the staff usually have their collective fingers on the collective pulse of the town and my gossip gene was hungry for a fix. I'd been away for a while and needed to hear the 'dis' on who was doing what to whom behind whose back...

Alex and I did a Laurel and Hardy thing at the door to the station, each in great haste, our shoulders wedging us into the opening. Egads.

The things you see when you don't have a video camera. We both ignored the sniggering behind us and proceeded in a more orderly fashion to the parking lot.

We went in Alex's police car and I had a moment of deja vu. I remembered the routine as if it was yesterday. You open the driver's side door and you're hit with the smell of cigarette smoke, fast food and sweat. Your arms are usually loaded down with all the sundry supplies you need for your shift. Your duty bag gets strapped in the passenger seat, overflowing with reference material, ticket books and other important cop stuff. Then you do your walk around. It's the same as flying and, like flying, one of the most important things you do. If your vehicle isn't in perfect condition you are risking your life needlessly. You take care of it and it will take care of you, it's that simple. Lights, tires, any damage to the vehicle, etc. Check the trunk for your flares, first aid kit, spare, cones, safety reflective vests and a shovel.

Once that's all done you climb in and hit the sirens, giving them and yourself a comforting blast of power and control. That's what it's like, you know. You drive around in your car and know that almost every person that sees you drive by notices you. If they're driving near you they will automatically check their speed, fasten their seat belts and pray that you just pass them by.

You feel a sense of omnipotence and security as you cruise around, the center of attention wherever you pass. It's an awesome and intimidating feeling all at the same time. As safe as you feel you also realize that by virtue of your uniform and your vehicle you are a target for any sick puppy out there that may have a score to settle. A tension begins to tighten the back of your neck and your hands grip the wheel so hard they feel cramped and swollen by the end of your shift. It's like a drug that you can't imagine living without.

That's why a lot of cops do what I did...staying in the game but playing by our own rules. We don't have the badge or the uniform but we have the attitude and it's that - the power coming from within - that drives us.

Most cops have an unfailing belief that the law is right and those that break the law are wrong. It's pretty black and white, I grant you that, but if you don't feel that way about it you should do something else. Cops need guidelines. You fight to enforce the rules, even if you don't always agree with them.

That was always the hardest part for me, too many shades of gray. On my own I could let the line between right and wrong blur to suit myself. The goal is still the same. Someone does something wrong and you see to it that they're caught and punished. Simple. Black and white.

As a cop everything you do is observed and monitored. It has to be that way. It protects you, your brethren and the citizens you represent. On your own the only people you are ultimately accountable to are yourself and your client. I prefer it that way. All these memories and thoughts whizzed through my mind as I climbed into the car with Alex.

We parked on Commercial Street, in front of Beachfront Realty. Good thinking on Alex's part. This way we could catch Tim and Muff by surprise, if only for a moment. We entered the bright interior of the restaurant. It smelled like breakfast. Bacon, onions, fresh muffins.
My stomach made a sound that should have come from a much larger person.

Speaking of muffins, Tim and his betrothed were seated at a table for four overlooking the street. I knew they must have seen us enter and I headed right over.

"Morning you two. What's the breakfast special?" I asked as I pulled out a chair across from the lovers and sat down.

If they were happy to see me they hid it well. Fortunately I'm kinda thick skinned that way. I realized that Alex and I should have discussed strategy for this face-to-face confrontation. Turns out I needn't have concerned myself with that. This kid knows his stuff, I'll give him that.

He knelt down in front of Muffin, blocking her view of Tim. Nice move. I noticed her noticing him. Her eyes swept across his broad shoulders and rested momentarily on his muscular forearms before they returned to his face. A slightly more than casual glance I think.

"Miss DeWitt...I know that you are under no obligation to do so, but I would appreciate it if you could just sit and talk with me for a couple of minutes. I don't want to intrude but, Ms. Ryan is a popular member of our community here and there's quite a bit of pressure on me to find out more about the attack on her. You may not know it, but you could possibly shed some light. Would you mind? Really, it'll only take a minute or two."

Smoothie. I saw Muffin trying to work herself around Alex, to no avail. Tim, for his part, was busy glaring at the back of Alex's head. Muffin rose uncertainly from her chair and, with a quick glance at Tim, moved to the bar with Alex. Perfect. I seized the opportunity.

Plonking myself down in the recently vacated chair I waited for Tim to acknowledge me. When he did speak he sounded, I don't know, weary somehow.

"Okay...you have me to yourself. What do you want?"

Hmmm. He had seen through the ruse. No matter. I plunged in.

"I don't think you had anything to do with the attack on Sydney. I wouldn't go so far as to say that you don't know more than you have told me, but I don't think you did it."

If I had expected him to be appreciative of my largesse, I was to be disappointed.

"And? I'm supposed to feel...what? Relief? Gratitude? Don't hold your breath. You want something. Why don't you just tell me what that is and I can get on with my life...if it's not asking too much."

Some people just make it so hard to like them...but I prevailed. I kept the image of the destroyed sixteen-year-old boy in my mind's eye and carried on.

"Here's what I think. I think that someone you know attacked Sydney and, further, I think you know who and why. If you don't know for sure I would bet that you have your suspicions. You may even be covering for them. I want your help...if not for Sydney then for Harley."

The last bullet hit the bull's-eye. Ryan flinched at the mention of his daughter's name. I was relieved to see it. I couldn't be sure about his paternal loyalty but it seemed there was some after all. I didn't want to use Harley as a pawn in this game but if I had to, to get to the truth, I would. Scruples, after all , is just a board game.

I thought about what Jennifer had told me, her belief that both families wanted to sweep the whole custody thing under the mat. I wasn't so sure about that.

I decided to strike while the iron was hot, whatever that means.

"I need you to level with me, about a lot of things."

He looked like he had eaten something nasty.

"Look, I'll answer your questions as they pertain to Sydney, but that's it. I will not, however, do your job for you. If you and the Keystone cop over there can't figure this out for yourselves that's tough shit lady."

Charming young fella don't ya think? I thought fast. I had prepared some questions in my mind and quickly rifled through them now.

I was pretty sure I would only have a minute or two with Tim and wanted to at least get answers to the top three or so questions. I went with the rapid fire approach.

"I need to know the truth about why you and the rest of your family are here. Did they all follow you or did you summon them here? What is the deal with Harley and the custody case? Have you had a change of heart about giving up your rights to her? Why did your fiancée come with your parents and not with you? Why were you at *The Shooting Gallery* yesterday when you attacked me? Who do you think did this and why?"

The last question was, I felt sure, not going to receive an answer but what the heck...if ya don't ask ya don't get, right?"

Tim took a breath and held it for a second or so. He closed his eyes. I imagined he was trying to decide what to answer and how without further arousing my suspicions. He may be wondering whether or not he could pull the wool over my eyes. I hope he realizes that I am allergic to wool and would not want to risk getting a rash on my face.

He took a long drink from his coffee, careful to set the cup back down in the exact same spot as before, as though seeking order for his actions as well as his thoughts. I sensed he was a meticulous man, if not a slightly obsessive one. This I can admire as I too have often been accused of being ever so slightly obsessive myself. Hah, that's an understatement, but now's not the time. I waited him out. I didn't have to wait long.

"Mizzz Shore, what my parents do and where they choose to spend their time long ago ceased to be a concern of mine. Why are they here? For me. I suppose, as strange as that show of support seems to me that's their story and I for one choose to believe it. The last several years my parents and myself have rarely seen eye to eye on much of anything...except Muffin. They adore her. She's like a daughter to them."

At this his eyes took on a brand new light. I knew he must be thinking about his own sister and the tragic circumstances of her death. The pain was so raw and naked in his eyes that I had to look away. I wasn't about to volunteer that I knew about the accident that took her life and spared, in a manner of speaking, his own but I did feel a slight pull to comfort him. It passed. He swallowed and continued.

"I told Muffin I was coming here to talk to Sydney. I assume, Mzzzzz Shore that by now you are aware of my history with Sydney. No doubt Jennifer Eastcott has filled you in on her version of events so I won't waste either of our time going over those details. Muffin has, ah, concerns, with respect to my handling of things. She was worried that I would let my temper get in the way of doing what's right for Harley. For us.

I also assume you've checked into my background...my history with the law. I can't remember a time when I wasn't pissed off at someone and I've tried, since getting together with Muffin, to get a handle on that. I had a chip on my shoulder that got in the way of anyone getting too close to me. I was lonely and being with Muffin made it okay to realize that."

I was afraid to breathe for fear that Ryan would hear himself and cut off this personal revelation session that he was engaged in. I didn't blink and in the back of my mind I sent a message to Alex to stay clear. I wondered if Tim knew that I knew about his sister...if that's what he was referring to about the legal troubles he had in the past. I would have to be on my guard here. I would bet my last Bugs Bunny Pez dispenser that his suspicions were pretty close to the truth.

The next statement out of his full-lipped mouth just about floored me...

"I can't believe what I'm about to do...and don't, even for a second, assume this has anything to do with you...I want to help you find who did this to Sydney. I want to hire you, but there's a couple of conditions..."

"Like?"

"Like, I want to know what you find out before you turn the information over to Deputy Dawg. "

I sat, stunned, and stared gape mouthed at Timothy Ryan. I couldn't agree to his terms yet I couldn't say no either. Hmmm...Did he say something about hiring me? Can you say 'rent money?'

I needed to hear all of his conditions before I responded.

"What else?"

"I want to go with you when you confront them. When you're sure. "

"Them?"

"Oh Christ... him, her, it...whatever."

Hmmmm. Hmmm. Hmm. Oops, I think I said that out loud. Ryan was glaring at me.

My gut, which by the way sounded like a lawn mower with the choke stuck, told me to walk away from the deal. I always try to color within the lines when it comes to involving the authorities. It wasn't just my own past with the department, though that was a significant factor. It was just good business, plain and simple.

The police have contacts and resources that were invaluable to me as a private detective. If at times the relationship was a tad acrimonious...who's stepping on whose toes kind of thing... the benefits far outweigh the disadvantages.

In Toronto where I spent about four or five months of the year, my hometown, I was on good speaking and working terms with most of the Metropolitan forces. I had friends in low, medium, and high places and my success was due, in part, to those relationships.

Having spent a lot of time in Provincetown over the years I had become friendly with several members of the force but, as yet, had never worked in an official capacity with them.

If Alex was any example, I had struck gold. The idea of cutting him out didn't really seem like an option. On the other hand...

Ryan was waiting for an answer and I assumed it was a limited time offer. In the suspicious quadrant of my brain I had to wonder if this wasn't just another ploy to distract me from the truth. Time would tell.

I gave him my decision. I may or may not live to regret it.

CHAPTER 20

Alex dropped me off at the station where I had left my car. Neither of us had said much after leaving Galerani's, both of us lost in our own thoughts about our chats with Muffy and Tim. His patience extended beyond his years and I respected him for it. Alex understood that he could trust me...I just hope that trust was not misplaced. If he had found out anything from Muffin I guessed it wasn't of much consequence. As for my deal with Tim, well, I kept that to myself for the moment.

We agreed to meet later, after Alex's shift ended at six that night. It was still early and I had lots to do.

My injuries from yesterday were sending red beams of pain all through my body. My head felt stiff and sore from the inside out. In some strange way having had migraines for years made the pain in my head seem insignificant. My leg, however, was a different story. Although the colors were pleasing to the eye the swelling was slowing me down.

My discomfort made me think of Catherine...and I mean that in a nice way. Since that first examination so many lifetimes ago, Catherine had advised me many times on how best to tend to my various aches and pains. I could never remember if it was heat for swelling, ice for bruising or Chardonnay for muscle damage.

I thought of calling Catherine. I sat there in the parking lot outside the police station and pictured her in my mind. A discomforting flood of heat rushed through me and I think maybe I was blushing. I wanted to call her, to hear her voice.

I imagined she had had little or no sleep since bringing Sydney to the hospital and my heart went out to her. Apparently, and inappropriately, so did my hormones. My mind wandered to our last meeting.

I had been at my home in Toronto. It was a hesitant Spring, late in May. The trees were just starting to come back to life after the long winter. I was sitting at my desk, filling out some reports from my latest case. Mostly I was staring out my window at Lake Ontario. It looked like a painting, all different shades of blue, and the sun was so bright I had to squint.

I noticed an airline limo pull into the driveway and assumed it was for my neighbors, Helen and Angelo. They were headed for a week of sun n' fun in Cozumel. No, I wasn't envious at all.

I didn't expect the knock on my door and considered playing possum. I couldn't remember if I had locked up or not until I heard the door opening. Buster, who until then had been unconscious on the couch bolted down the hall. I could hear the sound of his tail wagging as it whipped through the air.

"Leah? Is that you? Did you bring me a latte?"

"No I didn't bring you a latte. Can I still come in?"

My heart went into double time at the sound of Catherine's voice in my hallway. Last I had heard she was in San Francisco for some big deal doctor's symposium.

The grapevine in Provincetown kept me up to date on her comings and goings even if I didn't solicit the information.

Catherine and I had kept in touch but our conversations were usually strained. The unresolved feelings we had for each other always seemed to get in the way of the niceties. Our love affair had ended...sort of...before it really got started.

That first spring and summer with Dr. Hobbes had been the best and most frightening time of my adult life.

My relationship with Leah had been based on love, respect and shared misery. Our time together had been marred by too many tragedies and all-consuming, dark periods of intense mourning. We had been there for each other and still were. She was my best friend before and after our union.

In our years together we had both lost our fathers, my brother, and Leah's best friend Angela, all taken from us suddenly and painfully. It was the worst time of both our lives and we supported each other as best we could. In retrospect we did a good job of it too. When the pall began to lift we were left with barren earth where once our loved had bloomed. It was an impossible transition to make together so we had gone our separate ways.

What I felt with Catherine was different with a capital 'D.' I had loved Leah and I had loved others before and after her. I had never been *in love*...capital 'l.' Having Catherine in my life opened up a side of me that I had given up believing in. My whole being had become involved in the process. Physically, emotionally, spiritually. It was a wild ride and I had no idea how to get off or even if I wanted to.

The intensity of what I felt then had overwhelmed and intimidated me. It was exhilarating and terrifying at the same time.

The worst of it was that my free will had been overtaken by something stronger. I didn't feel in control and I didn't care. That was the strangest part for me. I gave into the feelings and I still hadn't recovered, as I realized when I heard her voice in my home.

It was the first time Catherine had been there and it was, I don't know, weird. She looked different somehow, surrounded by *my* world. Larger than life, or something. I wanted to rush to her...throw my arms around her, yet I remained frozen in my chair. I called out to her and she and Buster came into the room and stopped a few feet short of where I sat.

She looked too sexy for words. She was dressed uncharacteristically in tattered Levi's, flannel shirt and boots. She had a light tan and her hair was loose and wild about her face. Her green eyes were outlined with liner and they sparkled enticingly.

My heart was pounding in my chest and I was holding my breath. Right before I passed out I managed to croak out a more appropriate greeting.

"Who sent you?"

Her laugh was exactly what I needed to hear. I snapped back to some semblance of a conscious person and stood to embrace her. When she came into my arms it all fell away. Whatever the reasons for our not being together, and there were reasons, Catherine's arms around me felt like making love. All of a sudden she looked perfect in my home, like her presence had been missing all along. Buster stood attentively, ready to manipulate the situation in whatever helpful way he could.

She smelled amazing, and I breathed deep, inhaling her essence, feeling her breath on my neck. I wanted her then more than I ever had before. It made me dizzy.

My little inner voice was writing something on the etch-a-sketch in my subconscious but I erased it's misgivings as I took Catherine's face in my hands, my lips feeling hers long before they met.

"Can we do this?" Catherine asked me.

"Can we not do this?" I answered.

"No. I mean yes. I mean...kiss me Jess."

Who was I to argue with a Harvard graduate?

That night was magic. There was a full moon that illuminated my bedroom, the light from it bouncing off the still water and shining over our exhausted bodies. We had held each other for hours, not talking, dozing off and on. I remembered how much I had always loved sleeping with Catherine. Her body and mine fit perfectly together. Her skin against me was like a rare and exotic silk. I remembered how, always a light sleeper, I had passed long night time hours waking and feeling her there next to me and going back to sleep again. It felt that night that I hadn't really slept in the months since we had last been together. Exhaustion was replaced with a feeling of peacefulness that was new to me. That belonged to her.

When we made love that night we both let ourselves be carried away with the rightness of the moment. When Catherine's nails dug into the tender flesh of my back I closed my eyes and felt the colors explode in my mind. Making love with Catherine was always better than I remembered. It was passionate and unreserved. We had always communicated well that way, which was for me yet another anomaly.
In the past I had despaired for my sex drive.

The part of us that was unresolved and undiscussed rose with the sun. I got up from the bed and opened wide the windows so we could lie there together and watch the new day break over the expanse of the lake and smell the fresh spring air.

Catherine spoke first as I crawled back into bed and wrapped my legs around hers tucking her head under my chin.

"We have to talk Jess. It's time."

I felt a clenching in my guts at her words. They weren't unexpected or unwarranted but I dreaded them just the same. I was never good at inter-relational dredging.

As often happens, things go along at a certain pace for a certain period of time free from examination. You get so caught up in the sheer pleasure of falling in love with someone and having them fall in love with you...you just let it happen. Then, in time, it's like another step needs to be taken. All of a sudden where you're standing is no longer good enough. Forward motion is inevitable.

Is it time to discuss cohabitation, continued monogamy, hearth, home and family?

In the beginning it's fun to talk about forever. Who wouldn't want to feel that way...that falling in love way, and want it to never end? Nobody in their right mind, that's who. Certainly not me. I don't fall easy. Catherine was the first woman I had ever been truly in love with. I had known, intellectually, what being in love felt like and looked like but my heart had remained relatively unattached. I hadn't realized that until Catherine.

I finally knew why Hallmark was such a successful company. No longer schmaltzy or corny, their lyrical prose touched my soul. I was a goner.

I always knew that opportunities like this didn't come along often. Was this my one shot for the moon and the stars? It made sense to me. Having been immune to Cupid's arrow for so long could I reasonably hope to be struck more than once in my lifetime? Some people went their whole lives not knowing what love like this feels like.

Even though it had been months since Catherine and I had been together, I still felt the same intensity of love for her. I just didn't know if we could make it last a lifetime.

We both had discussed options and were painfully aware of our chances for survival. Any couple, no matter the gender combination, had the statistics working against them. Divorce has replaced counseling as a way to deal with discord. It was easier to split than stay and fight it out .

The battle between my head and my heart had been fought and re-fought many times and my head always won out.

Even with Leah, who I had loved as well as I could, my head had been more involved with her and our relationship than my heart   It wasn't that I hadn't experienced hurt before. I had, and plenty of it. Funny thing was, it wasn't until I had fallen in love with Catherine that I had glimpsed the potential for falling into the deep, dark depths of despair. This knowledge frightened me more than running into the pointy end of a .45. Having felt the sting of a gunshot, I knew that pain. That searing blast of heat that came even as the sound of the gun firing still echoed in your ears.

A broken heart was another cup of Darjeeling all together.   Catherine had entered my life and left me vulnerable. If I thought I'd had trust issues before, and I knew I did, this was a big 'ole can of worms for sure.
Bravely, or so I thought, I began. "You go first."

"Okay I will. I need to know what's going on with us. Now don't panic...I can see you grinding your teeth Jess, for heaven's sake. It's me, remember?"

She still lay in my arms and I made a conscious effort to separate my upper and lower jaw from each other.

"What's going on? Should I know what that means? What's going on???"

I sounded defensive even to myself. I took a deep breath and Catherine waited for me to compose myself. I knew Catherine wasn't attacking, it wasn't her style.

"Okay. Sorry. Let me try this again. Here's what I do know. I fell in love with you that first day, out on the beach. I looked into your eyes and it was like diving into the middle of the ocean. I remember everything about it. My heart was beating so hard it made my hands tingle. I couldn't breathe. It felt like when you're really scared and your adrenaline pumps through you like thunder." I felt Catherine shift in my arms. "Jess, that was two years ago. I need to talk about now, honey. Today." "I know. I was getting to that...what I was going to say is that I felt that again...yesterday when you walked in here. It was as overwhelming and shocking as before. Maybe more. I haven't figured out what that means, in the long run I mean, but I know that I want to keep feeling this way. I'm still in love with you Catherine. That hasn't changed." She shifted enough so that we were facing each other. Her eyes were moist from un-shed tears and I kissed her lips gently. I surmised that I had said the right thing and I felt good about that. I wasn't one to say what I didn't mean and in saying what I did mean, to Cat, I realized the truth of it all. I was in love with her and I did want her in my life. What I hadn't said, and what would now wait until I had finished exploring each and every magnificent inch of her body, was that I didn't know how we could fit this feeling into our lives.

The last coherent thought I had was wiped away by the sting of her teeth biting into the muscular flesh of my shoulder. Someone moaned and Catherine's mouth traced the line of my neck, gently, then insistently then gently again. I pulled her body on top of mine and felt the full weight of her. Wherever our bodies touched felt feverish. I kissed her long and deep and she met me halfway to heaven. Catherine broke away from my mouth and continued her exploration of my body, kissing all the spots that caused me to groan with pleasure. She had my left breast in her mouth and her tongue was teasing my swollen nipple into an engorged tight peak. I felt my hips rolling against her. I felt her body parting my legs, the round hardness of her hip bone rocked me towards paradise. I was melting inside and our bodies writhed against each others with urgent hunger.

My breathing was ragged and I cried out with the explosion that made all the light in the room vanish. I heard Cat's own desperate cries in my ear and we held so tight that I knew I would be sore and tender for days after.

I reached blindly for my bottle of water and poured some in the vicinity of my mouth. Before I could swallow Catherine sucked the now warm liquid from me to quench her own thirst. We laughed then and lay in the tangle of sweaty sheets as the sun rose fully in the sky outside my bedroom. It had been months since I had felt this peaceful and then, too, it had been because of Catherine. The die was cast and all I could do now, all *we* could do, is figure out the future. No sweat.

I have been accused of being cynical about love and, to a certain extent, life in general, but I didn't believe this to be true. I did believe in everlasting love, though for the life of me I didn't know why. My own upbringing had been typically atypical.

My father had been a workaholic, his life was ruled by internal forces that I knew nothing about. In retrospect I suppose he had been a very unhappy man who never knew real peace. If I could tell him one thing now it would be that I loved him and knew that if I had needed him I could have trusted him to be there for me.

I hadn't known that growing up. He hadn't been there for me and I hadn't known that I could call out for help. Better late than never. Knowing it now made a difference to me and gave me a comfort that I hadn't known or felt before.

I never knew any of my grandparents, and aunts and uncles were simply faded photos in a dusty album.

There was an unwritten code of silence about my parent's past lives. I had gleaned certain facts from both my mother and father and surmised that neither of their childhoods had been happy ones. To what extent I couldn't know and likely never would. I was sorry for them both.

I didn't blame them. There's nothing to be gained from that. My parental baggage had been neatly folded and packed away for the most part and this was a huge relief for me.

My mother drank. For as long as I remember. It got worse the older I got and it could be pretty ugly. I was afraid *of* her and *for* her. I felt responsible for her obvious unhappiness. I didn't know it at the time but have come to realize that I never felt that I had any control over my own life.

We, my brother and I, had never wanted for anything in the material sense. We always had food to eat and clothes to wear and an obsessively clean house to live in. What we didn't have was parents who liked each other very much.

Their animosity towards each other often boiled over and left either my brother or myself scalded and raw.
As a child I didn't think of myself as unhappy. Words and feelings like that had no meaning for me. I felt lonely and distrustful. Each time I entered our house I could never know what to expect. I could never know if it was a good day or a bad day.

That uncertainty clung to me still, though not as much. To say I had trust issues would be a gross understatement. I knew that Catherine suffered because of that sometimes and that her own trust issues were equally invasive. It was something else that we accepted in each other and it wasn't always easy.

I devoted myself to trying to make everyone else in my family happy. An impossible task I now realize. The class clown without the big red nose and floppy shoes.

I gave a silent thank you to my therapist who helped me find my way and made me realize that I had done my best and that *I* was okay. That what had happened wasn't my fault. I'm still learning to tune out the 'merciless voice.' The one that tells me I'm not good enough. That I'm not a good person. It isn't true and though I know it in my head I'm still working on convincing my heart. A lifetime of negative messages takes awhile to reprogram. As the saying goes...'it's not where you start but where you finish that counts.'

In spite of, or maybe because of my past, I do believe in love. The kind you read about and see in movies, if not real life. I would be walking along the boardwalk in The Beach, Buster and I, both of us lost in our own thoughts. From the corner of my eye I would spot a couple.

White haired, their faces maps of all the places their hearts had been. They would be holding hands and talking to each other...listening to each other, and I would get a lump in my throat the size of an MG.

They had what I wanted, or at least it appeared that way and that was good enough for my abundant female hormones. There were moments like that one, lying with Catherine in post-coital bliss, that I felt like I actually would have it. Catherine *knew* me. Knows me. I've hidden nothing from her.

Sometimes it hasn't been comfortable for either of us. I was determined this time, with her, to be myself. Warts and all. I am who I am and Catherine loves *that* me and I love her for that. I'm not easy to be with and we both know that, but then neither is she. She knows that, too. We accept each other and love each other. We don't *like* everything about each other and that's okay too.

We have learned that in our own lives, and our life together, nothing is perfect and that isn't our goal. Our goal is to give each other a safe place to live and grow. A place where love is unconditional and kind. A place where mistakes can be made and will be forgiven. We were striving for excellence, not perfection.

We both have our lives to live and, though they may look different on the surface, we have the same dreams and challenges.

We believe in the same things, and in the important stuff we're a lot alike. We love and respect our friends and fiercely defend their right to be wrong. We believe in honesty and integrity, and mistrust anything that comes too easily. We don't believe we're better than the next person - only different. We come from different worlds but live in the same one now. We have learned that there's nothing we can't resolve in a hot bath with lots of bubbles and even more love. I wasn't prepared to let that go and I knew it more at that moment than I ever had before.

I wasn't concerned with the geographical difficulties. I had never believed that one had to live in direct vicinity to one's lover in order to have a successful relationship. Catherine had deep roots in the New England community and that suited me just fine. My own roots were mobile and could adapt to all sorts of soils. I loved my home in Toronto. It was where I had been raised. It was where my family, both chosen and birth, still lived. Wherever I went I seemed to feel at home.

Florida, Provincetown, Toronto...all occupied a space in my domestic heart. Have dog, will travel. I was willing to go where my heart led me and worry about the details when I got there.

I realized Catherine was watching me and my arms drew her closer. Okay...here goes.

"Anyway, as I was thinking...I say, Goddess help me, that we give this a shot. No pun intended. I can't imagine being with anyone else and I certainly am mightily repulsed at the idea of you being with anyone other than me. So, that's it. I love you. I want you. What happens next? You tell me 'cuz I think I feel a migraine coming on."

"Oh poor baby, do you really?"

The naked concern and love on her face made me want to cry. Truth was I did feel a migraine coming on. Either that or there was a pre fourth of July fireworks display getting underway right next to my closet. I did feel nauseous and I was pretty sure it wasn't my conversation with Cat. I was a tad premenstrual so history dictated that the migraine was lurking in the wings.

My face felt both numb and aflame, my left eye squeezed from within by some demented and evil elf. If I moved my head too quickly the whole room would spin. I probably only had about a half an hour or so before the onslaught and Catherine knew this. She reached over me and opened my underwear drawer where I kept nine pairs of black Jockey underwear and all my prescription drugs.

She shook out a Fiorinol and two Gravol. The breakfast of champions. She was about to go to the kitchen, probably for an ice pack, bless her, when I pulled her back to me. It always came as a surprise but the onset of a migraine made me either want to vacuum or frisky...go figure. Since I didn't think hauling out the Hoover was a good idea...

"Yo Billy Jean, I believe the ball's in your court?"

I meant to sound lascivious but by now I was slurring my words and had a slight stammer. Sex on a stick, that's me.

"Jess, know this. Whatever it takes, I want to be with you, now and forever. I know the odds, I know you, and I know me. I say the hell with the odds, let's go for it."

And we did, so to speak. An hour or so later I fell gratefully into a drugged stupor that passed for sleep. Catherine had given me a massage that lost its medicinal intent somewhere along the way and I was spent. She had darkened the room as best she could and I felt her cool lips gently kiss me on the forehead. Three times for luck.

Often getting a migraine meant feeling guilty. Canceled plans, disappointed friends, sulking yet concerned dog. The pain arrives and life leaves. I knew I couldn't help it but I also knew it was a bitter pill, at times, for others to swallow, as if I was using it as an excuse.

Catherine understood and this was always a great relief to me. I heard the bubbles pop and snap from the Vernor's ginger ale she had left by the bed as she and Nurse Buster tiptoed from the bedroom. I drifted off in love and woke up some hours later with the feeling intact. This was a good sign.

It was a comfort to feel her nearby. I squinched my eyes open and instantly regretted it. Yup, I was in for the long haul. I reached for my drink and missed by about and inch knocking the glass to the floor. It sounded like an explosion and I groaned. I heard the door open and felt Catherine sit gingerly next to me on the bed. She whispered gently, telling me that she was there. She knew it was a bad one.   I heard the drug drawer open and knew that Dr. Demento was about to shoot me up to the heavens for awhile.

I was a big sissy when it came to giving myself injections and welcomed the intervention. I bared my cowardly butt to her and felt the sting of the syringe.
The Imitrix would work quickly and was the only chance I had to get rid of the now entrenched migraine. I think I told her I loved her and I remember wanting to ask her not to leave me but I passed out before the words could find their way out.

When I finally came to it was freshly dark outside and I felt weak but better. I slowly navigated myself out of bed and felt my way to the bathroom. I brushed my teeth for about an hour and felt way better. I staggered back to the bedroom and fell in love all over again.

The bed was crisp and fresh with new sheets, ginger ale replenished and a plate perfectly set with three Saltines and Jif peanut butter sat next to it. I realized I was crying lightly when I spoke.

"Okay I'll marry you."

"Good, I accept, now get back to bed."

"Alone?"

"Not if you don't want to be."

Now I was really crying.

"No Cat. I think I've been alone long enough."

CHAPTER 21

I shook my head like Buster does after swimming in the Bay, trying to clear away the Catherine cobwebs.
Having made my bargain with Beelzebub Ryan, I had to shake a leg. Thoughts of Catherine needed to be filed away for the time being. My talk with Timothy Ryan had been illuminating and I was anxious to dig deeper in the dirt that he had overturned for me.

I whipped down Bangs and parked, illegally, in front of Kristen's Diner for a quick bite and some insight. Like Meg and Karen, Kristen was a longtime resident of Provincetown and if something happened she usually knew the details and more. I tucked ravenously into my egg white omelet and told her that I was working on Sydney's case. I didn't mention who my employer was and she didn't ask.
She had heard about the attack on Sydney and I filled her in on what I knew about her physical condition. She looked pissed off and I knew that her anger would be an asset to me.

Kristen had recently taken in a foster daughter and Sydney had been one of the first to drop by and offer whatever support or counsel she could.

Harley and Sara had become good pals over the months and as a consequence so had Kristen and Sydney.
She leaned her considerable bulk across the narrow booth and her dark eyes flashed dangerously.

"If I were you Jessica I'd lock myself in a room with that lawyer from Boston...that Eastcott woman, and do whatever needs doing to get her to spill her guts."
I chewed thoughtfully, my silence encouraging her to continue. She did.

"Sydney was having some problems with her for awhile now. She liked her well enough, at first, but lately she started worrying about how involved she was getting. Sydney thought Jennifer was getting a little too emotional with her case, if you know what I mean..."

"No, actually Kristen, I don't know what you mean."

"Oh come on. How hard can it be? Sydney is a beautiful, successful, kind, generous, talented woman. Jennifer Eastcott is a too bright, too beautiful, too insecure woman. Put two and two together and you get a mess."

Such a way with words...and math. I ventured a question.

'So, if I hear you correctly, you think Jennifer was after Sydney for more than her retainer? Is that right?"

"Now we're on the same page honey. Yeah, Sydney talked to me just a couple of weeks ago about it. The kids were in a baseball tournament in Wellfleet and Sydney was pretty quiet the whole time. Usually she's the main cheerleader at these things so I was curious. Sydney's a private gal, I'll grant you that, but maybe because of the kids, I don't know, but she knew she could talk to me. And she did. She didn't know if she was right...if Eastcott was getting romantic or not...but she didn't want that kind of complication anywhere near the custody battle."
Kristen filled me in on her conversation that night with Sydney and subsequent chats since that time.

I listened intently as I mopped up the last globs of Swiss cheese with my toasted bagel and rose from the bench before I had finished chewing. I reached in my pocket to pay for my meal and Kristen froze me with a look.

"Thanks Kristen. For the breakfast and especially for the information. I'll let you know when I nail this thing down. Meantime, give that little one of yours a big squeeze from me."

Kristen walked me to the Jeep clucking her opinionated tongue at the sight.

"For cryin' in the sink Jess...when are you going to let this thing die a dignified death?"

"Too late for that I'm afraid. 'Sides...rust is a good color on me."

She waited while I hopped in. Something was on her mind, I could tell. Kristen didn't usually wear her emotions on her sleeve and I watched as she wrestled with her thoughts. I bailed her out.

"Don't worry about Sydney or Harley. Catherine will do everything humanly possible to get her better and Harley is fine, for the moment. I'll tell her you two send your love. If Harley can be persuaded to leave the hospital I might suggest that she hang out here. That okay with you?"

Her relief was as obvious as my false optimism.

"Yeah, that's good Jess. Now get out of here."

I swung by Beachfront to use Meg's phone. I wanted to arrange a meeting with myself, Jennifer and Muffin but I didn't want them to know that the other was coming. The element of surprise could never be underestimated.

I called up the *Provincetown Inn* and asked for Tim Ryan's room. I didn't want his parents to know what I was up to and I figured, in light of our recent pact, that he'd be pleased as punch to work with me.

Sure enough he answered the phone. Muffin, it seems, was having a stroll around the Salt Marsh but Tim promised to track her down and deliver her to the meeting place within the hour. I could hear his clenched jaw but have to admit he was as civil as I imagined he could be.

Jennifer Eastcott was another pot of pasta altogether. She was a slippery noodle and it took several attempts before I tracked her down at Sebastian's Bar.

Miss Lynnie was on the bar and she discreetly confirmed that indeed Ms. Eastcott was currently sitting on the business end of a very dry martini and that she would see that the message was delivered. Lynnie also mentioned that Ms. Eastcott was not alone. Apparently there was some fellow with her and she was picking up his tab.

It seemed to me a tad early in the day for cocktails but figured this would work to my advantage. I encouraged Miss Lynnie to pour liberally should another round be ordered and rang off. I also asked her to keep an ear on the conversation between the two. I knew after years in the business that Miss Lynnie would give me a better report than if I had videotaped the whole exchange.

Whoever Jennifer's date was would have to remain unknown for now. I thought of calling Alex and having him swing by and have a look see but I hesitated long enough for the thought to vaporize. An accomplice? A client? A pick up? Time would tell.

That done I took a fresh piece of paper from Meg's desk and wrote her a note. I secured it under her telephone and headed out to *The Shooting Gallery*.

True to her word Gillian, and the gang had carried on in Sydney's absence. There were a few diners in the main room and Sharron was handling the small crowd with her usual finesse. I guessed that some of the customers may be there for the gossip factor as opposed to the clam strips but knew they would find Sharron tight-lipped about Sydney's attack.

I waved a quick hello and Sharron hustled over. She hoped I may have some information about Sydney and I had to disappoint her for the moment. I had left myself enough time to put in a call to Cat and promised to update when we connected.

I went back to the kitchen and unfortunately startled Gillian just as she was about to crack open the large claw of a freshly boiled lobster.

The appendage jumped from her hands and landed with a splash in her hollandaise. Any other time and she would have doubled over with laughter but now was definitely not that time. As she fished the fish from the sauce I saw fresh tears spring to her round dark eyes.

"Jessica George Shore...you scared the bejesus out of me. What's the matter with you?"

I didn't know how she had gotten hold of my full name and decided not to encourage future use.

"Jess will do Gill, thanks. Sorry about the start. I'll be more careful next time."

Then I did laugh. I couldn't help myself. Gillian was a professional and dressed the part no matter what or where. Her white linen stovepipe hat was starched to attention and her tall as it is wide body was lost in the folds of her chef's whites. Her brown, round face was shiny and spotted with flecks of today's lunch special. As soon as the sound was out of me I realized my mistake. She glared at me which, sad to say, made me want to laugh even harder. I resisted the urge.

"Carry on Gill, I want to use the phone in Sydney's office for a second. I haven't checked in with Catherine since early this morning and I think we could all use an update."

"Oh yes, please do Jess. Can I get you something to eat?"

I didn't want to tell her that I had eaten already so I sidestepped the question by saying I didn't have much of an appetite at the moment but maybe later. Gillian fed people instead of hugging them and I didn't feel in the mood for either.

I sat behind Sydney's desk and waited until Gillian was once again consumed in consommé.

For the first minute or so I just sat there. I always liked to spend a minute or two in the skin of the person or persons that were involved in my cases. To see their world from their perspective. Desks are the best. Whether it's the big cheese at Mega Computer, a customer service representative at a courier company or a tray table crammed into a kids playroom...workspace is inner space.

At home in Toronto, or here in Provincetown, my workspace spoke volumes. I spent too much time just sitting there, staring out at whatever body of water I was on. I would look around me, wander and wonder about the truths that were revealed there. The pictures I had on the walls, scattered here and there; comics clipped from the newspaper, ragged edged and yellowed with age; my dad's favorite fountain pen. To some, just something more to dust. To another an abridged profile of the person that sat there and thought there. Dreamed and worried there. Planned and lived a life.

That's what I was looking for as I sat at Sydney's desk, taking my time as I glanced around me. I tried to clear my mind so as better to feel my way around. What was important and why? Was it important to me and my investigation? I could have rifled through her files or electronic diary but that could be done at any time. Okay, I didn't know squat about operating an electronic diary...whatever.

I did the 'clock check' like when you're flying. You can't just scan the horizon because you may miss the odd seagull or parachutist.

You take a position, say twelve o-clock, hold it for three seconds and move on by the half hour. That way if something is in your field of vision you have a chance to spot it.

I went from the far to the near, beginning with the walls. A couple of Cape Cod prints, framed and signed by local artists and photographers showed Sydney's love of her adopted home.

Bookshelves, another cornucopia of insight, were jam packed with a variety of reference books, biographies and a multitude of cook books: French to Fusion and everything in between.

Her reading tended to the cerebral as opposed to myself who loved a good mystery. Sydney was the kind of friend I could rely on for political or historical stuff and that suited me fine. Why read every book out there when somebody else has, I say.

She also had a mini law library. Family law mostly. That seemed to make sense considering what she had been through with Tim the last couple of years.

I was just about to shift my gaze when something caught my eye, something protruding slightly from the pages of one of the legal tomes. I swung out of Sydney's chair and pulled down the book. 'Custody and Adoption in the State of Massachusetts.' Not a top ten on my reading list, but then why would it be? I opened the encyclopedic sized pages to the paper. I turned down the page, a bad habit, and tossed the book aside for the moment.

It appeared to be written in Sydney's hand, the paper torn from a spiral ringed notepad. There was a name, Marilyn Dickinson, and phone number. The area code was for Boston and I was dialing before I had a chance to think about what I was doing. Another bad habit.

"Massachusetts State Bar Association, how may I direct your call?"

"Marilyn Dickinson please."

"One moment."

Strains of Neil Sedaka's 'Breaking Up Is Hard To Do.' I was just about to join in on the bridge when a pinched, nasal voice cut in.

"Mrs. Dickinson's office, this is Ruth speaking, how may I help you?"

Get your mind engaged before you put your mouth in gear, I cautioned myself. I went for the honest approach. What the hey...it could work.

"Good morning, my name is Jessica Shore and I'm a private investigator licensed to operate within the State of Massachusetts. I am currently investigating an attempted murder and Mrs. Dickinson may have valuable information. Is she available?"

Silence is not always golden. Purse face voice took her sweet time.

"Mrs. Shore..."

"Miss."

"Hmmm. Yes, well then, Miss Shore, Mrs. Dickinson is attending hearings in Washington until the end of the week. She does receive messages throughout the day and I will pass yours along. I can't promise she will get right back to you, however. Mrs. Dickinson is extremely busy. Perhaps this matter would be best directed elsewhere."

I was losing her, I could feel it in my bones.

"I understand completely Ruth, ah, by the way...what position does Mrs. Dickinson hold within the Bar Association...if you don't mind my asking?"

"Not at all Miss Shore. Mrs. Dickinson is the head of investigations into reports of unethical practice amongst her brethren."

Brethren? Yikes stripes.

"May I have your phone number please Miss Shore?"

I gave it to her, also, Alex Thorne's pager, the restaurant and Karen's office. That oughta cover it. I was sure I had scant moments to get in a question or two.

"Ah, Ruth, I wonder...do the names Jennifer Eastcott and/or Sydney Ryan ring any bells for you?"

"I'm really not at liberty to say Miss Shore. As you can imagine, much of what Mrs. Dickinson does is highly confidential."

"Yes of course Ruth, understood...however, Sydney Ryan is clinging to her life by a thread and her eight year old daughter is watching her grip loosen by the second. Please Ruth, I implore you...does the name Sydney Ryan mean anything to you? Is there an investigation in the works that has her name on it? Is Jennifer Eastcott involved?"

I don't usually 'implore' anyone to do anything and I think this was implicit in my tone.

Come on Ruthie...you can do it.

"Miss Shore really, this is quite inappropriate, I don't mind telling you. Honestly. I could lose my job."

"Ruth, I swear to you this goes no further than me, at least for the moment. If it ever becomes necessary to make this information public I'll make sure I receive Mrs. Dickinson's assent. For the child, Ruth?"

"Miss Shore, I don't appreciate this type of pressure, from you or anyone else. Mrs. Dickinson...well, never mind about Mrs. Dickinson. This Sydney Ryan and her daughter, Harley...I take it they're good friends of yours then?"

Hey. I never mentioned Harley's name, I was sure of that. I do believe Ruth was giving me a little clue, bless her pointy head. I responded with like subterfuge.

"Yes Ruth, they are. Thank you Ruth."

"Good-bye Miss Shore. I'll see that your message is delivered."

I felt as elated as I had since landing in Provincetown. I surmised that whatever dealings Sydney had with Mrs. Dickinson must surely involve Jennifer Eastcott. An investigation for unethical practices hmmm? I checked the time.

I had an hour or so before Muffin and Jennifer arrived. I tucked Marilyn Dickinson's number in my pocket and went back to my post behind Sydney's desk.
Lots of bills and accounting type stuff.

If I read it right, *The Shooting Gallery* was in good shape financially, no large deposits or withdrawals to pique my suspicions, nothing untoward about her tax filings either. I dug deeper, glad to move on from the math part of the test. I was coming up empty and leaned back in Sydney's chair, staring out at nothing...until, what's this now?

A yearbook from Tonawanda High in Buffalo, circa 1975. By my calculations this would have been grade ten or so for Sydney. Well, as it turned out it was this and so much more.

Since I didn't know Sydney's birth name I had to flip through every page. I found Sydney easily enough. Her last name was Attridge and she was quite a looker back in her teen years. Her hair appeared dark, probably auburn, and disappeared below the line of her shoulders, full and curly. Her light gray eyes were a stark contrast to her Mediterranean skin tone and they seemed to dance with secret amusement. Next to her picture was an arrow pointing down three rows to another winsome lovely named Janet Evans. Rather than the usual arrow head point, each end of the line had a heart attached. The meaning was clear. Seems young Sydney had her sexual ducks in a row at an early age. I took my time with each page. I wanted to know more about Sydney.

She played senior basketball and in the team photo she was head and shoulders above the other girls, her height adding to the overall leanness of her form. She also played tennis, ran the school darkroom and was assistant editor of the yearbook.

I scanned the autographs throughout the book and found nothing of great interest. Some really bad poetry, many wishes to have a great summer, life, whatever. Sydney was and still is an accomplished woman. No news there, but it was fun to look.

My own high school memories were sketchy. It seemed so long ago, and those days had never been all that carefree for me. I knew nothing about Sydney's past, family-wise, and decided I'd have to dig a bit deeper in that dirt if something didn't turn up soon. I put back the yearbook and went back to my scan.

There were plenty of photos of Harley on her own, with Sydney, the restaurant staff, even Buster posed fetchingly in one. Most shots were black and white and I assumed that Sydney still dabbled in the photographic arts. The shots were wonderfully candid. Obviously Sydney had an eye for that sort of thing and there was nothing to pique my interest in their content.

Off to the file cabinet then. I said a silent apology to Sydney for the violation I was about to commit, and dug in. I flipped through the business stuff. I could come back to that if need be. I found the file I was looking for in a separate drawer and it was thick as Gill's clam chowder. Ryan vs. Ryan...in the matter of Harley Ryan. On top of the stack of papers was an envelope that was postmarked just the week before.

I was just about to get comfy when Jumpin' Gilly whipped in, slamming the door behind her. Never underestimate the speed and agility of the vertically challenged.

"Hey Shoestring, you've got company."

"That's Gum Shoe, and pray tell to whom do I have the honor of greeting?"

Gill sat heavily in a low slung easy chair on the other side of Sydney's desk and removed her mountainous hat. The top of her thinning head, thinning hair that is, was barely visible. I sat forward and waited for the guest list.

"Well, first off Miss soon-to-be Muffin Ryan arrived, delivered, if you don't mind, by her fiancé. She looks a little the worse for wear but otherwise she was friendly enough. I sat her at the back bar. Just as I was heading back here, in spins Sharron with a sloppy looking Jennifer Eastcott."

"Define sloppy."

"Well if it wasn't before noon I would've said she was a bit tipsy."

Oh goodie. Loose lips sink shits, or something like that.

"Was she alone, Gilly? Jennifer, I mean."

Gill scrunched up her face as if she had only to leaf back a few pages in her head and look beyond Jennifer's entrance to the street.

"No. I mean, yes. Yes she was not with anyone."

Grammatically I knew we were both in trouble but now was not the time. What Gill had done when adapting to English as her second language was between her and Webster. I had been hoping for an ID on the swarthy fellow that Miss Lynnie had mentioned but I could get to that later.

"Okay Gill. Tell the ladies that I'll be with them in ten minutes or so. Maybe you could fix them something to eat...or drink, in the meantime."

Gill looked like I had asked her to take a dip in Clorox. I understood. There was a chance that one of the two ladies out front was responsible for what happened to Sydney. A good chance. I'm sure that preparing a tasty repast for either of them was anathema to her.

I heard her swallow down her objections, took note of the glare that was meant to wither me and watched her spin on her white nurse's Wallabees and huff out of the office.

That done I turned my attention back to the file that I had dropped in my lap. My two years of law school gave me just enough knowledge of legal-ese to skim through the jumble of briefs and motions and stuff.

What I was looking for was going to be somewhere between the lines. The letter proved to be the most interesting tidbit of all. It was from Timothy Ryan, Sr. of all things. Handwritten, the old boy was asking Sydney for permission to see Harley...on the sly. No family, no lawyers, no kidding. It wasn't a begging kinda tone but it was contrite to be sure.

The sound of the phone ringing somewhere under the stack of files made my heart skip. Geez, could I be any jumpier? Gotta watch that caffeine intake. The phone kept on. I grabbed for it finally, assuming the staff was tied up.

"The Shooting Gallery, may I help you?"

Her voice sent shiver's down my crooked spine.

"Jess? It's Catherine."

"Cat. How are you?"

I think that my first question was concerning her well being and not her patient's spoke volumes and I wished I could snatch the words back before they sped along the fiber optics and into her perfectly lobed ear.

"Oh Jess. I don't think I've ever been so tired in my life. I haven't been able to close my eyes since this whole mess started. She's the same, Jess. Holding her own for the moment but no signs of coming out of the coma yet."

"That's not good, is it Cat?"

"Not good. Not bad either. Sometimes it's just a matter of waiting, Jess. There's really nothing else I can do."

I could hear the pain of frustration in her voice and pictured her deep green eyes filling with the unshed tears that threatened. I couldn't do much about Sydney but maybe I could give a bit of a boost to her doctor.

My heart felt all soft and squishy towards Catherine anyway and hearing the tremor in her voice made my arms ache to hold her. I could feel her waiting for me to say something.

"Listen honey..." 'Honey?' Did I just say 'Honey?' Shit. Color me crimson I think I just rolled up my sleeve and knocked my heart off it. Oh well. I stammered on...

"...I know that you've done...and will do...everything medically possible to help Sydney. Don't forget who you are and how good you are. You're the best doctor Sydney could have and I know that, deep down inside, you know that."

Her words came out in a deep sigh. "Thanks Jess. I think I just needed to hear your voice...Is it okay to say that?" Should I tell her that her words...her voice...gave me chicken skin? Nah.

"Of course it's okay to say. I feel the same. It's been a long time Cat. I've missed you. I didn't even realize how much."

"I know what you mean." I could tell she was smiling. I smiled back at her.

"Catherine? I have to go. I've got a couple of gals waiting for me out front and I don't know how long Gill can be trusted alone with them."

Her smile was gone from her voice. "A couple of gals Jess? Sounds like the old you. Shouldn't you be working on Sydney's case?"

I could have been pissy. She was using her oh so sarcastic voice but neither of us needed that kind of conflict right now. Ah maturity...ain't it grand?

"For Pete's sake honey...they're suspects. I only have eyes for a certain winsome physician that I used ta know."

"Who's Pete?"

"Wouldn't you like to know?" We were back on solid ground and I was relieved.

"I'll check in with you soon. Call me here if you have any news. How's Harley doing anyway? Is Kelly still better'n Barney?" Now who's being sarcastic. Yep. Me.

"Harley's sound asleep in the lounge...head in Kelly's lap. She's okay Jess. You do your job and I'll do mine."

"Deal. You okay?"

"No. But better. Thanks. Jess..."

"Hmmmm???"

The smile was back..."never mind...it'll keep...talk to you soon."

"Yes...you will."

I sat for a second and held my thoughts close to me. Seeing Catherine yesterday had been a shock. Since things never really ended with us and since we never *didn't* want to be together I guess she would have seemed more...I don't know...familiar to me. As it was, when I actually saw her again ... I didn't recognize her in a way. I mean of course I knew it was her but it was also a woman that wasn't her too. Like seeing a stunning stranger. It had been like that the first time. There was an instant spark. Interest. Attraction. Still was.

Well, time enough for all that later. Meantime I decided to move my butt outta the chair and mosey on out to chat with the girls. I was looking forward to it in a 'maybe I quit analysis too soon' sorta glee. Whatever was in Sydney's file would have to wait.

What I saw as I came out of Sydney's office made my Docs dig in. The two were so engrossed with each other I would have had to set my hair on fire to get their attention...and I wasn't going to do that.

CHAPTER 22

I approached their table warily. What a queer alliance this would make, I thought. Jennifer and Tim's Bit. Oooh. Icky. I remembered the information that Alex had gotten, the youthful alliance between the two ladies before me. Details please.

Their heads swiveled as if on the same stick as I sat myself down with them. Jennifer looked a little bleary eyed but seemed far from tipsy. Too bad for me.

"Ladies. Thanks for coming by. Can I order you something to eat or drink?"

Muff looked as though she had something very unpleasant in her mouth as she replied to my generous offer. "I don't plan on being here long enough to have a drink, Ms. Shore. Could we just get on with this?"

"Squirtenly. Jennifer, how 'bout you? Cocktail? Crab cake?"

She didn't have a chance to answer before Sharron popped into the circle of blight with what appeared to be a mostly vodka Bloody Mary.

The stock of celery would have been suitable for decorating at Christmas time. When Jennifer pulled it out a fine spray of Tomato Juice hit Muffin right in her Yves St. Laurent. Uh oh.

Sharron was snickering as she moved quickly from the table, an impish wink in my direction.
Jennifer made like she was going to dab at Muff's boyish chest and then, wisely, thought better of it.

"Sorry Muffin," she muttered through the straw in her glass.

"Don't worry about it. It's no big deal." Muffin actually smiled at Jen Jen. I mean really smiled...right up to her crystal ice-blue eyes.

I felt like I was at a tennis match as my eyes darted between the two gal pals. I dove in figuring the waters were more than deep enough for the plunge.

"So. I understand you two are friends from way back. What a coincidence...I assume?"

Jennifer sucked noisily on her already nearly empty drink in response to my revelation.

I turned to Muffin and raised my eyebrows in what I hope looked to be an expectant manner. She caved.

"So what?"
Hmmm. I had hoped for more.

"So lots."

"And you actually make a living doing this?" Jennifer laughed. I was prepared to take umbrage when I saw that her laughter was genuine. She was right after all. I was grasping at straws and it showed. I smiled back at Jennifer.
"Fair enough. So why don't you just tell me what I need to know. What's the deal with you two? Did you know that the other was going to be here?"

It was Jennifer who took the bullshit by the horns.
"It's true Jess. I mean the part about me and Muffin knowing each other. We met in the summer of '79. I had moved to Boston in July.

A friend from my neighborhood had a cousin that had a neighbor who was renting out an apartment in her house. All I knew was that the location was perfect for school and the rent was ridiculously low. The woman who owned the house was in her seventies then and on her own. Her family wanted to have someone around in case anything happened. I met Mrs. Stephenson and we hit it off. I moved in the next week."

Muffin chortled. Honest.

"God. I remember when Aunt Jane called me about you. She was worried that you might feel lonely in a new city and wanted me to come around and befriend you. It was like a play date! What a laugh."

Jennifer was grinning now.

"Yeah. I was the last thing you wanted hanging around you that summer."

I was losing my place of dominance as the two traipsed down memory lane and that just won't do.

"Right. So...it's a world of laughter, a world of tears. Muffin, tell me about you that summer."

Her glacial orbs softened a weensy bit as she cast herself back.

"It was the greatest time of my life. I had taken a year off before starting college and done the debutante hustle across Europe. It was fabulous. I discovered cheap wine, poor boys and open-minded girls."

I tried to hide my surprise but felt like I may burst with the effort. Who was this French pastry that sat before me? Wine women and sarongs? Saucy, don't ya think?

Muffin was watching me watch her. Think, Jess. Take charge for Pete's sake. Alrighty then. Your aunt summons you to her mansion on the Hill and you and Jennifer meet. Next?"

"What can I tell you? I was prepared not to like her. I was...still am I suppose, a snob. I'm not proud of it but there it is. "

Jennifer looked up at Muffin and smiled fetchingly.

"Muffin swept into Mrs. Stephenson's place and managed to keep one foot on the accelerator of her Porsche so she could greet and run.   I had expected to feel...I don't know, intimidated or something.

Muffin seemed to be everything I wasn't.   She was rich of course, and beautiful.   For some reason it just felt...I don't know...not awkward.   Muffin and Mrs. Stephenson clearly adored each other and the three of us ended up having a wonderful afternoon.

We clicked.   That night Muffin took me to a party out on the Cape.   We got smashed on Singapore Slings and the rest...at least what I remember...was history."
Muffin picked up the story.

"We spent a lot of time together that summer.   It's true we seemed opposite on the surface but really we're quite a lot alike.   Jennifer has always been an inspiration to me.   She made it on her own.   There was no trust fund, no strategic introductions.   No family, really.   Aunt Jane, Jennifer and I became closer that summer than I had ever been to my own family.   I admired her ambition.   Still do."   Muffin turned to Jennifer and their eyes locked in a warm optical embrace.   Brother.

There was a part of me that wanted more details about the nature of their 'friendship' but it wasn't really important.   If there had been anything intimate between the two it was in the past.   I think.   Hearing the story of how they met shone yet a different light on Muffin.   Less harsh somehow.   Poor little rich girl with spunk.   And Jennifer...well...jury's still out on that one.

"So ladies..."   I began ...   "fast forward to present day would you?   Since I don't hold much with the concept of coincidence I'm guessing seeing each other here is no big surprise.   Am I right?"

Jennifer sighed and Muffin nodded slightly. Apparently permission to speak had been granted.   Jennifer lead off.

So here's the scoop.

Jennifer began her career at Harvard late that summer. Muffin, much to the chagrin of her family, decided to head for New York to try her hand at acting.

She wasn't good but she wasn't bad either and managed to earn her Equity card and make a living for herself.

The next summer Jennifer was taking classes and, although she still lived with Mrs. Stephenson, the girls didn't see much of each other. Their friendship faded with the years. It wasn't until Sydney Ryan entered Jennifer's office, and life, that Muffin re-appeared. It was a coincidence after all. Sort of.

Jennifer had been working on Sydney's case for a couple of weeks. Her first meeting with Tim Ryan had just passed and she was doing some digging into his background. Turns out he had just announced his engagement to Muffin DeWitt. Uh oh. Can you say 'conflict of interest?' Me too. Once Jennifer found out about the connection she contacted Muffin. What happened next blurs the lines of ethics almost beyond recognition. It's just my opinion but...Jennifer should have handed over the case to a disinterested party. She didn't.

What happened instead could lose her any and all opportunity to ever practice law again. No wonder Mrs. Dickinson and the Massachusetts State Bar had a file on her. Methinks Jen is in big doo doo. Could make her a tad desperate. Unpredictable. Unreliable. Dangerous? Maybe. Muffin and Jennifer realized they had a mutual interest in Sydney gaining full and sole custody of Harley. Tim, for his part, seemed to agree with Muffin that this was the best course of action. The pressure to pursue the case came from the elder Ryans. Tim had gone along with them for a time, mostly for financial reasons. As long as he did as he was told he would continue to receive his more than generous allowance.

For a time this worked for the Tim man...then came the Muffin of Oz and he found his heart.

Muffin had her own ideas about family ties and she found the Ryan's hold a wee bit too tight for her liking.
Muffin didn't care about Tim's past and she didn't want him caring about hers either. Neither of them had lead exemplary lives but both were ready to put that all behind them. They had no secrets from each other and Harley was part of the whole package. As far as they were both concerned Harley was best off where she was. With her mother.

They both agreed that Sydney could tell Harley whatever she thought best for the child with respect to her father. He wasn't going anywhere and if the opportunity presented itself they wouldn't object to being in her life. What they wouldn't do was make waves in the shallow end of her young life. Tim and Muffin had plans for their own family someday and if Sydney thought Harley could be part of that, swell. If not they wouldn't press it.

Muffin kept one crucial bit of information from her hubby-to-be. Guess what it was? Yep. She never did tell him that Jennifer was a bosom buddy. I asked, Muffin why the lie?

"I honestly don't remember what it was in the beginning. What reason I gave myself for not telling Tim everything. It was stupid. I know that now. I just wanted to make things a little easier for him, you know? I mean the poor guy, believe it or not, has not had a great life."

I believed her. I thought about the accident that had claimed the life of his sister. I wondered at the hold his folks had on him. Nope. I doubted that being Tim Ryan was as much of a picnic as I had originally assumed. If his beloved wanted to spare him some angst...misguided as her actions turned out to be...I was on the same page. Whatever...she kept mum.

Speaking of mom...seems Mrs. Ryan was a frequent flyer to Jennifer's office too.

She shook, rattled and rolled her way in there on a half dozen different occasions, according to Muffin. Seems the farther Tim and Muffin backed away from the whole custody thing the more involved Mommy bleariest became. Pa Ryan only tagged along once and even then he left after a few minutes, preferring to wait in the lobby for his missus. There didn't seem to be any lines this family wouldn't cross in order to get what they wanted.

Jennifer had finally had to call Muffin, on the sly of course, to persuade her future mother-in-law to cease and desist with the face to face. Mrs. Ryan was a puffy woman. A water retaining Margaret Thatcher look alike. Jennifer didn't care for her and didn't want any more one on one with her under any circumstance. Muffin had come through and the visits by Mary not so contrary had stopped.

Jennifer and Muffin had their heads together from the get go. Jennifer was concerned about the pressure she was getting from Mrs. Ryan. It was Sydney after all who was her client. Any correspondence between the Ryans and her should have been done through their lawyer. Yet another breach of conduct. Tsk tsk.

I didn't say it out loud, believe it or not, but I had to wonder if Jennifer wasn't a tad reluctant to do the right thing because of the little scandal of yesteryear. Bigwig, Behemoth and Bitter, partners at law, weren't likely to give a warm howdy doo to their former workmate. Still, not an excuse *not* to do the right thing far as I was concerned.

If Muffin and Jennifer had thought they could keep the lid on their collusion they were barking up the wrong jar. Secrets like theirs always rise to the surface no matter how deeply you bury them.

My head was crowding from all the new info.

I was about to fire off a fresh round of questions when who should darken *The Shooting Gallery* doorway but Mr. and Mrs. Ryan.

He looked like he hadn't slept for days. Mr. Ryan was a pooped papa. His wife, in stark contrast, bounced and gurgled away like a school girl, clinging to papa's arm...I suspect more for balance than anything else.

They both seemed genuinely surprised to see me and the girls. I heard a not so silent groan escape from Muffin and Jennifer patted her hand consolingly.

I waved the two over to our table and to my absolute horror and slight amusement felt Muffin kick me under the table. Had we bonded? Was it me and Muff against the world? Nah. She must have been aiming at Jennifer and miscalculated. My immediate instinct was to boot her back but I restrained myself. For now.

As soon as Mr. and Mrs. Ryan reached the table Jennifer attempted an exit. Seems she was prepared to play the ethics card when it suited her. Her words sounded practiced as she said,

"Hello Mr. Ryan. Mrs. Ryan. You'll have to excuse me. It would be inappropriate for me to join you at this time while Sydney's case is still pending. Muffin."

I couldn't help it. I snorted. What a hypocrite. Try as I might I just couldn't get a warm and fuzzy thing happening for Jennifer. She didn't seem like a bad gal but she didn't seem like a particularly good one either. I tried to regain my composure.

"Jennifer give me a break will ya? Sit down for a minute. I'm sure your professional boundaries won't snap if you hang in. For Sydney's' sake."

Gotcha. She froze in mid lift and plunked back down into her seat. Mr. Ryan had pulled up a couple of chairs to the table and was trying to negotiate his wife into one of them. She didn't seem to notice.

She glared bleary eyed at Jennifer, then Muffin, finally resting her rheumy gaze on me. She looked not well. Her speech was deliberate but otherwise clear.

"Well now. Isn't this cozy. I didn't realize you ladies were all acquainted with each other. Muffin. What is this all about?"

If Mrs. Ryan thought she could intimidate her future daughter-in-law she was obviously mistaken. Muffin didn't flinch in the least.

"Mother Ryan. Timothy. Please. Join us." Pop looked relieved.

This was a guy who was probably used to a lot of confrontation on the family and business front and may just be over it all by now. He wasn't a young man but seemed pretty fit and firm just the same. If I had to guess at the expression on his face I'd have to say he was a tad embarrassed. He was the first to break the ice.

"Miss Shore. I'm glad I...we...ran into you. I wanted to ask how Sydney was doing...and..." His voice trailed off.

I was thinking about the letter I had just read when I asked,

"And Mr. Ryan? And what?"

"My granddaughter. How is she?"

At the word granddaughter Mrs. Ryan made a sound like her upper plate was lodging in her esophagus. She sputtered in the direction of her husband.

"*Your* granddaughter? She's my granddaughter too, Timothy. Have you forgotten that?"

"No I haven't forgotten. I stand corrected. Miss Shore, please, how is *our* granddaughter?"

Being in the presence of these two gave me the heebie jeebies. That aside, I guess I never really took in the fact that they were indeed Harley's grandparents. I wondered if she even knew about them. More questions and, unfortunately, with Sydney still unconscious, Jennifer was the only one who could answer many of them and I was wary about her.

"Well Mr. and Mrs. Ryan, as far as I know Harley is doing as well as can be expected, given the circumstances. Her mother, by the way, is not doing very well."

Mr. Ryan looked genuinely pained at this.

"I'm sorry to hear that Miss Shore. If there's anything I can do..." His voice trailed off.

Muffin picked up the ball and lobbed it right back in their faces.

"For heaven sake...Harley's eight years old. Don't you think your concern falls under the too little too late heading?"

A small gasp escaped from Mrs. Ryan, accompanied by a tiny bubble of spit in the corner of her mouth that I really wanted to wipe away. I don't know what the deal was with this woman but she looked like she could use some help. Muffin wasn't one for the gentle touch when it comes to her future in-laws.

Mr. Ryan seemed unaffected by Muffin's harsh words.

"You're right, of course, Muffin. Still, I do care what happens to her. It was never my choice that Harley *not* be a part of our lives and you're well aware of that. You too, Ms. Eastcott. You know that Mrs. Ryan and myself have always maintained an interest in her well-being. It's your client that has kept us at arms length all these years."

Jennifer looked about ready to pop a vein. Oooh. This was getting good. I hoped they would all just forget I was there and air out all their dirty little family secrets.

But no...it was not to be. Muffin took the reins yet again, bossy little baked good that she is. She turned to Jennifer and said,

"I think it would be best if you left, Jennifer. Whatever we Ryans have to discuss, it should be in private. I know you understand."

Jennifer was off like a prom dress. She nodded a brief see ya to the Ryan clan and whispered warmly in my ear. "Watch your back Jess. I'll wait for you at your place. We need to talk."

With that, she was gone. I turned my attention back to the Ryan clan.

Sharron was hovering nearby so I waved her over. Mr. Ryan ordered a coffee for himself and a glass of wine for his wife. Muffin stayed pat with her water. I sat in eager anticipation. Mrs. Ryan leaned across the table and got within hissing distance of my face.

"Miss Shore we need your help..."

Squeeze me? Did I hear that right?

"How so Mrs. Ryan?"

"We want this whole business over with. We want to go home and we want to be left in peace. "

"Well Mrs. Ryan, there's no reason that I know of that prevents you from going home at any time. To the best of my knowledge, none of you are being detained. Is there some other reason you feel your departure being impeded?"

Wow. Don't I sound mature and dignified. Can't last. She fidgeted with the humungous bow in the back of her platinum blonde hair.

"Of course we don't feel like we can leave now, for heaven's sake. You've practically accused all of us of having some sort of involvement in this whole Sydney affair. I know what you're thinking."

Her voice became shrill and thin. There's an hysterical edge to this lady that could cut brick. Her husband patted her knee in a distracted kind of way. Muffin rolled her eyes and thunked back in her chair wearily.

"What is it that you think I'm thinking?"

"Enough of these games, Miss Shore. You obviously think one of us did this. Well, young lady, that's just bullshit and you're walking a very dangerous line. Do you have any idea who we are?"

Mrs. Ryan said "bullshit." Had she stripped naked and played a kazoo I would have been less shocked. Spunky ole gal. I kinda lost what else she said in my amusement. I buried my chuckle for the moment but I couldn't wait to relay the details to Leah. Whew! Okay. Regroup.

"Why yes, Mrs. Ryan, I do know who you are. What's your point?"

"My point little lady is this. Back off. Get out of here and do your job and leave us out of it. Am I making myself clear?"

"Yes. And you're making my face damp.
Mind backing up the attitude bus an inch or two?"

Ooh. That was harsh. Tough. I couldn't be sure if it was her outburst or mine but Mama Ryan seemed to deflate like a week old balloon before my eyes. Sharron whistled in with the drinks and Mrs. Ryan gulped hers down like a pro. Must have been a good month, vintage wise. She nodded to Sharron for another. I hope I wasn't going to get stuck with this tab.

And now a word from the Muffin gallery.

"Mother Ryan, this isn't going to help anything. I suggest you calm down and listen to what Jess has to say.

I know that she has questions for all of us and I don't see how we can avoid answering them. We all have the same goal in mind...to get the hell out of here. Agreed?"

"Mmphf."

"Good. Go ahead Jess."

"Gee, thanks Muff. Okay. Let's start with you, Mr. Ryan. You flew into Provincetown yesterday morning, is that right?"

"Yes. You can confirm my flight times with the local airport. I filed a flight plan from Boston and a copy of it is on file at Logan."

"Yes, I have that information. Odd though. It took you almost an hour longer than usual to make the trip. How come?"

He seemed surprised by my question and I caught him glancing over at Muffin before he re-composed himself. Hmmm.

"Well Miss Shore, I don't know how much knowledge you have about flying but it's not unusual for a flight to take longer than scheduled. There's headwinds to consider...and routing."

"I see."

I kept my own aerial qualifications and what Karen had mentioned to myself for the time being. Let him think he has a leg up on me, so to speak. Can't hurt. I knew he was lying but I didn't know why. I had my suspicions, though.

"Alright then. So, your flight arrived late. You, your wife and Muffin all left Logan together and landed in Provincetown together. Right?"

"Yes. That's right. It's all in the flight plan Miss Shore."

"No stops on the way?"

"Of course not. If there had been there would have been records. There aren't."

Lying again. I could smell it like a tuna sandwich left over the winter in a forgotten pocket of my golf bag.

"No sir, that's true. There is no record of any other landings. Okay. Let's move on. Explain to me, in your own words, why exactly you're here."

His smile was thin and tired and he gazed over my shoulder, seemingly lost for a moment.

"I'm here, Miss Shore, because my family needed me to be here. I'm here for Tim, not that he would ever believe that. I'm here for my granddaughter, although she'll probably never know that. I'm here because I really believed we could all work this out."

"Work what out, Mr. Ryan? "

"The custody issue. This case has been dragging on for months and it's taking its toll on all of us. I never got a chance to know Sydney when she and Tim were together. Their marriage was a mistake. He was acting out his anger at us. I understand that now, but didn't at the time. If there ever was any genuine affection between those two it was friendship, not love. The child...Harley...she isn't a mistake. I want to know my granddaughter. I know that Tim and Muffin have agreed to relinquish his paternal rights to the child but I haven't.

I have no intention of causing trouble in her life or that of her mother. I came here to tell Sydney that.

Jennifer Eastcott made it perfectly clear to our lawyers that any contact I may have with Harley would be highly inappropriate. I don't care, frankly. Enough of the goddamn lawyers.

Miss Shore, I'm not a young man. I've made mistakes in my life but overall I've done well. My relationship with my son is no different from the one I had with my own father. I know Tim feels I was hard on him. Not there when he needed me. Maybe that's true, and if it is I'm sorry for that. Losing his sister...my daughter...was hard on all of us. Nothing was the same after that..."

He never had a chance to finish. His wife turned on him like a wild banshee. She clawed at his face with her blood red talons. He looked horrified and not a little bit frightened. Then she started to screech.

"You bastard. You fucking bastard. How dare you? How can you even say those words? You don't have the right to talk about her....do you understand? Never. You killed her. You ruined everything. I hate you...."

I was frozen in my seat. It was kinda like what you're supposed to do when a bear approaches you...or is that when a skunk is about to spray? Whatever...I didn't move. Don't let them see your horror! Muffin obviously didn't read the same Cheerio's guide to the wilderness manual that I did. She lifted herself from her seat, leaned across the table and slapped Mrs. Ryan across the face so hard I could hear her upper plate rattle. She then sat down, oh so calmly, took a refreshing sip of her water and said,

"Shut up Mary. You're making a scene."

Apparently making a scene is the code word or maybe it was the slap. Either way Mrs. Ryan snapped out of it. Surprisingly, Mr. Ryan seemed totally unaffected by the incident.

I was certain this wasn't the first time he'd been the recipient of his wife's hysteria and likely wouldn't be the last. Family. You can't pick 'em but you should be able to have them committed with a minimum of fuss.

I smelled food. I turned my head and was eye to ample breast with Gillian. She stood next to me with a cleaver the size of an oar in her meaty hand.

"You alright Jess?"

"Yeah Gilly. Sorry about the fuss. Mrs. Ryan here was just having a bit of a spell. We're all fine though. Thanks."

She took a moment to glare at each of my table mates and made her way back to the kitchen.

Muffin was laughing. At me? Surely not.

"Interesting friends you have, Jess."

"Interesting family *you* have, Muffin."

"Tell me about it."

I think I was starting to like this gal. Spunky and apparently not without a sense of humor. Going to the altar with this group would require a strong constitution and I suspected she had this. Tim Ryan was a lucky man. I hope he realized that. I didn't want to let Mrs. Ryan calm down too much. I guessed that she had two speeds. Stop and rage. I'd seen the rage and wanted to dig in before she checked out.

"Mrs. Ryan. Are you feeling alright now?"

"Bitch."

"I'll take that as a 'yes' then, shall I?"

She said nothing but I could tell she didn't want to ask me to be a fourth for bridge. Darn. I plugged on, 'cuz that's what us detecting folks do.

"So, I know why Mr. Ryan is here. Could you tell me why it is you decided to accompany your husband?"

"Someone has to keep an eye on him. Damn fool. He thinks he's too good for the rest of us. Well he's not.

Sydney has no intention of letting him see Harley and never will. He knows that but still thinks he can just come here and make everything the way he wants it. It's always like that with him. I know about her kind...about this place."

"Her kind, Mrs. Ryan. Help me out."

"She's a lesbian. You know how they are."

Oooh. The hole in my tongue was gonna be huge. Bite Jess. Bite hard.

"No Mrs. Ryan, I'm not sure I do know how *they* are. Enlighten me."

"She's not going to let us be part of that little girl's life unless we make her."

Muffin stirred next to me.

"That's enough Mother Ryan. I think I should get you back to the Inn and you can lie down. Jess, please excuse us."

"Oh no. Not so fast. Plant it Muff. You all are tough enough to pin down. I'm not done here. Go on Mrs. Ryan."

She looked vindicated and cast a smug look at her husband. Wherever he was at this moment he looked at peace. It was like his brain had a hearing aid attached and he had long ago cut the volume to filter out his wife's diatribes. I thought about Buster's snoring and wondered if I could get me one of those things.

Mrs. Ryan went to take a slug of wine and missed her mouth by about an inch. A crimson stain spread across Sydney's lovely linens. She didn't seem to notice. I dabbed at the spot reflexively and she knocked my hand away. Not a good thing. I bit down harder on my poor tongue.

"Leave it alone for Christ sake."

Mrs. Ryan has potty mouth. Who knew? I struggled to remain calm. I didn't count on having much time before Mrs. R. left the planet so I made nice. Yeech.

"Sure. Sorry. Go ahead. You were saying something about making Sydney let you see Harley?"

"It wasn't going to happen. I knew that even if my fool of a husband didn't. You can't reason with her kind. Everyone knows that. Lawyers. What a joke. Nobody's going to keep me away from my little girl. Not any more.

They tried to tell me she was dead. He tried to tell me she was dead. That Tim had killed her. Liars. All of you are goddamn liars. She's here. She's been here all along."

Oh my. Get me a map, I'm lost. I turned to Muffin.

"Help?"

"I'm sorry Jess. Mary gets confused sometimes. The past few years haven't been easy on her. You see, Tim had a sister..."

"I know about that already. What does that have to do with Harley?"

Potty mouth butted in.

"Tim had a sister. My baby girl. They said he killed her and then I find out that she's here with that awful woman and they're all trying to hide her from me. Well it won't work I tell you. She's mine..."

"Enough!" Mr. Ryan looked on the verge of an apoplectic seizure. "Shut up Mary. For once in your pathetic life shut up. I'm sick of this. Of you. Sarah is dead. She's been dead for almost twenty years. You can pop pills and swill booze until the day you die...she's still not going to come back to life.

"Muffin, get her out of my sight. Take her back to the hotel so she can pass out and I don't have to listen to her insane babbling anymore. Please."

Man. This group made my family look like The Brady Bunch and that ain't easy to do.

I checked out Mrs. Ryan. She looked pretty much spent.

"Go ahead Muffin. I'm done with her for now. I can't insist but I would ask that you not leave town without letting me know. Alex Thorne my have some questions for you as well. I'll let him know where you are. You have my number?"

"Yes Jess, I'll call you. Come on Mary. I'll take you back now and you can have a rest."

"Assholes. All of you. Assholes."

"Yes Mary. That's right. Here we go. Tim, I'll see you later."

"Thank you my dear. I'll be along shortly."

Mother Ryan went quietly with Muffin. The other diners gawked after them, then turned their attention back to our table. Ah, the delights of a small town. This oughta make the front page of *The Banner*.

" I apologize for my wife, Miss Shore."

"I suspect you've had to do a lot of that. Please, call me Jess. Can I get you anything Mr. Ryan? A drink maybe?"

"Thank you, no. I don't drink. Haven't had a drop since Sarah's accident."

"I understand. More coffee then?"

"That would be nice, thank you."

I waved at Sharron and gave the universal signal for a refill. She bustled over...which is not something she's well known for...and topped us up. Mr. Ryan took a grateful sip and sat back. If his wife's outburst had disturbed him in any way he sure didn't show it. Maybe he had a honkin' hole in his tongue too. I'd wager he had a good sized one in his stomach.

"So what's the deal here, sir? Any clues as to what your wife was talking about?"

He actually laughed out loud. A surprising sound. Like your voice when you first try it out in the morning, it sounded hoarse and unused. This was not a man who had a lot of chuckles in his day.

"Oh, Jess, it's no mystery really. My wife is nuts. She's been like this since I met her. Back then I thought it sweet and charming. She was a wee slip of a girl then. Bright and charming and terribly fragile. I liked that. It made me feel, I don't know, *needed* I suppose. Over the years she got worse instead of better. I thought that my love for her would make her strong.

I believed that having a family of our own would force her to grow up. Mature. I was wrong.

She was never cut out to be a mother or, for that matter, a wife. She remained that girl that I first knew so many years ago. When Sarah was killed she lost whatever uncertain grip she had on reality. It's been a downhill ride since then." He sighed and took up his coffee.

"I'm sorry for that Mr. Ryan. Still, it doesn't explain what she was saying just now. Help me out, would ya?"

"Quite simply, my wife is delusional. She has gotten it into her head that Harley is really Sarah and that there's been a conspiracy all these years to keep her apart from her beloved daughter. What a laugh. When Sarah was alive Mary couldn't have been less interested. In Tim either. Like I said, Tim had every right to resent his family. We haven't been good parents. I'm not proud of it but I can't change the past. I'm trying now. I want to be there for Tim and Muffin. They deserve a chance."

"And your wife?"

"Ah yes. My wife. I honestly don't know anymore Jess. I just want some peace in my own life. I want to enjoy what years I have left to me. I can't go on living like this. Mary has problems. She needs help. It's not her fault, I know that. I don't blame her for being as she is. She is delicately balanced. I don't know what will happen next, but I will see to it that she gets the best care possible."

"What are you saying Mr. Ryan? Are you going to institutionalize your wife?"

"I will if I have to. I don't know what else to do. Her doctors agree with me. She can't survive in this world anymore. She's lost her grip, you've seen that now. It's my fault really. I always thought I could keep her safe. Make her well. I can't.

I've made millions over the years. I'm considered a great man. I'm not. I'm just as fumbling and inept as the next fellow, especially when it comes to my family.

That's why I want to get to know my granddaughter. I know it may sound terribly selfish but I think I can be a good influence in her life. I don't want to interfere, honestly I don't. I know I don't have the right to even ask. As I said, I never took the time to get to know Sydney, but I have learned things about her..."

"You hired people to investigate her is what you mean, isn't it?"

He looked sheepish. "Yes, that's it. What I have found out is that she is a good businesswoman and a great mother. There is nothing in her past that is questionable or suspect..."

"She'll be relieved." I know I sound testy but I can't help myself. The guy seems nice enough, but honestly. What an ego.

"I understand why you may question my motives. I can't say I blame you, but I can promise you that I only have the girl's best interests in mind, and those of her mother as well. I had actually written her a letter not long ago. I wanted her to consider letting me meet Harley. Get to know the child. The timing of this whole mess...the attack on Sydney, is pure coincidence."

I was relieved to hear him own up to the letter writing. Maybe he didn't have anything to hide but I doubted that.

"I don't believe much in coincidence, sir. Never have."

"No I suppose you wouldn't...your line of business I mean."

These Ryan folk were tough to get a handle on. I started out not caring a hoot for the whole clan then, like fungus, they started to grow on me. 'Cept for the matriarch of course. She's a berry scary lady and it was hard to know if she was more dangerous to herself or the world at large.

Certainly she'd made victims of her family all these years. Her insanity was intense and the thought of her anywhere near Harley made me iggly all over. It couldn't happen and that's all there was to it.

"Mr. Ryan, do you have any thoughts at all on who may have attacked Sydney?"

He stared at that spot over my right shoulder again as he answered.

"I'm sorry Jess. You're going to have to figure this out on your own. I can't be involved."

"Can't or won't?"

"What difference? The fact is I have to protect my family and I will. I haven't been very successful before, but I plan on sticking by them now."

"Sounds to me like you do have some suspicions. Care to share?"

"Again...no. Sorry. I really should get back. Please let me know as soon as you resolve this investigation. I need to get my wife back to Boston where she can get the help she needs. I promise you we won't leave until then. I hope you're good at what you do Jess."

"I am. Mr. Ryan...?"

"Yes."

"About Harley."

His face turned mushy.

"Ah yes. Harley. What a treasure."

"Yes, that's true."

"You know her then, do you Jess?"

"Yeah I know her. I've known her for several years now. She is a treasure. See here, Mr. Ryan.

"I can't stop you from getting involved in this whole mess but I can speak my mind. Sydney has made a wonderful life here for herself and her daughter. Your son seems to get that and has decided to do the right thing. Tim and Muffin will stay out of Harley's life and I believe that may be best, at least for now. This horrible attack on her mother is more than she should have to handle. Back off sir. Please."

His eyes turned to ice and flashed a warning, then, just as quickly, the look passed.

"I can't promise you anything Miss Shore. Harley is my granddaughter and I want to get to know her. I won't push it. When her mother is fully recovered I will speak to her about this. That is, assuming..."

"Don't even say it. Sydney will be fine. So I have your word then? You'll butt out, for now?"

"Yes. For now." He unclipped a fifty from a sizable wad of other large denominations and put it down on the table.

"This should take care of our bill. Good luck Miss Shore. Jess."

"Thanks. Oh, Mr. Ryan. One last thing. Do you consider your wife to be dangerous? She said something about 'making' Sydney do something about Harley. Care to speculate?"

"No I don't. She's not a well woman, Jess. Let her be. I'll see that she isn't a problem to anyone here again. I'll do it my way."

"Well sir, that's all well and good, but if your wife had anything to do with this I will find it out."

"I understand. Good day Jess...and again, good luck."

Good luck the man says. Sure. With his family involved I'd need that and a whole lot more. I was exhausted. My brain felt like a bag of microwave popcorn. I barely had a chance to breathe before a shadow loomed over me. Tim Ryan, Jr. Swell.

"Mind if I sit down?"

"Oh please do. I was hoping the Ryan express hadn't pulled out of town yet."

"I did it."

"Squeeze me?"

"I did it. I attacked Sydney. You were right all along."

Goodness gracious. This is getting good.

"I see. Ah huh. Okay. Mind if I ask why?"

"Why not?"

"Why not? Come on Timmy, you can do better than that surely."

"I'm confessing, alright. Call your little tin soldier to come and arrest me and let's just get this whole thing over with."

"No, I don't think so."

"What kind of detective are you anyway? Look, I'll pay your fee. How much? I'll give you a check right now."

"No Tim. It's not the money. It's about the truth. I don't believe you hurt Sydney. I'm pretty sure you're covering for someone else and I will find out who and why."

"Forget it. I'm the one. It finishes now. Got it?"

"Still no. Sorry." I needed to re-group. "Excuse me for a sec will ya? I have to make a phone call."

"Good. Tell the cops to hurry. I want this wrapped up as soon as possible."

"Just sit tight. I won't be long."

I almost knocked Gillian over in my mad dash for Sydney's office. She spun around and followed me in.

"What's wrong Jessica? You look awful."

"Thanks. I feel a bit green around the gills, Gill."

Gillian looked worried.

"I'm fine. Really. I just need a minute of quiet."

Oops. Judging by the 'hey you took my last gum ball' look on Gillian's face, I'd said the wrong thing.

"Sorry Gill. It's not you. Honestly. It's those Ryans. They're wearing me out. Tim just showed up to confess that he is, after all, the culprit. Like as if..."

"I'll kill the bastard. Where is he, Jess? Give me two minutes with him..."

"Whoa there little lady.   None of your sous chef justice. Besides, he didn't do it."

"How do you know?"

"I just do. Trust me. "

"I do Jessica. I do. Okay, I'll leave you to your figuring. Can I fix you something to eat? You've been here for hours and I know that you think better on a full stomach."

"Sure honey, that would be swell. Surprise me."

She just got her last gum ball back and looked as happy as I'd seen her since I arrived. Nothing like a good feeding to make her day. Ah, that my needs were so easily met. Speaking of Catherine...

I picked up the phone. Old habits die hard. When we had first gotten together she had quickly proven to be a voice of reason and inspiration for me. Her calm and logical thinking, her unconditional love and support. There was never any bad day that couldn't have been made better by just hearing her voice.

I needed that now and I knew she needed me. I guess that should answer any questions about what our future looked like.

Of course we would be together. I've always known that. Whatever it takes, we'd make this work. This epiphany made me feel calmer than I had in months.

Ah, love. Ain't it grand? Now I only had to convince her to see the same light and walk toward it with me.
I would have loved to bounce some ideas off her now, have her help me make some sense of what I had just experienced with the Ryans. Her plate was full, though, and I knew that her energies had to stay with Sydney.

CHAPTER 23

■ tried Catherine's cell phone. No answer. I left a message for her at the nurse's station with the number of *The Shooting Gallery*. The nurse on duty told me that there was no change in Sydney's condition. I hoped that was just the party line. After all, she didn't know me from a hole in the wall and patient updates are confidential.

It would have been great to hear some good news for a change. Ah well. I put in a call to Alex Thorne. He answered just as I was about to hang up.

"Jess, what's going on? I was just about to track you down."

"Got something?"

"Maybe."

"I'm at Sydney's restaurant. Tim Ryan's here too. Oh...and he's confessed. "

It was impish of me but I couldn't help myself. Oh to be a fly on his tie clip.

"What did you just say? Tim Ryan confessed?"

"Yup. But he didn't do it."

"I'm on my way."

"Okay. See ya in a minute."

I only hoped he could keep his youthful zeal down to a dull roar. Oh, what a tangled web we weave when we don't get what we need.

Okay Jess, think. First of all, no way did young Tim attack Sydney. He did, however, attack me and I wouldn't be heartbroken to see him suffer a little time in the clink for that. Muffin knew more than she was telling me; I was pretty sure of that. Jennifer was still a puzzle and I didn't care much for the picture that was being revealed there. Then there was Mr. Ryan.

Well, probably just a pooped old guy who woke up one day and realized that he'd pissed away most of his life in a boardroom. Mega bucks don't wrap you up in their arms in the morning and tell you that you're loved. Too bad, so sad. Of course I knew he hadn't flown straight here from Logan. Dorothy and Toto could have made better time. So he was lying about that, I just didn't know why.

Then we have Mrs. Ryan. Whew. And I thought my mother was bad. Nothing like a little perspective to brighten one's past. What I wasn't sure of was whether she was nutty enough, or sane enough, to be a threat to Sydney or Harley. I didn't trust her, that's for sure. If she really believed that Harley was her beloved Sarah brought back from the dead she could be daft enough to try to bring her home.

Ow, my aching pea brain. I was stalling. I hoped to hear the phone ring and have Catherine tell me that Sydney was fine and she was coming home. Hope springs eternal.

I had time for a quick call home before Alex arrived. Leah picked up as if she had been sitting on the phone, which, knowing Leah as I do, is entirely possible.

"Leah, it's Jess. What's shakin'?"

"Besides my thighs, not much."

"Are you alone?"

"Nope."

"Jennifer?"

"Yup."

"Everything okay?"

"Sure."

"I need your help."

"Of course you do. It was just a matter of time."

Count to three Jess. Your tongue's suffered enough for one day.

"Grill her, Leah. She knows a lot more than she's saying. I've already caught her in a couple of lies and I suspect there are more. I really think she holds the key to this whole mess. Find out what you can. Also, Miss Lynnie said she was chatting up some swarthy fella at the bar earlier. Try to find out who he is."

"Will do. Anything else?"

"Yeah, how's Buster?"

"Thrilled to be spending time with his nice mom."

One. Two. Three...

"Alright. I'll be home in awhile. Don't let her out of your sight."

"With pleasure. In case you didn't notice our little lawyer is...."

"Please Leah, I don't want to hear it."

"Grump."

"Flake."

"Love you."

"You too. Bye."

No more stalling. Might as well find out what Timmy boy has up his sleeve besides one of the biggest biceps this side of Muscle Beach.

Fortunately Gillian was temporarily swamped in the kitchen so I didn't have to disappoint her again with the lack of news about Sydney.

I snagged Sharron for a word. I told her that if anyone called for me to please interrupt, otherwise give the table a wide berth. She looked relieved. The place was jammed.

Late lunchers or rubber neckers...who could say for sure? Either way business at *The Shooting Gallery* was hopping. I arrived at the table the same time Alex did. Ryan looked smugly from one to the other of us. If he thought he was going to have his way he had another think coming.

"Hi Alex. Glad you could join us. Have a seat."

"Jess. Ryan."

"Officer Fife."

"Knock it off Tim." Geez. Didn't this guy know the old quit while you still have a behind theory?

I gently laid my hand over Alex's and my eyes implored him to be patient. A tough request for a young stud with a squeaky new leather belt and shiny new badge, but this kid was wise beyond his years. He nodded slightly at me and I dug in to Ryan.

"So Tim, about your confession. As I mentioned, I don't buy it."

He was a grumpy guss this afternoon and that's not his best side. His voice was tight and I doubt you could have gotten a wisp of wind between his clenched teeth.

"Hey detective...you deal in facts right? Well here are the facts from where I sit. You're looking for the person that attacked Sydney. I hired you to do that, but only to throw you off my trail. I did it. I was there when you arrived so I can't see why you have a problem with this.

"She pissed me off. She was dragging her feet on this custody thing and I just got a little carried away. I didn't mean to hit her. Something just came over me. I have a lousy temper. Okay?"
He turned to Alex.

"You're here, so arrest me. I'll sign whatever you want. A confession...whatever. Lock me up and let my family get on with their lives. Either of you have a problem with that?"

Alex couldn't help himself. Ah youth.

"Nope. I don't have a problem. Timothy Ryan you're under arrest..."

Oh pooh. Now what was I going to do. I couldn't very well not let Alex do his job but I knew that Tim Ryan no more beaned Sydney than Leah did. I did, however, have to play straight and narrow with Alex. He was the law here and I sure didn't want to ruffle his downy soft feathers. So what's the worst that can happen? Ryan goes to jail and the rest of the clan feels relief. That may make someone sloppy. I'm sure it's not what Tim had in mind, but this little confession of his may well be the catalyst to flush out the real evil-doer.

"You're right, of course Alex. Mr. Ryan, I leave you to officer Thorne. If you want to talk to me, let Alex know. He can track me down."

Ryan looked dumbfounded at my turnaround, then he looked really suspicious. Yup. That's right. You made a boo boo. He knew it and I knew it.

"Hey wait a minute..."

"Sorry, no can do. Alex I gotta go. Good work here. I'll drop by your office later. Meantime you and your prisoner have a nice day."

Alex seemed a little confused but kinda pleased with this turn of events. An arrest in this case would be a gold star on his record whether the confession was false or not. Good for him.

"No worries Jess. I'll take it from here."

"Bye boys."

I would have given my Silly Putty keychain to have seen Ryan being cuffed but duty called. I waved a quick good-bye to Sharron. I knew I should go and say bye to Gillian but I didn't have the time or, frankly, the energy.

I wanted to go home for a bit. I wanted to hug my dog and sit on my porch. I needed space to think and home was that space. And Jennifer Eastcott. Ah yes. I wondered how Leah had made out, so to speak, with Miss Stiff Upper Lip. I pulled into my driveway and stood for a second to take in the beauty of my surroundings.

There hadn't been time since my arrival to adjust to being back on the Cape. There's something about Provincetown. The bay, the beaches, the people, the life. Whenever I was here I wondered why I would want to be anyplace else. And of course there's Catherine. Maybe it was time for me to make a commitment to her...to us. Maybe it was time to consider staying put for awhile. Give things time to settle between us.

Since we had met, my life had been here, there and everywhere. We grabbed moments as we could but never more than a few precious weeks at a time. Seeing her again made me realize that I wanted to be here with her. I wanted to wake up every morning and know that she was lying next to me. I wanted to go to sleep at night with her back curled into me. Yikes! When did this happen? Well, whenever, fact is my heart was taking charge and for once in my life I was going to let it. One day at a time.

I made my way to the door and when I tried to open it my heart froze. Something...or someone was blocking the way.

I, of course, immediately imagined that Leah was lying on the other side in a pool of her own blood having been bludgeoned by Jennifer.. I pushed harder, my panic giving me extra umph.

The door gave a bit then slammed back in my face. I pushed again and heard a yelp of complaint. Buster! He was sound asleep on the other side and simply taking his sweet time about getting up. Oh my poor shattered nerves. My relief was quickly replaced by something else. At that moment, I had believed Jennifer Eastcott capable of murder. My instincts are usually pretty dead on, so this was no small enlightenment.

I hadn't really had a good feeling about her from the get go, but now I realized my guts thought even less of her.

Ooh boy. Maybe she had told Sydney how she felt and Sydney had blown her off. Maybe she had attacked Sydney in a rejection rage. It's possible. More than possible. The timing was all off, though. I remembered the bracelet I had found outside *The Shooting Gallery*. It could well have been a piece that Jennifer Eastcott would wear. I hadn't thought of that before, but now...

Buster finally gave way and I inched into the cottage cautiously. Ah shit. Leah! I had left her here alone with a woman who may well be a homicidal maniac. Good job, Jess.

"Leah? Leah are you here?"

No response. I pulled my 9mm from my waist and, with my back to the wall, began to check out the interior. I nudged Buster out the door and he took off for the water. No signs of life. I felt sick to my stomach.

"Leah!"

"What for goodness sake. Why are you screeching at me? And put that evil looking thing down, will you. It makes me nervous."

Leah emerged from the bathroom looking like she was dressed for the Alien Invader's convention. Her hair was festooned with foil and the smell of hair bleach made my eyes water.

"What the hell are you doing?"

"Language, Jess. Language."

"Sorry. You scared me."

"Does it look that bad? " She fingered her twisted bits and pouted endearingly.

"No no. You look...ah...swell. I just got scared for a second. Paranoia getting the best of me. Are you alright?"

"Well of course I am, silly. Sit down now and take a breath or two. I'll make you a cup of Blueberry Tea."

Oh goodie. Herb tea. That oughta help.

"Thanks Leah. Hey, where's Jennifer?"

"Hay is for horses, Jess. What's happened to your language skills?"

Through clenched teeth I threatened. "Leah please. Where's Jennifer?"

"I don't know?"

"Why don't you know."

"Well she was here awhile ago. We had a lovely chat and then she had to go somewhere."

"Where?"

"I think she went to The Provincetown Inn to see a friend of hers."

The Provincetown Inn? Uh oh. This can't be good.

"How long ago did she leave?"

"Oh I'd say about ten minutes after you called to say you'd be right home."

I asked Leah to give me the short version of her chat with Jennifer. First of all, the guy she was with at Larry's Bar is her law clerk. Seems Jennifer had been conducting a little investigation of her own.

She had told Leah that she was digging through all the files she had on the Ryans, looking for the needle in the haystack. She had her own suspicions and convinced Leah that she was hot on the trail of the bad folk.

What I did next may have been a tad left of ethical but I did it anyway. I rummaged through Jennifer's briefcase. I know it was an evil thing to do but it had to be done. My misdeed did not go unrewarded. I snatched a bundle of papers and ran for the door.

"I gotta go."

Now Leah was pouting for real.

"You just got here. Let me come with you at least."

"Like that?"

"What? Oh right. Can you wait another," she consulted the timer on the counter "thirty-two minutes?"

"No."

"Of course not."

"Leah, please."

"Sorry. Go on then. I'll be fine here."

"I know. I need you here in case Jennifer comes back or Catherine calls. Also, call Alex Thorne and have him meet me at The Inn. I'll explain it all later. If Jennifer does come back, don't let her leave. Got that?"

"Yes ma'am."

"And another thing..."

"For pity sake, Jess, what did your last secretary die from?"

I ignored that for the time being.

"Call Karen and ask her to get my plane fueled and a flight plan for Logan done up A.S.A.P."

"Done. Go."

I hugged her quickly which I regretted since one of her bar-b-que hair bits stuck me in the eye. She hugged back and shooed me out the door. I owed her big and we both knew it. Friends. Don't ya just love them?

CHAPTER 24

I got to the Inn in record time and went directly to the room the Ryans had been in yesterday. I banged a few times and got no reply. The emptiness of the room on the other side of the door was palpable.

I ran to the front office and scrambled through my brain for the name of Alex's gal pal.

Barb? Bitsy? Annie? Nuts. She wasn't on duty anyway so I needn't have worried.

The young studly on duty told me that the Ryans had checked out about twenty minutes ago. Unbelievable. So much for 'all for one and one for all.' Tim Ryan was in jail and the family beats it out of town on the first tail wind that blows towards Boston.

I was dashing for the Jeep when Alex peeled into the lot.

"Alex, thank goodness you're here. Where's Ryan?"

"Locked up Jess, like you said I should."

Sweet boy.

"Good work. Any word from his family?"

"Yeah. I was going to call you and tell you. They pulled into the station about five minutes after I did. There was a lot of whispering and stuff, then his mom and that Muffin girl left."

"And Mr. Ryan?"

"He's back at the station calling around to get a lawyer to fly down here."

Time was against me now. If my suspicions were correct Sydney was in danger again...or still. I had to act fast.

"Alex, I need you to radio the airport. Find out from Karen if Muffin and Mrs. Ryan managed to get a flight out.

Tell her I'm on my way now. Give me about fifteen minutes."

"What else can I do Jess?"

"Nothing for now my friend. Keep an eye on things and I'll stay in touch."

Alex grabbed my arm as I was hoisting myself into the Jeep.

"You know who did this, don't you?"

"I think so Alex. I think so."

"Good luck."

Just my luck, it was rush minute in Provincetown. The traffic leaving the beach was pokey and my blood pressure was reaching seizure levels. It would have been faster to jog there but I wasn't wearing the right shoes. I finally arrived at the airport half an hour later. Karen was waiting for me.

"Jess. About time."

I was going to need a new tongue when all was said and done. My bad nerves threatened to snap all over Karen and that would have been a very bad thing.

"I know. I got held up. Please tell me they're here."

"Sorry. No can do."

She urged me through the terminal to my plane and filled me in on the way.

"First of all, Mr. Ryan calls me up this morning to let me know that his pilot would be arriving soon and to ask him to wait here for instructions.

I assumed that he did all his own flying but I was wrong. He's got a company plane as well as his own and a hired fly-boy on salary. Company man gets in around ten and I give him the message. He asks for the number of The Inn and goes outside to use the pay phone. He comes back in and makes arrangements with me to fly back to Logan early this afternoon. Then about an or so ago your lawyer friend arrives and catches the Cape Air flight to Logan. It arrived in Boston about five minutes ago.

About five minutes after *she* takes to the sky, Mrs. Ryan and Muffin wheel in here and roust their fly boy outta his seat. They took off about the same time Alex called me or I could have stalled them. I did your pre-flight for you so you can take off now. You're cleared right through. Can you tell me what's going on? "

"Karen trust me. I don't have time right now to explain. I need you to get hold of Catherine. Do you have her cell phone number?"

"I do."

"Good . I'm worried about her and Sydney. Tell Catherine to get security to have someone watch Sydney's room and tell her to stay in there with Harley. They're both in danger."

I didn't wait for a response. I knew I didn't have to. Karen would take care of things from here.

I felt my blood pressure mount as I awaited clearance to land at Logan. I could be circling here for hours waiting for the 'real' planes to land.

Muffin. Jennifer. Mrs. Ryan. 'I don't like it. I don't like it at all,' I thought as I began yet another circuit above my intended runway. I thought of the documents I had read from Jennifer's briefcase. They say one's past doesn't equal one's future. Not so this time, I feared.

After what seemed like years I was able to land my plane and made a mad dash for the terminal. As I flew out the doors to grab a cab, I ran smack dab into Kelly.

"Where's your car?" I barked.

"Follow me." Kelly shouted over her shoulder. She must have seen the urgency in my face and knew this was not the time for questions.

If I was a praying sort of gal I would have begged the divine one to make sure that Karen had been able to get a message to Catherine. I didn't know what to expect when I got to the hospital, but I had a pretty good sense that it wasn't going to be a picnic.

The idea of any harm coming to Catherine made me physically ill. I already felt as if I hadn't done my job very well. I realized now that I had missed some pretty big clues. That, in and of itself, can happen...no biggie. What pissed me off was the reason I had missed them.

I had made certain assumptions about Jennifer that had kept me away from the facts. Her alliance with Muffin had lead me down the wrong path, and I knew I would kick myself for that for years to come. The papers I had scammed from Jennifer's briefcase had tipped me over the edge. If she knew what I now knew there was no question that Sydney, and anyone else around her, was in danger. Jennifer was the fuse leading to a big stick of dynamite.

Kelly made record time en route to the hospital and we squealed up to the entrance in a cloud of dust. The car was still moving as I jumped out and just about knocked over a couple of smokers and their I.V. stands as I crashed through the doors.

The elevator took four days to arrive and when the doors opened to Sydney's floor the sound I heard made my blood run cold. There is no mistaking a gun shot. Not once you've heard it up close and personal. I heard myself cry out in terror. As I ran past the nurse's station I told the blur in white to call the cops.

I got to the door of Sydney's room just in time to fall head first into the flailing body of Mrs. Ryan. She's a sturdy gal and her weight knocked the wind out of me.

I couldn't see past her bulk as I tried to roll her off me. Just as I was struggling to my feet another gun shot blasted and something bigger than a bread box fell on top of me again.

Jennifer Eastcott. And she didn't look at all well. I again struggled to upright myself and saw Catherine firmly planted in front of Sydney's bed. Her hands were shaking so badly that the gun she had just fired waved crazily in the air. Behind me Mrs. Ryan groaned and tried to make her way down the hall. I looked past her and saw Kelly just getting off the elevator.

"Stop her, Kelly."

Before Kelly had a chance to register what was going on, Muffin blasted around the corner and planted a solid jab right in the center of Mrs. Ryan's puritan jaw. She went down in a heap.

I shouted down the hall at her.

"Don't let her move Muffin. The police are on the way."

"She's not going anywhere Jess."

I went back into Sydney's room. Jennifer wasn't moving and Catherine looked like she was about to go down for the count. I walked slowly toward her and gently removed the gun from her hands. As soon as I did she fell back onto the bed, missed, and landed on the floor.

"Catherine. Catherine." I was shouting now. The combination of shock and the blast from the gun would be making it almost impossible for her to hear anything. I crouched down in front of her and took her face in my hands.

"Catherine. Are you all right? Tell me what happened."

Her voice, when it came, was a squeak.

"Jennifer. Help Jennifer."

By the time the words were out the room was being overrun with medical personnel and paraphernalia. I turned my attention back to Catherine.

"Can you tell me what happened honey?"

Tears ran down her face as she filled me in. Karen had gotten hold of her around the same time I was on my way from the airport. Catherine had headed straight for Sydney's room and intended to sit guard until I arrived. Harley had been sleeping in the lounge next to the nursing station so she was well out of harm's way. I would lecture her later about not notifying security.

Catherine was checking Sydney's vitals when Mrs. Ryan barged into the room. As clearly as I can make it out now Mrs. Ryan had a gun and ordered Catherine to stand aside. She threatened to shoot her as well as Sydney and may well have if Jennifer hadn't arrived when she did.

Having read the files in Jennifer's briefcase I knew that it wasn't the first time Mrs. Ryan had been violent. Seems the old bird had a habit of being naughty. Apparently Mrs. Ryan waved around her Saturday Night Special the way most women her age waved around their compacts. Mr. Ryan himself had been forced to call for help on one occasion some years ago. Anyway...on with Catherine's tale of the harrowing harridan.

Jennifer jumped on Mrs. Ryan but wasn't bulky enough to get the weapon from her hand. Mrs. Ryan, whether she meant to or not, had shot Jennifer. The shock of the gun going off must have made her lose her grip because Jennifer managed to get it from her before she herself faded to black. Mrs. Ryan had been making a waddle for it when I fell into her.

Jennifer had handed off the gun to Catherine who panicked when I came in. The gun went off in Catherine's hand but the bullet embedded itself in the wall, well over any of our heads.

CHAPTER 25

The service for Jennifer was simple. We all stood silently by as Muffin cast the ashes to the four winds at Race Point. Tears ran down her face and softened her features more than I would have thought possible. Jennifer, I suppose, had been her one and only true friend. Real friendships were not dimmed by the passage of time. I thought of my own friendship with Leah and felt the lump in my throat grow. Fear of loss? You betcha.

Catherine held me so tightly from behind that I saw cartoon stars. I didn't mind. Since the shooting I hadn't let her out of my sight and didn't plan to in the near future, either. In front of me Harley stood, stoic and silent, a drooping bunch of daffodils clutched in her tiny hand.

Her grandfather held the other hand and she leaned slightly into him. If Mr. Ryan was at all concerned about the welfare of his long-suffering wife he sure hid it well. When I had spoken with him yesterday he had almost sounded relieved.

"At least now maybe she will find some peace." He told me.

Mrs. Ryan had never been the same since the death of their daughter. Tim Ryan had inadvertently planted the seed in his mother's head when he began making noises about getting custody of Harley. His mother saw this as a second chance and the lines of reality blurred for her. She really hadn't been right in the head since then. Once she had convinced herself that Harley was her long lost daughter, she herself got lost.

Whether or not she ever really intended to physically harm Sydney, we may never know.

My guess is she didn't even think about that. She was lost fully now in her psychosis and it would likely be months, at least, before she was fit to answer any questions

I doubt she was capable of rational thought by the time she arrived in Provincetown, and the attack on Sydney was just another outburst from her fevered brain.

I had managed to weave together all the bits of information in the days since the shooting.

Muffin had been keeping a close eye on her mother-in-law to be. She was an unstable woman and Muffin didn't trust her. For her and Tim, the whole Harley issue had been resolved. They had gone to Jennifer and told her they wanted the whole thing dropped. That had been the news that Jennifer was bringing to Sydney that fateful day that I had flown her into Provincetown.

In Jennifer's files, the ones I had pinched from her briefcase, there were copies of squashed records pertaining to Mrs. Ryan that went back some fifteen or so years. Some was minor stuff, was more serious. The files also contained psychiatric reports that began just months after the accident that claimed the life of her daughter. It seemed there wasn't a pill or potion that hadn't found their way down her throat. I suppose if I had gotten close enough to her I would have heard the ticking. Mrs. Ryan was a woman on the edge, about to blow. I hadn't picked up on that and I would regret my oversight for many months to come.

Jennifer had finally put it all together after our little lunch at the restaurant. I assumed that once she witnessed Mrs. Ryan's madness first hand, she had realized the extent of the threat she posed to Sydney. She may well have intended to fill me in eventually, but had made getting to Sydney, protecting her, the priority.

I couldn't fault her for that. Mrs. Ryan had been ranting of late that if it weren't for Sydney, Harley would be home with them where she belonged. Muffin was supposed to have an early breakfast with Mrs. Ryan the day of the attack on Sydney to discuss plans for the wedding.

Instead of going to the restaurant in Boston, Mrs. Ryan had hired a car from the livery service and headed for Provincetown.

Muffin stuck to her like glue and convinced the old bird that she was on her side. "Keep your enemies close at hand" was more than just an old war adage. If a quick trip to Provincetown would assuage Mrs. Ryan then Muffin would go along for the ride.

I had talked lots with Muffin since the shooting at the hospital and believed her side of the story. She figured Mrs. Ryan just wanted to confront Sydney and that would be the end of it. Muffin assumed they'd both be back by supper and no one need be any the wiser. The Ryan family secrets piled up ever higher and there didn't seem anything unusual about that. Some families operated that way.

Muffin called Tim from Hyannis when they stopped for gas and told him to meet them in Provincetown. She knew that getting his mother back home would not be an easy task.

When they arrived at *The Shooting Gallery* Muffin figured they would just wait out back for Sydney to arrive. The driver left them there at Mrs. Ryan's request.

I had asked Muffin about breaking into the restaurant that fateful morning. What she told me would have to remain my little secret to the grave. Apparently Mary Ryan had been content to wait out back and confront Sydney in the parking area. They had been waiting there for some time, and Mrs. Ryan was getting antsy. Taking a chance, Muffin had tried the back door and it had opened. It may or may not have been locked but it hadn't closed properly. I didn't dare question Gillian about this. There was a lot of coming and going in the restaurant this time of the year and it did seem possible that someone had dropped the ball. No point in making everyone feel worse than they already did. Let them think Mrs. Ryan had broken in somehow. It seemed a small lie and I wasn't bothered about telling it.

Provincetown isn't a mecca for crime and it's not unusual to leave your door open when you go out. It turned out to be a costly and dangerous mistake. Muffin and Mrs. Ryan slipped inside and waited for Sydney.

When Sydney did arrive she came face to face with Muffin. They had been introduced at Jennifer's office one day some months back. Before Muffin could explain their presence Mrs. Ryan bonked Sydney on the head and down she went. Seems she carried more than tissue and breath mints in her bag. Muffin, by her own admission, panicked and dragged Mrs. R. out of the restaurant.

Tim arrived just moments after his mother had attacked Sydney and he and Muffin made some fast decisions. Muffin and Mrs. Ryan jumped into Tim's car and made a beeline for Orleans. Tim was left behind to fend off the authorities. Muffin used the car phone to call Mr. Ryan and he had snagged them from Orleans on his flight to Provincetown. Hence the missing hour on his flight manifest. What a grand conspiracy it had all become.

It was Mrs. Ryan's bracelet that I had found in the kitchen. The Ryans drew together to cover up for their own. It wasn't the first time either. Both Tim and Mrs. Ryan had had their run-ins with the law yet neither of them had criminal records. Once Muffin and Tim realized the seriousness of what Mary Ryan had done they closed ranks.

I still wasn't satisfied with Tim's excuse with respect to his attack on me. He said that he panicked and thought he could frighten me off. He'd seen me arrive with Jennifer and wanted to make his escape before she spotted him. Possible, I suppose, but I decided that if I ever had the misfortune of running into him again I'd give a wide berth.

The irony is if Mrs. Ryan had come clean at the get go she probably could have walked with a slap on her liver spotted hand. As it is...

Tim Ryan went to his fiancée and held her as she wept into his shoulder. Muffin had been charged as an accessory after the fact and was currently out on bail. She would be alright and Tim was being a great support for her. They'd be okay, I suspected.

Meg, Karen, Leah, Kristen, Sharron and Alex made up a makeshift choir and were walking us slowly into the valley of the shadow...or something like that.

My family. I looked at them there. Old friends and new. I am rich because of their presence in my life and I know it. I hoped that Jennifer too had known such love as I did. Another twinge of regret shot through me and I shivered as though cold. Maybe she and I would have become close in time. Who knew?

Mrs. Ryan had been officially charged with both Sydney's attack and Jennifer's murder. She wouldn't be seeing the light of day again. I felt sure that a psychiatric assessment would keep her in Librium for the rest of her life.

As for Harley, well, in spite of everything, she seemed the same as before. She was tickled to have a grampa and the idea of staying with Catherine for awhile was, apparently, pretty cool too. I would have to agree with her on that.

Sydney was slowly making her way back to us all. It would take time but Catherine believed she would enjoy a full recovery. She didn't remember the attack and that was just as well for the time being. Otherwise she was all right. I guess prayers do work.

We made our way back to *The Shooting Gallery* to enjoy a celebration in Jennifer's honor. She had turned out to be one of the good guys after all and had saved Sydney's life. I still felt kinda guilty about the way I had treated her but would come to terms with that in time.

As for Catherine and me...well...we had taken some tentative steps along the road to togetherness. I was planning to stick around P-Town for a couple of months and we would take things one day at a time.

We love each other. That's a pretty good start.

More Fiction to Stir the Imagination
From Rising Tide Press

CLOUD NINE AFFAIR $11.99
Katherine E. Kreuter
Christine Grandy – rebellious, wealthy, twenty-something – has disappeared, along with her lover Monica Ward. Desperate to bring her home, Christine's millionaire father hires Paige Taylor. But the trail to Christine is mined with obstacles, while powerful enemies plot to eliminate her. Eventually, Paige discovers that this mission is far more dangerous than she dreamed. A witty, sophisticated mystery by the best-selling author of *Fool Me Once*, filled with colorful characters, plot twists, and romance.

STORM RISING $12.00
Linda Kay Silva
The excitement continues in this wonderful continuation of *TROPICAL STORM*. Join Megan and Connie as they set out to find Delta and bring her home. The meaning of friendship and love is explored as Delta, Connie, Megan and friends struggle to stay alive and stop General Zahn. Again the Costa Rican Rain Forest is the setting for another fast-paced action adventure. Storm fans won't want to miss this next installment in the Delta Stevens Mystery Series.

TROPICAL STORM $11.99
Linda Kay Silva
Another winning, action-packed adventure featuring smart and sassy heroines, an exotic jungle setting, and a plot with more twists and turns than a coiled cobra. Megan has disappeared into the Costa Rican rain forest and it's up to Delta and Connie to find her. Can they reach Megan before it's too late? Will Storm risk everything to save the woman she loves? Fast-paced, full of wonderful characters and surprises. Not to be missed.

CALLED TO KILL $12.00
Joan Albarella
Nikki Barnes, Reverend, teacher and Vietnam Vet is once again entangled in a complex web of murder and drugs when her past collides with the present. Set in the rainy spring of Buffalo, Dr. Ginni Clayton and her friend Magpie add spice and romance as Nikki tries to solve the mystery that puts her own life in danger. A fun and exciting read.

AGENDA FOR MURDER $11.99
Joan Albarella
A compelling mystery about the legacies of love and war, set on a sleepy college campus. Though haunted by memories of her tour of duty in Vietnam, Nikki Barnes is finally putting back the pieces of her life, only to collide with murder and betrayal.

ONE SUMMER NIGHT $12.00
Gerri Hill
Johanna Marshall doesn't usually fall into bed with someone she just
met, but Kelly Sambino isn't just anyone. Hurt by love and labeled a
womanizer, can these two women learn to trust one another and let love
find its way?

BY THE SEA SHORE $12.00
Sandra Morris   avail 10/00
A quiet retreat turns into more investigative work for Jess Shore in the
summer town of Provincetown, MA. This page-turner mystery will keep
you entertained as Jess struggles with her individuality while solving an
attempted murder case.

AND LOVE CAME CALLING $11.99
Beverly Shearer
A beautifully told love story as old as time, steeped in the atmosphere of
the Old West. Danger lights the fire of passion between two women
whose lives become entwined when Kendra (Kenny), on the run from
the law, happily stumbles upon the solitary cabin where Sophie has
been hiding from her own past. Together, they learn that love can
overcome all obstacles.

SIDE DISH $11.99
 Kim Taylor
A genuinely funny yet tender novel which follows the escapades of
Muriel, a twenty-something burmed – out waitress with a college
degree, who has turned gay slacker living into an art form. Getting by
on margaritas and old movies, she seems to have resigned herself to
low standards, simple pleasures, and erotic daydreams. But in secret,
Muriel is searching for true love.

COMING ATTRACTIONS $11.99
Bobbi D. Marolt
Helen Townsend reluctantly admits she's tried of being lonely...and of
being closeted.   Enter Princess Charming in the form of Cory
Chamberlain, a gifted concert pianist. And Helen embraces joy once
again. But can two women find happiness when one yearns to break
out of the closet and breathe free, while the other fears that it will
destroy her career? A delicious blend of humor, heart and passion – a
novel that captures the bliss and blundering of love.

ROUGH JUSTICE $10.99
Claire Youmans
When Glenn Lowry's sunken fishing boat turns up four years after its
disappearance, foul play is suspected. Classy, ambitious Prosecutor
Janet Schilling immediately launches a murder investigation, which
produces several surprising suspects-one of them, her own former lover
Catherine Adams, now living a reclusive life on an island. A real page-
turner!

NO CORPSE $12.00
Nancy Sanra
The third Tally McGinnis mystery is set aboard an Olivia Cruise. Tally
and Katie thought they were headed out for some sun and fun. Instead,
Tally finds herself drawn into a reunion cruise gone awry. When women
start turning up dead, it is up to Tally and Cid to find the murderer and
unravel a decades old mystery. Sanra fans new and old, won't be
disappointed.

NO ESCAPE $11.99
Nancy Sanra
This edgy, fast-paced whodunit set in picturesque San Francisco, will
keep you guessing. Lesbian PI Tally McGinnis is called into action
when Dr. Rebecca Toliver is charged with the murder of her lover
Melinda. Is the red rose left at the scene the crime the signature of a
copycat killer, or is the infamous Marcia Cox back, and up to her old,
evil tricks again?

NO WITNESSES $9.99
Nancy Sanra
This cliffhanger of a mystery set in San Francisco, introduces Detective
Tally McGinnis, whose ex-lover Pamela Tresdale is arrested for the
grisly murder of a wealthy Texas heiress. Tally rushes to the rescue
despite friends' warnings, and is drawn once again into Pamela's web of
deception and betrayal as she attempts to clear her and find the real
killer.

DEADLY RENDEZVOUS $9.99
Diane Davidson
A string of brutal murders in the middle of the desert plunges Lt. Toni
Underwood and her lover Megan into a high profile investigation, which
uncovers a world of drugs, corruption and murder, as well as the dark
side of the human mind. Explosive, fast-paced, & action-packed.

DEADLY GAMBLE $11.99
Diane Davidson
Las-Vegas-city of bright lights and dark secrets-is the perfect setting for
this intriguing sequel to *DEADLY RENDEZVOUS*. Former police
detective Toni Underwood and her partner Sally Murphy are catapulted
back into the world of crime by a letter from Toni's favorite aunt. Now a
prominent madam, Vera Valentine fears she is about to me murdered-a
distinct possibility.

RETURN TO ISIS $9.99
Jean Stewart
It is the year 2093, and Whit, a bold woman warrior from an Amazon
nation, rescues Amelia from a dismal world where females are either
breeders or drones. During their arduous journey back to the shining
all-women's world of Artemis, they are unexpectedly drawn to each
other. This engaging first book in the series has it all-romance, mystery,
and adventure.

ISIS RISING $11.99
Jean Stewart
In this stirring romantic fantasy, the familiar cast of lovable characters
begins to rebuild the colony of Isis, burned to the ground ten years
earlier by the dread Regulators. But evil forces threaten to destroy their
dream. A swashbuckling futuristic adventure and an endearing love
story all rolled into one.

WARRIORS OF ISIS $11.99
Jean Stewart
The third lusty tale is one of high adventure and passionate romance
among the Freeland Warriors. Arinna Sojourner, the evil product of
genetic engineering, vows to destroy the fledgling colony of Isis with her
incredible psychic powers. Whit, Kali, and other warriors battle to save
their world, in this novel bursting with life, love, heroines and villains.
A Lambda Literary Award Finalist

EMERALD CITY BLUES $11.99
Jean Stewart
When comfortable yuppie world of Chris Olson and Jennifer Hart
collides with the desperate lives of Reb and Flynn, two lesbian
runaways struggling to survive on the streets of Seattle, the forecast is
trouble. A gritty, enormously readable novel of contemporary lesbigay
life, which raises real questions about the meaning of family and
community. This book is an excellent choice for young adults and the
more mature reader.

DANGER IN HIGH PLACES $9.99
Sharon Gilligan
Set against the backdrop of Washington, D.C., this riveting mystery
introduces freelance photographer and amateur sleuth, Alix Nicholson.
Alix stumbles on a deadly scheme, and with the help of a lesbian
congressional aide, unravels the mystery.

DANGER! CROSS CURRENTS $9.99
Sharon Gilligan
The exciting sequel to *Danger in High Places* brings freelance
photographer Alix Nicholson face-to-face with an old love and a murder.
When Alix's landlady turns up dead, and her much younger lover, Leah
Claire, the prime suspect, Alix launches a frantic campaign to find the
real killer.

HEARTSONE AND SABER $10.99
Jacqui Singleton
You can almost hear the sabers clash in this rousing tale of good and
evil, of passionate love between a bold warrior queen and a beautiful
healer with magical powers.

PLAYING FOR KEEPS $10.99
Stevie Rios
In this sparkling tale of love and adventure, Lindsay West an oboist,
travels to Caracas, where she meets three people who change her life
forever: Rob Heron a gay man, who becomes her dearest friend; her
lover Mercedes Luego, a lovely cellist, who takes Lindsay on a life-
altering adventure down the Amazon; and the mysterious jungle-
dwelling woman Arminta, who touches their souls.

LOVESPELL $9.95
Karen Williams
A deliciously erotic and humorous love story in which Kate Gallagher, a
shy veterinarian, and Allegra, who has magic at her fingertips, fall in
love. A masterful blend of fantasy and reality, this beautifully written
story will delight your heart and imagination.

NIGHTSHADE $11.99
Karen Williams
Alex Spherris finds herself the new owner of a magical bell, which some
people would kill for. She is ushered into a strange & wonderful world
and meets Orielle, who melts her frozen heart. A heartwarming
romance spun in the best tradition of storytelling.

FEATHERING YOUR NEST: An Interactive Workbook& Guide to a
Loving Lesbian Relationship
Gwen Leonhard, M.ED./Jennie Mast, MSW $14.99
This fresh, insightful guide and workbook for lesbian couples provides
effective ways to build and nourish your relationships. Includes fun
exercises & creative ways to spark romance, solve conflict, fight fair,
conquer boredom, spice up your sex lives.

SHADOWS AFTER DARK $9.95
Ouida Crozier
While wings of death are spreading over her own world, Kyril is sent to
earth to find the cure. Here, she meets the beautiful but lonely Kathryn,
and they fall deeply in love. But gradually, Kathryn learns that her
exotic new lover has been sent to earth with a purpose – to save her
own dying *vampire* world. A tender, finely written story.

SWEET BITTER LOVE $10.99
Rita Schiano
Susan Fredrickson is a woman of fire and ice – a successful high-
powered executive, she is by turns sexy and aloof. From the moment
writer Jenny Ceretti spots her at the Village Coffeehouse, her serene life
begins to change. As their friendship explodes into a blazing love affair,
Jenny discovers that all is not as it appears, while Susan is haunted by
ghosts from a past that won't stay hidden. A roller-coaster romance
which vividly captures the rhythm and feel of love's sometimes rocky
ride and the beauty of life after recovery.

HOW TO ORDER

Please send me the books I have checked. I enclosed a check or money order, plus $4
for the first book and $1 for each additional book to cover shipping and handling.

NAME (Please Print) _____
ADDRESS _____
CITY _____ STATE _____ ZIP _____
Arizona residents please add 7% sales tax to total.

Send to: Rising Tide Press 3831 N. Oracle Rd. Tucson, Arizona 85705
Or visit our website: www.risingtidepress.com